THE DEVIL OUT THERE

Julie Keith

THE DEVIL
OUT THERE

*A Novella
and Stories*

Vintage Canada
A Division of Random House of Canada Limited

VINTAGE CANADA EDITION, 2001

Copyright © 2000 by Julie Keith

All rights reserved under International and Pan-American Copyright Conventions. Published in Canada by Vintage Canada, a division of Random House of Canada Limited, in 2001. First published in hardcover in Canada by Alfred A. Knopf Canada, Toronto, in 2000. Distributed by Random House of Canada Limited, Toronto.

A slightly different version of "Knowing" was published under the title "Kevin" in *The Hudson Review*.

Vintage Canada and colophon are registered trademarks of Random House of Canada Limited.

Canadian Cataloguing in Publication Data

Keith, Julie Houghton
    The devil out there : a novella and stories

ISBN 0-676-97358-2

I. Title.

PS8571.E4458D48 2001   C813'.54   C00-932425-9
PR9199.3.K44D48 2001

www.randomhouse.ca

Printed and bound in the United States of America

10 9 8 7 6 5 4 3 2 1

for Mireille

CONTENTS

THE DEVIL OUT THERE

THE DEVIL
OUT THERE

PART 1

I CAME TO MONTREAL IN THE FALL. A brown-eyed girl from the townships. It was the year I'd lost all my feelings. I didn't cry any more, not even at the movies. Nothing struck me as funny. Nothing made me mad. When I visited my mum, I didn't feel like bashing my head on the door frame. I forgot how to hate my dad. I stopped missing my brother. And weirdest of all, in the rooms of our apartment, I watched my husband come and go as if he were a goofy stranger. What was he to me? What were any of them to me? What was I to myself?

Before I left Claudeville, I told my mum I'd be going. This was not right before—I left in a rush—but ten days or so previous to my leaving, when I didn't know just how soon I'd be on my way or what exactly would cause me to go. At the time I told her, my mum was having her mid-afternoon sherry. She drank quite a few glasses each day, always politely. Her voice would thicken a little but never enough that anyone could call her tipsy.

We were standing by the big front window that gave out onto the garden. Beyond the square of grass, the cedar hedge made a wall of darkest green. "I think I'll be pulling out one of these days," I said. I gave a little wave, not at her but towards the gate in the hedge and the walkway that led down to the road, so she'd know I meant I'd be leaving town.

She gave me a look and took another sip of sherry. The glass was shaped like a coneflower with a long stem, and it was decorated around the sides with triangles and circles cut into the glass. We had five more like it on the sideboard. They had come from my grandmother. (She'd died one winter from a "woman's complaint." They wouldn't tell me what it was, but I supposed a kind of cancer.) In my mum's roughened hand, the frail old glass had the sparkle of a snowflake turning through the air. After a moment she nodded. I didn't think she agreed with me so much as she simply knew I'd do it and meant to indicate she'd understood my meaning.

My mum was a dreamy sort of woman with pink, sun-destroyed skin and the kind of hair people called "strawberry blond," though it seemed more the colour of carrot soup to me. "God's favourite colours, red and gold," our neighbour Mr. Pritchard used to say to me in a rhapsodizing voice. I ignored him. Who wants to hear such stuff about their mum? "There goes the truest, finest hair God ever made," he'd say in this worshipful way, while she pottered in the back gardens, kneeling among the plants or moving slowly back and forth along the burgeoning rows of green as she worked her way down past the radishes and zucchini and lettuce, and on to the onions and the pole-beans and spinach. The gardens ran as far out as the horse barn. The rest of our property, which was all pasture land, was leased to a couple of farmers down the road. My dad worked at a clock factory over east of Drummondville.

Mr. Pritchard was sweet on my mum, from the day he moved in next door, most likely, though I don't remember so far back. In summer he hung around her garden, and in winter he dropped by as much as three times a day, for whatever reason or none. She perked up in his presence, and her back seemed to straighten. As though she became in that instant a younger person. I've thought about it since. Did they ever come flesh to flesh, my mum and Mr. Pritchard? I suppose they probably did.

My dad wasn't a big man, being narrowly made and thin enough that the skin of his face stretched tight over his bones. But his brown eyes could turn to slits and righteous rage transform his face, and at such times he seemed to loom over all of us. A punishing voice was what he used. And sometimes a punishing hand. He was a big-time member of the Lutheran Church. Luther the Reformer was his hero. My dad whacked my brother around, with words more than with his fists, telling him he was worth less than a barn rat and reforming him one way and another, until my brother up and left one spring morning. (He hitched out to Calgary, and then north and west some more; these days he's up around Prince George.) Dad whacked me around a bit too and made me pray aloud in front of him and told me what a wilful, sluttish girl I was. But I was made of tougher stuff than my brother, and I'd got myself so I didn't hear the words but halfway into my head. He went specially furious when he caught me wearing makeup, said I had the devil's eyes.

Sneaking in late was another thing that got to him. But for all he yelled and whacked us two around, I could never say he beat us, for he hardly ever left a bruise. And never, never did he raise a hand to my mum. He couldn't shout her into misery either because whenever he got to yelling about one or another sin and the devil out there, waiting, she'd just up and collect her sewing or her garden books and walk into another room. It was more the boredom of his ways that came to mind when I thought of reasons for my mum having it on with Mr. Pritchard. All Dad's Lutheran heaviness. I could imagine what lengths a person might go to just to get out from under such a weight.

I myself had been bored living there on the outskirts of Claudeville for as long as I'd been alive. When I was a kid, there were times I needled my dad just to see him blow and smash a plate or a bowl or even send me flying. Once he cracked the kitchen table with his fist, and a bowl of eggs fell off and smashed thrillingly on the floor. My punishment began with me being the one to scrape up the eggs.

Later, when I'd just turned seventeen and was dating Albie, my dad would come and stand in my bedroom doorway while I was getting ready to go out. His hair, which had once been dark like mine, was pretty well silver by then, and with his pale skin he looked like a vengeful ghost standing there, his eyes slitted and the creases beside his mouth gone white. I could hear his every breath like a judgment, and I knew he'd sensed somehow that I was having sex with Albie.

It was the week before commencement that he walked into my room and took my white tulle graduation dress from the closet and tore it into four pieces. I'd been brushing my hair, and I stood there screaming at him, brush in hand, while he shouted back that I didn't deserve to wear white, a slut like me, just as if the dress was meant for a wedding and not my high-school graduation. The four white pieces he left lying on the floor.

I screamed and cried in my bedroom until I could hardly breathe at all, but of course none of that mended my destroyed dress. The next day during study hall, I found myself drawing a picture of my dress in my English notebook, and then and there I decided I would see what I could manage by way of repairs. I didn't hang around the drugstore with my friends after class let out, but came straight home on the first bus.

When I walked into the kitchen, Mr. Pritchard's barn boots were standing just inside our door. I banged the door shut and shouted hello up the stairwell, loud as I could, and then I went to the fridge for a glass of milk.

I heard a lot of scurrying up above and some thumps, and after five minutes or so they came down the stairs looking kind of flushed and my mother kind of annoyed too. "It's barely four," she said, glancing at the clock on the wall. "You always stay in town."

"I have to fix my dress," I told her. "On your sewing machine."

"Oh," she said and turned to Mr. Pritchard. "Her dress got a trifle torn, you see."

Mr. Pritchard said hello to me then, as if he'd just noticed me standing there, not five feet from him.

"Hello," I said back, without giving him a glance, which for some reason made it easier for me not to picture exactly what he might have been doing with my mum.

The mending took me most of the afternoon. I stopped twice to try on the dress and make adjustments, and, when I was through, the job seemed quite neatly done. It was true that the tulle skirt did not hang evenly from front to back. All those extra seams, I guess. Still, at the dance no one noticed. After all, every girl there wore white, and, as I could have told my dad, most of them weren't virgins either.

The day after the dance, Albie and I got married over in Granby. At first I liked marriage all right, how everything was calm living with Albie, and how we could have sex in a bed and most any time we wanted. But after a while, I got to thinking of all the wild moments at home when my dad would lose his temper and everything around us would get crazy. I knew I didn't miss the out-loud praying or being smacked and told I was a slut or the feelings I had when he ripped up my dress, but I missed something.

Albie was always talking about some problem at the store, the failures of their suppliers or the shoddiness of customers' morals or else about his bowling team. Once I had big bruises on my elbows and bum for near to a couple of weeks—I'd slipped carrying laundry down the stairs from our apartment—and Albie never noticed. The truth was, high school had been more fun than this. Learning had been easy for me. And we'd had parties and football games to go to, and winter skating at the town rink when the boys weren't playing their hockey, and dances in the gym and lots of boys to flirt with. Now all that was over, and what I had left was a job tending the cash register at Tremblay's Hardware Store and a three-room apartment on a side street around the corner from the main grocery store in Claudeville, and of course, Albie, my husband.

We'd been married just over one and a quarter years when he announced it was time we got started on making Albie Junior. His dad had given him a raise and promised him a share of the profits at the end of the year, and this, Albie figured, would make us able to afford a four-room apartment and let me quit my job.

"You can keep working up to when you have the baby," he told me. "Tremblay can get a stool or something for you to sit on when you get fat. We'll use the money to buy furniture, baby stuff... Your mother will know what." While he went on talking, Albie was smiling at himself in the bathroom mirror (maybe he was seeing a little Albie), and then he grabbed up all my pills from the shelf, three months' supply, and flushed them down the toilet. I remember his face in the mirror and the sound of the toilet gurgling down my pills like some hungry baby suckling. The next day I was gone.

After I bought my ticket for Montreal, I called my mum from the bus depot's phone booth. She sounded clear-voiced for mid-afternoon and not too surprised. She wanted to know if I'd taken the new navy gabardine suit she'd bought me down in Sherbrooke. I said I had. I had also left a note for my boss at the hardware store, emptied my savings account and picked up a new supply of pills at the pharmacist's, though I didn't bother to mention all this to my mum. I promised I'd give her a call from Montreal, and then I ran out and caught the 4:17 semi-express.

We rumbled into the city over the Jacques Cartier Bridge, the big bus swaying in what felt like cross-currents of wind. To the left and right stretched the huge river. Below us lay the islands that had housed the world's fair two summers previous to now. I had come to Expo 67 four times that summer, three times with Albie and some other friends, and once with my mum and dad and brother. My parents had had a fight in front of the Czech Pavilion, my dad shouting and my mum turning her back on him and inspecting the leaves of a potted bush. We'd already waited near to an hour in the lineup, so I guess she didn't want to walk away. My brother did though, just walked away, his shoulders hunched like our dad's shouting was rocks being flung against his back. Later, a day or two before he left for good, he told me he'd spent the rest of that afternoon riding the elevated train from island to island, getting off here and there and walking around, looking at all the futuristic buildings. He said it had been fine, like visiting a comic-book city. Now, rising from the water, those same spikes and spheres and polygons of steel and Plexiglas and concrete looked more to me like ruins of a city abandoned to the river.

We reached the Montreal side of the bridge, and after a series of turns headed towards the skyscrapers downtown. I could see them coming closer, Place Ville-Marie and C-I-L House and others whose names I didn't know, and right at that moment I felt life speed up. This was now, and I was here. I knew how life should be led; I read magazines, after all. I watched television. Desire and nothing else ruled the modern day. If you thought of it, you did it. Some people wanted war to end, and some people wanted sex with everyone in sight, and some people just wanted to trash whatever came their way. In the big nation to the south of us, the Americans burned their cities and shot their leaders and fought a war no one could understand. This, it seemed to me, was modern. Even here in Montreal, black students had wrecked a university's computer room just last winter, for reasons I'd forgotten. Their lives, too, were modern lives. And like them I wanted to know unrest. I wanted to know wickedness and chaos. As I gazed down on Dorchester Boulevard and the rush of cars and the crowds of people waiting to cross at the intersections, I felt quite sure I could find it all.

I was not the first person from Claudeville to leave in search of something modern. Three of my classmates, a girl and two boys, had grown their hair and bleached their jeans and gone on the road. We heard the girl got sick and then that all three of them were living on a commune in British Columbia.

I myself had never fancied the road. I wanted sensation, but I also wanted sexy, stylish clothes, lamb chops and steak, an apartment with soft, cushy furniture and wall-to-wall carpeting. And, as I stepped down into the Berri Street station and waited for the driver to pull my two suitcases from the belly of the bus, I knew that in my immediate future not any of this awaited. The YWCA was what awaited, a subway ride away. And after that, the matter of a job. That was where things stood on my first afternoon as a city girl in downtown Montreal.

After a bit of hunting—there wasn't much I knew how to do—I got myself hired to sell sweaters at a department store called Cardiff's. I'd been at this job for a little over a month when I repacked my two suitcases and said goodbye to the girls on my floor at the Y. An apartment downtown would have suited me fine; I'd had in mind a high-rise with a view of the river or the mountain, but the prices in the rent ads in *The Star* had erased that hope. My parents had friends in Montreal West and a cousin in Saint-Laurent, but they seemed unlikely to know anything useful, and certainly I had no interest in looking them up.

I heard about the room in Freddie's house from a woman at the store. Mrs. McPherson was an older lady of at least fifty who worked sometimes in Ladies' Gloves, sometimes in Men's Socks and Suspenders. The counter where I worked was, like both of hers, on the main floor. I sold thick, hand-knit sweaters imported from Ireland and later on from Portugal and somewhere in South America. They were the colour of sheep, slightly dirty-looking, and the cardigans had rough buttons like chunks of bone. At first I admired these sweaters, their foreignness, their absence of delicacy, but the thick wool gave off a smell that gradually came to nauseate me, and the cheaper ones left a sheen of grease on the palms of my hands. A job, however, was a job.

Following this Freddie person's instructions, which she'd delivered in a breathless trill over the phone, I took the bus west along Sherbrooke Street. After a few stops I slid into a window seat and, propping my feet on my suitcases, settled back to admire the old brick apartments and houses, all crowded together, not grand but solid and properly cityish. My appreciation for those ordered streets may seem strange for someone who wanted to know chaos, but I was not myself a chaotic person. I liked the stone town hall sliding by on my right and then the big park stretching away to my left, its sweep of grass and trees presided over by several fancy-looking buildings. We passed into a shopping district, and as instructed, I got off just before the bus turned around. There I switched to another bus that carried me further west into Notre-Dame-de-Grace, N-D-G as I already knew it to be called. After I got off that bus, I walked north up a slanting street, away from the shops and into a neighbourhood of red brick, terraced houses.

Climbing, I stopped here and there to set my suitcases on the sidewalk and rest my arms. These houses were not important like some of the ones I had spied from the bus. They offered for beguilement only the occasional lead-paned window or bit of carved wood above their doorways. In their small front yards, a few Michaelmas daisies and purple and yellow chrysanthemums bloomed among the ravaged leaves and made me think of my mother's garden.

Freddie's house stood halfway up the block, plain as any other, except for a panel of stained glass set high in the front door. The glass was green and blue mostly, and though her sidewalk was broken in a dozen places and the porch stairs were shaky beneath my feet, my eyes stayed on that small window, shining green and blue in the after-noon sun.

I pushed the bell button and waited. After a moment, the door was opened by a woman with grey curls and a waist as stout as my mother's ancient tub washer. Old, was my first thought, at least as old as Mrs. McPherson, but the face gazing down at me had something of a baby in it as well, the button eyes and nose, the little crimson mouth buried in a bulge of cheeks. It was the face of a fat doll, if you didn't count the sag. And she was wearing doll clothes too, a crimson blouse that matched her lipstick and a pleated, red plaid skirt.

"I'm Nancy Jean Marchand," I said.

"Do come in," she said. It was the voice I'd heard over the telephone. "I'm Freddie." She smiled at me and pulled the door open wide. There was lipstick on her tiny teeth.

I carried my suitcases across her foyer into her front hall. Here the floor seemed to be covered with several thicknesses of rug, laid one on top of another. "Mind the rugs, dear," she told me. "I've ever so many too many."

She shut the door then, and in the sudden gloom I could smell old cloth and furniture wax and baking. As my eyes got used to the dimness, I saw two squat chests standing further along the hall and, between them, a table. On the walls, pictures in thick gilded frames hung one above the other, as did a pair of large mirrors. The glass of both these mirrors was so murky I could see no sensible reflection in them, not my own face nor the paintings opposite nor any other object in the hall, only a kind of rippling shadow such as might be seen in the muddiest swamp water. Above our heads a lopsided brass chandelier cast a tarnished light.

Freddie was smoothing the offending rug with her foot, causing more wrinkles to form behind her heel. "I've

got ever so many too many rugs in this house," she said
again. "My parents, don't you know, they were mad
about Turkey rugs."

They must have been mad about furniture too.
Through the doorway to the front parlour, I could see
a quantity of dark chairs and tables. White crocheted
doilies hung like cobwebs over the chair arms, and in the
far corner a secretary desk loomed against the wall. Rugs
covered the floor in there as well, corners sticking out
from under corners, like in a rug store. The high walls,
what I could see of them, looked to be hung with more
paintings and mirrors.

"Now I expect you'll want to come right up and
see your room." Freddie had picked up one of my suitcases and was heading for the stairs. "My friend Mrs.
McPherson tells me you've come to town only just this
past month . . . "

I followed Freddie's red plaid rump up the stairs and
along a narrow back hall into a bedroom with a big back-
facing window. Here we set down the suitcases, and I
stood a little aside and folded my arms as I'd seen my dad
do when someone was trying to sell him a load of wood
or a new mower. On one side of the room stood a dark
wooden dresser and a small wooden rack with two white
towels hanging from it, and on the other a narrow bed
covered with a pink-and-yellow quilt, and, of course, laid
on the floor was a carpet, dark blue and beige, covering
all the space between the bed and the dresser. Freddie
pointed out the switch on the bed lamp and the radiator
knob and the shades that pulled down to shut out the
view of a telephone pole and tree branches and through
them the backs of houses across a lane.

"It gets to be all leaves out there, come spring," she told me, and moving to the doorway, she smiled and clasped her hands over her plaid stomach in the manner of a peaceable child, the kind that trusts whoever comes along. She stood there and talked all the while I moved about the room putting away my skirts and blouses, my two pairs of shoes (the black ones new and fashionable with their chunky heels), the navy gabardine suit my mum had chosen.

Under a layer of tissue paper at the bottom of my suitcase, I had packed my two new dresses. These dresses had not come with me from home but had been acquired just the previous week, in a way that I will explain later. One was a dark green jersey, beautiful with my white skin and dark hair, and the other a deep red and near as handsome as the first. In both I felt like someone not quite myself.

Now, while I hung them up, Freddie's voice informed me that this house had been her parents'. Her mother had died first. "A touch of indigestion, that's all we thought. She'd gone to lie down after lunch..." Her voice quivered. "It was a shock, I can tell you. I was the one went to wake her. Going to have an egg for her supper, she'd said... You could see she wasn't there at all, just her body, don't you know. We held the funeral up at St. Michael's on the Côte Road." I nodded. I had no idea where this was. "And then my father, he just kind of shrunk and died himself, and after that, well, I took in boarders. It seemed the thing to do, with all these rooms and just me." She smiled at me, as if this and I myself, being here in her spare room, were the happiest and luckiest of endings.

After I'd put away my underwear and stockings and sweaters in the bureau drawers, she led me back along the hall to the bathroom. There was no toilet in this room, only a sink and a tub with claw feet and high, curving sides. On the metal soap rack sat a pink rubber duck. The floor was tiled with little black and white hexagons, the high, white ceiling split by a glass-panelled trapdoor. From this hung a knotted rope. I had never seen such a thing and stood staring up at it.

"Now just you pull on it like so," said Freddie, and she gave it a tug. The trap door groaned and lifted a few inches; there was stir of cool air, and a shower of paint particles fell down on us. "Of course, that's only in the summer," she said cheerily, as if the fact of it being autumn would explain the bits of paint I was dusting out of my hair.

Next door to the bathroom was the watercloset. Like the bathroom it had little black and white tiles on the floor and a skylight. A chain flush-pull hung from the water tank on the wall above the toilet.

"Now then," said Freddie, shutting the doors on both conveniences, "I expect you'd like a cup of tea. I always want one myself come late afternoon."

I said I supposed I would, and we descended to her big, white-painted kitchen. In the centre of this room was a wooden table with a pile of magazines on it and on top of them a yellow sugar bowl. I seated myself while Freddie stumped about, filling the electric kettle, pulling a box of tea from a cabinet, cups and saucers from another and spoons from a drawer.

She went on talking too. Her real name was Frederica. "After the kings of Prussia." I nodded, having no idea of this history. Her father, she said, had admired royalty. Mine was not her only spare room. She could take three boarders at a time, if she'd a mind to have them.

"But only nice ones, don't you know." In the three years, there had been girl students from McGill and a boy from Sir George Williams University, a school teacher and a comptometer operator, and several salesladies and a secretary. "A doctor's secretary, she was. Lived with me for near a year, bless her heart. She got herself engaged to a widower, one of the doctor's patients. It was a sweet wedding, I can tell you. Two kinds of cake—I'm partial to spun sugar myself..."

The stories went on. The school teacher, too, had left to marry; his had been the room down the hall from mine. All this was told to me amid the clinking of crockery and the opening and closing of cabinets and drawers. From their titles and front covers the magazines looked to be about food and housekeeping. Presently the kettle began to scream, and she unplugged it and set about making tea. This was a process more elaborate than I, being used to tea bags, could have imagined. First she poured a bit of the boiling water into the teapot, swirled it around and poured it back out into the sink. Next she measured in the loose tea, scooping it by spoonfuls from the box, and poured in more boiling water from the kettle. Finally she clamped on the teapot lid. And all the while she did each of these things, she went on talking.

"The boy I've got in there now, in the front room, don't you know, he's the son of my sister's friend. She died, pneumonia, when she was just in her forties. They always said she drank, but then they do talk, and who's to know the truth of things? He came to me last year. He's an actor when he can be." She set the pot of tea down on the table, and I leaned forward, breathing in the steam and trying to sort out what she'd just told me.

"The others didn't take to him after a while. But me, I like having a boy around." As she said this, her little round baby eyes sought mine, and she smiled at me in a such a silly way, I thought to wonder if she was all there.

She started to sit down, clapped a hand to her cheek and got up again. "Biscuits, for goodness' sake! And milk. I do forget this and that." From a shelf above the stove, she pulled down a big red tin and pried off the lid.

The cookies were large and rocky. I tasted cinnamon and raisins, as if the chunk in my hand had once been a bun or spice cake. It was like gnawing on a fossil. She was pouring milk into a pitcher when I heard the front door open and then shut. At the first click she paused, pitcher in hand; by the second click a flush bright as her blouse was spreading up her fat neck and into her cheeks, as though she'd acquired a fever. The kitchen door swung open.

A painted angel was my first thought. The boy walking into the room had wings of red-brown hair sweeping either side of his brow. His eyes, pale as daylight, were outlined in sooty, red-brown lashes and together with his high cheekbones and deep curved mouth gave his face the calm look of a seraph. He was my height, no more, and so light on his feet as he crossed the room that it seemed any greater size or weight would have been excess. I remember thinking I had never seen a man so beautiful.

While I was staring, well beyond the rule of proper manners, he kissed Freddie on both her pudgy cheeks. She giggled and he backed away from her.

"Tea time, Freddie?" His voice was deep and resonant, the voice of a large man.

She giggled again and fluttered her hand at him, as though he'd said something outrageous. "Oh, Stephen... it's always about now. You know that." She beamed lovingly at him and began to rush around the room. A cup was set on the table, a large, beautiful cup, cream and rose with gold edges. (The two she'd already set out for herself and me were plain white and normal size.)

"It's Dresden," she said noticing my interest. "A man's cup by its size. We always used it for my father's tea." Her cheeks were now bright red. She glanced from me to him. "Oh, goodness. Oh, Stephen... my manners! This is Nancy Jean. Nancy Jean, this is Stephen."

He had not glanced once in my direction. Now his eyes flicked over me, and he looked uninterested. "Hello, Nancy Jean," he said. He did not smile.

"Hi," I said, cool as anything.

Sitting down across from me, he eyed Freddie's headlong progress as she hustled breathlessly from faucet to stove to table to stove again. He glanced at me once more, and this time he smiled. The smile lit his face and, like a flash of lightning, was gone so fast I registered its meanness only in the startled aftermath. Then he did something I would never forget. He reached out and picked up the cup. I had just enough time to notice his beautiful gold wristwatch, which I would later learn had been Freddie's father's, when with a twist of his thumb and forefinger, he snapped the gold handle off that lovely cup. The noise was sharp. His hands must have been strong.

"Oh, sorry, Freddie," he said as she turned to look. He held the cup up in one hand, in the other the little arched handle; it looked like a tiny golden elbow.

Freddie's baby features crumpled. "Oh, heavens," she cried. "Oh, goodness." She looked as though she was going to weep, but what she said next was, "Oh, never mind, Stephen dear. Never mind. They're so old, don't you know. My mother's and all. Bound to break sooner or later."

I was still staring in shock at him and Freddie and the cup, when he turned and gave me a wink. His eyelashes fluttered like a girl's. "So you've come to share Freddie's happy home?" he said. "No one loves you more than Freddie." He glanced back at Freddie. "Right, Freddie?"

"Oh, Stephen." Freddie stood pressing the palm of her free hand to her cheek. Her face was still bright red, and she still appeared close to tears. She looked horrified, and yet she looked thrilled too, and rather as though she was going to burst apart with all these feelings. There was something comical about it. I thought of the county fair we'd sometimes gone to over in Regent, where they always had a cow or pig dressed up in ladies' clothing.

"By the way," he said. "Did Nancy Jean get old cowlips' room?"

"Oh, heavens, Stephen," Freddie said. "The poor lady couldn't help how she looked . . ."

"Oh, heavens," Stephen said back to her, mimicking her tone. "Heavens, heavens. Oh, what a bitch that boy is." She giggled, and he glanced at me. "Give Stephen a cookie?" he said, still in her voice. I shoved the tin over to him. His eyes, silver more than grey, stayed on me for a second, and I thought he knew everything I was thinking—which was all about what it would be like to be in bed with him. And I thought he didn't give a damn what I was thinking because he knew sex was what everyone thought about when they looked at him.

Sex was something I thought about a lot, to tell the truth. With Albie it had been a pretty patchy business. Especially before we'd got married, when nothing so sophisticated as undressing had figured in it. More like unzipping and unbuckling and unbuttoning. And sometimes ripping too. We'd had no place to go either. There were some motels on the roads outside of Sherbrooke and Lennoxville that we could have gone to, the kind where you paid cash and no questions were asked. But they cost money, and besides, someone was sure to spot Albie's father's pickup truck. I knew about small-town news. My boss at the hardware store, where I worked Saturdays, went to those motels with the lady who helped out at the bakery. The two of them were cool as anything with each other when they met on the street, and they must have thought no one knew. But the fact was everybody knew. The word shot up and down Main Street whenever someone spotted the boss's car. I'd laughed along with the others. But a picture of their bodies, my paunchy boss and the flabby, large-assed bakery woman, heaving among the sheets stayed in my brain and gave me a queasy feeling. At least Albie and I were lean, my breasts up where breasts were supposed to be and Albie's gut concave instead of hanging over his belt like an uncured ham. Even if we were stuck with doing it in the truck—or else, in summer, in someone's field, with me ending up scratched and bug-bitten—even so, we didn't resemble a pair of rutting pigs. Albie's arms were handsome, I will say that, and I liked feeling the muscles in his back. It was the sex itself that bored me, his sweaty, snorting satisfaction, the stupid things he said; and there came the hours afterwards when shadows quite often clouded my mind, as if something of mine, I could not quite remember what, had been erased.

In Montreal sex would be different. Altogether sexier, like in the magazines. Working at Cardiff's, I had begun by eyeing male customers. I was not an especially pretty girl nor a plain one either, but I was very slim with high round breasts and good legs. I knew how to move and how to look at a man so's he'd notice me. Two or three times I went out for a drink with a salesman from Men's Sportswear and other times with one and another customer, hoping one of them would be fun. But the salesman was full of nothing but bragging and complaints, and the customers were a dry, business-suited lot, all except for one. I met this man the first week I was working at Cardiff's. He was buying perfume for his girlfriend and walked over to the Sweaters counter to ask my opinion. I gave him a look and tossed back my hair, which I was growing long, and I told him I couldn't say about her, but I myself preferred Chanel 22, which in fact I did because I'd been testing the perfumes over in Cosmetics during my coffee breaks. He laughed and bought me a bottle and took me out to dinner.

His name, he said, was George, George Martin. It wasn't, of course. The second time I went out with him, I snuck a look into his wallet. R. Charles Weymouth, his driver's licence said. He was thirty-three, bespectacled and lean. His front teeth stuck out just enough so he seemed, like a little boy, to be perpetually biting his lower lip. His dark hair had thinned at the top, and I liked that he clipped it

short there, didn't try to pretend, and had just let his side-
burns grow so as not to look uptight. Behind the thick
lenses of his glasses, his eyes were dark and shiny and un-
wise, as though despite his businessman ways, he had a
wild side or at least hoped to have one soon. He seemed
intelligent too, if a little overenthusiastic. He was nice to
go to bed with, being interested in how things went for
me, which was not at all like Albie and caused me to
enjoy myself in ways I had not before, and he rented a
hotel room each time, so I knew he had some money and
also that it wasn't his girlfriend he'd been buying the perfume for, but his wife.

It was he who bought me the dresses, the red one and
the green one. He did this after I'd worn my navy gabardine suit three times in a row to the fancy restaurant he
said was his favourite. (I was pretty sure he'd chosen it
as his so-called favourite because it was north on Park
Avenue and quite far from Cardiff's and Place Ville-
Marie, which was where he said he worked, and also
from Westmount, where he hadn't said he lived but did,
according to the papers in his wallet.)

Luckily he couldn't see me but once a week at most,
so I didn't have to make up any lies to explain how I
needed to keep free. The truth was I had in mind someone jazzier and more modern than George (whom I
sometimes called Charlie in my mind, though George did
suit him). I did not fancy the dirty hippie boys, all ragged
and overgrown with hair, who hung around smoking
dope in the parks and city squares. It was difficult to
imagine anything glittery or hard-edged about those
earnest, druggie boys. Sex of another sort was happening
in the bars along Ste-Catherine Street, but this crowd did

not attract me either. Men who said they were race-car drivers or hockey players dropped in and were set upon by the cruising girls. The hockey players were mostly stuck on themselves, and the drivers were hooked on cars, and they weren't, most of them, real hockey players or race-car drivers either, and nothing they said was something an interesting person might say. Late at night and on weekends, the college boys from McGill and Sir George Williams came by, and I looked them over with more interest. The University of Montreal boys hung out further east and north, in the bars on the Main and along rue St-Denis. I thought them handsome and sexier to look at than the English boys, but my French wasn't up to any decent smart talk, the kind you need for flirting, so mostly I stuck to the English boys.

When I moved to Freddie's I'd been seeing this George for a whole month. He spoke French quite well. His father was a senator, and his parents, intending him for a career in finance or politics, as he said, had sent him and his older brother to French school in Outremont when he was young. His brother was a bigwig in some investment house in Toronto. George laughed at my accent when I spoke French, and he was crazy about my stories of Claudeville and my mum and dad and Mr. Pritchard. And he was crazy about going to bed with me. It was my opinion that he had never tried anything interesting to do with sex before, as he acted like I was some kind of genius and had invented electricity or the internal combustion engine when all I did was what I felt like doing. I hadn't told him about my being married or about Albie, and he hadn't told me anything at all about himself. What he told me were funny stories about politics and business mostly. He seemed to know a lot. He told me about "the three wise men" who had gone to Ottawa to be members of Parliament and about "la Révolution tranquille" of Jean Lesage and Eric Kierans and René Lévesque and how life was changing in Quebec and Canada. And he fed me in wonderful restaurants, real French food, nothing like any food I'd ever eaten. Of course, I tried whatever he suggested— why wouldn't I?—and I listened and asked questions when he talked. I didn't think this was something special to notice. After all, I was a girl from the townships and had a lot to learn.

But one evening when we were in the Park Avenue restaurant, sitting at a table in an alcove that was closed off by a curtain of beads, he said to me all of sudden while I was dabbing a piece of French bread in my blanquette de veau, "You know, you're really quick. You're the quickest girl I ever met."

The gravy of this dish was the creamiest I could imagine and made the most delicious stew I had ever tasted. That's what I'd been thinking about when he said I was quick. Plus the next day I was due to move out of the Y and head for Freddie's, so I'd been thinking about that too, and now I couldn't figure what he was getting at. "Quick like smart?" I said between bites of bread.

"You have a flexible mind as well," he said. "You should go to university."

I glanced up from my plate. George's face hovered above the candle. The room was quite dark, what with the curtain and being lit mainly by this little candle, but I could see how, behind his glasses, his dark eyes had fixed on me. The truth was no one had ever said such things to me before, my teachers being too concerned with stopping my smart-ass tongue to praise me for my good head and high marks, and my mum and dad being without such a notion altogether.

"Well, thanks," I said. "But university doesn't exactly pay a living wage."

"You could go nights," he said, leaning so far into the candle I thought his chin would catch on fire. "Sir George has a lot of night courses; even McGill might have some. I could find out for you. You'd like learning. You'd be good at it." He leaned back and rubbed his chin.

I began to get annoyed. "Well then, George, that's a nice life, working all day and spending my money on university courses so I can study all night. How would I ever have any fun?" I pushed back my hair and looked across the candle at him in the way I knew made him want to go to bed with me.

"I can't see you next week," he blurted, as though this had something to do with all this talk about me going to university. "Maybe not even the week after."

"Oh, yes?" I said. He was still looking wild-eyed, so to soothe him I added, "Here, want my last mushroom?" He was crazy about mushrooms. I picked up the mushroom in my fingers and reaching around the flame pushed it into his mouth. He caught hold of my hand and, sucking in the mushroom, sucked on my finger and thumb too.

"That tickles," I said.

He let go my hand then. "It's for business," he said.

"What's for business?"

"I have to go away for business." Now he was giving me one of those looks again, and I could tell he wanted to know something. Whether I cared, maybe.

I didn't. The French food was nice, and so was this snooty restaurant with the waiter in his short red jacket, fussing his way in and out of our little alcove like we were king and queen. And so was George nice. I felt relaxed when I was with him, and cheerful. After sex the darkness didn't grow up in my mind the way it had with Albie. But I still didn't mind if George went away somewhere. Or even if he was lying, which I thought he was. And if I wanted more sex, I didn't mind picking up an extra boy or two at one of the bars.

I had some new short white boots I'd bought on my Cardiff's discount, and I'd already shortened all my skirts to mini length. That meant I'd had to throw out my garter belt and stockings and buy pantyhose, so I'd done that, and now with the boots and most of my nylon-covered legs showing, I figured I could attract enough interest to take my choice in any bar.

"I'll call you as soon as I'm free," George was saying. "As soon as I get back, that is."

"A trip sounds nice," I said, teasing him. Probably his wife was turning the screw. I'd seen her name in the paper, Mrs. R. Charles Weymouth. She was on The Committee, it said, for some ball to do with a hospital. Tickets were sold out. I'd seen his father's name too, the Honourable Reginald G.C. Weymouth, Q.C. A senator, according to the newspaper. "Have yourself a good time, George," I said.

But George was busy calling for the bill. I supposed he couldn't wait to get to the hotel, and I remembered I hadn't told him I was moving the next day. I hadn't even told him the store was transferring me into Junior Dresses on the third floor. It seemed boring to mention such details now. Tonight was tonight. I'd sleep with George, wherever he'd got us a room, and tomorrow morning I'd head back to the Y, pack my two suitcases and take the bus to my new home. Those were my plans up to the night before I moved to Freddie's, and they seemed to me simple and clear and entirely complete.

That first night at Freddie's, I took a bath in the funny old tub with feet. Then I did my nails in a new frosted peach, and after that I got into bed with a copy of *Cosmopolitan* magazine. Most of the articles were about how career women could get men and keep them. Why anyone would want to keep men for ever and ever I couldn't imagine. I read until I got sleepy and then turned off the light. I was almost asleep when the door opened and Stephen came into the room.

"It's me," he said in his deep voice, shutting the door, not being the least bit quiet.

"I know," I said.

"Take off your nightgown," he said. I did, and I threw it on the floor and moved over to one side of the bed, and he got into my narrow bed with me. He was naked, and smooth to touch, even the skin on his chest, and I could feel the heat of him passing into me. There was a city smell to his skin, like burnt matches and smoky jazz bars late at night. His hair smelt more specifically of cigarette smoke. He surprised me by turning on the light. The brightness made me squint for a minute, but after that I was glad of the chance to look at him. His face was weary and I saw he had dark shadows under his eyes and was older than I'd thought that afternoon. But still his face was something beautiful to see.

He did not kiss me, then or on any other night, and to tell the truth I did not, even that first time, think sex much interested him, though he performed it with a kind of hunger that was near to violent and took away my breath. All the time he was in my room I said nothing more to him.

Just at the end, he put his fingers on the pulse at the side of my throat, as though to remind me of something. It occurred to me that, if he'd a mind to, he could strangle me there in my bed, and if he were quick enough, I would not even have the chance to scream. My body would lie there all night long, and no one would be the wiser.

He got out of bed then and stood for a minute with the lamplight shining on his torso, sleek and graceful as I imagined an acrobat or a dancer might be. Rubbing the back of his neck, he arched his back and stretched and after a moment tipped back his head and began to laugh. The sound was like something he made up for a prank, a screech almost. I put my hands over my ears. Freddie had to be hearing it.

After he left, I wondered how many times she'd heard it before. Those students who'd been her boarders, for example. And I wondered, too, whether she'd already known that she would be hearing it again tonight.

He came in a few nights later, after that not for a week, then twice in a row. He did it not out of desire, I thought, but to prove something. As for me, the sex did not provide much pleasure. His treatment of my body was too rough. The truth was I thought he disdained me. Yet I liked the idea I got from him that sex was just a thing to grab, like candy or an apple in a bowl.

He didn't laugh like that again, but he made enough noise each time that Freddie had to know what we were doing. She was still nice to me, but on the days after he'd been in my room, she gave me sad sideways looks. She seemed sad around Stephen too. Once when I came into the kitchen, he was sitting at the table eating an apple, cutting it into slices and eating them one by one, and Freddie was standing by the sink washing pans and crying. Her fat cheeks were pink and streaked with tears, and her button nose was even pinker and shiny too. Neither of them looked at me, and I got myself a glass of milk and left.

George found me on a Sunday afternoon. It was three weeks to the day after I'd moved in, and Freddie had just come back from church when the front doorbell rang. I heard her baby voice. "Oh, heavens, oh yes. Oh, I don't think she's gone out. I mean, I saw her come in, don't you know." I could hear the lower tones of a man's voice and then Freddie calling, "Nancy Jean! Nancy Jean! There's someone here for you." I'd just washed my hair, and I had on my old blue bathrobe and a towel wrapped around my hair. I was halfway down the stairs before I could see the tall man in glasses standing in Freddie's hall. A lean man. Dark. A bit foolish looking, though well set-up. Pleased with himself. Weak. Those were my judgments, made in those seconds before I recognized him. He was looking all around, at the mound of rugs and at the table and the two chests and the high walls covered with the big, blackened mirrors and the paintings of moustached men and lace-collared women.

"George," I cried, running down the rest of the steps.

He turned and glared. "You," he said. Uh-oh, I thought, and threw my arms around him.

He pried me off him and held me at arm's length. "No thanks to you," he said, very severe.

"Well, you went away; how could I call you?" I said and opened my eyes wide. His face softened then, and he hugged me. "And where would I call you anyway?" I added when he had let me go. Drops from my hair had begun trickling down the back of my neck.

"You might have left me word——," he began.

"Some tea then?"

We both glanced around and saw that Freddie was still there, standing off to one side of us, her hands folded over her stomach, her little eyes bouncing from him to me to him.

"Here," I said to George. "Say hello to Freddie. Freddie, meet George. He's an old friend."

She beamed at him, looking more than ever like a fat-cheeked doll. "Ever so pleased to meet you..." He shook hands with her, and that seemed to please her even more. "Come right in. Do come in." She was speaking in her most breathless voice. "I mean, do sit down. Nancy Jean, do take your friend into the living room. Wouldn't you care for tea? Biscuits too? I..."

He glanced into the parlour, and I saw him choke back whatever he really thought of it and of Freddie's offer. His face took on a stifled, automatic politeness, like something that had been made part of him a long time ago. "No, thank you," he said to her. "That's kind of you, but I won't keep you. I just need to talk to Nancy Jean."

"Well, of course you do," she cried, as if this was the very course of action she'd have recommended. "Of course you do." Still beaming, she rushed off towards the kitchen.

I led George into the parlour, stepping from rug to rug. We sat down facing each other on the plush-covered sofa. When Freddie's friends came calling, they used to sit in here sometimes, but neither Stephen nor I ever came in. To me it felt like a roped-off room in some dusty old historic house out on the edge of town. Now, with George eyeing me, I wrapped my towel turban tighter. It had got knocked askew when I'd hugged him. And then I got all comfy, tucking my feet under the hem of the robe and folding my hands into the sleeves.

As soon as I'd done this, George stood up. Then he sat down again. "You could have left me a note," he burst out. "At the Y, addressed to me. Would that have been so hard? An envelope with a piece of paper in it and an address written down. A telephone number. You could even have told me you were moving. No one at that sweater counter knew where you'd been switched to either. They all thought I was some sort of pervert." He shook his head and ran his hand over the top of it, where the hair was clipped short. "I had to bribe the desk clerk at the Y to give me your forwarding address."

"Oh, poor George," I said, nearly laughing now. I could see him in his beautiful suit and his English raincoat, begging the idiot desk clerk. "Well, now you've found me. Would you like some of Freddie's tea?"

"Jesus no," he said and sneezed. He glanced around at the walls, which of course were mostly covered with paintings in heavy frames. "This place smells like my great aunt's house used to. There's a thousand years' worth of dust in here."

"I know. Freddie keeps it sort of untouched, with all the old stuff, because of her parents. She says she imagines them sitting in here. The rest of the house is clean enough."

"What's the matter with her parents?" he said.

"They're dead."

"Jesus," he said and stood up. I realized I had never heard him swear. "Let's get out of here," he said. "Get dressed, and I'll take you to dinner. Filet mignon, foie gras, sole Armoricaine, anything you like."

"It's early afternoon," I said, staring up at him. He was wearing chinos and a sweater, ordinary weekend clothes, yet he still seemed all formal.

"I'll get a hotel room," he said. "We'll go out afterwards. We'll..." He went quiet because I'd begun to laugh. I stopped myself because I could see he was going to get into a snit again.

"Wait twenty minutes," I said, swivelling my feet out from under me and jumping up to face him. "I have to dry my hair. And I have to get some things. Take a walk if the house makes you sneeze." I headed for the door. "Or you could go have tea with Freddie," I called back. And I ran upstairs.

I hummed under my breath while I was drying my hair. Silly George, who was, of course, silly R. Charles Weymouth, had made me happy. Why was that? While I

was painting eyeliner around my brown eyes, I realized.
The truth was I liked George. It was as simple as that.
Even though I hadn't missed him, even though I hadn't
thought to let him know where I was going, I did like
him. If he wasn't exactly a friend, he was more of one
than any other person I knew.

After that I saw George one or maybe two times a week. I
went on letting Stephen into my bed too, though I did
sometimes ask myself why. For one thing I didn't sleep
very well, not knowing when or if my door would open.
For another I didn't in any true way like him. He never
talked to me, nor I to him, except sometimes in Freddie's
kitchen, usually with Freddie there too and the three of
us drinking tea and gnawing on her cookies. He teased
and baited her most all the time. At first I found this
funny, her squeals and bleats, the twittering protests and
flights around the kitchen, but after a while it began to
make me nervous. I'd begun to understand that in some
peculiar way he actually hated her. I watched her bathe
his every move in a worshipful gaze, as if he were a movie
star or the angel he resembled, and I saw how, whenever
her eyes came to settle on him, his face would twist and
clench as if she'd slid a knife between his ribs.

His meanness was simple-minded. He smashed things.
He insulted her looks. We were drinking tea at her kitchen
table the time he said to her, "I heard about a good diet.
Just the ticket for you, Freddie. Lose all kinds of pounds."

She was scrubbing a cookie sheet with scouring powder and steel wool, and she glanced around all bright-
eyed. "Oh, what's that, Stephen?"

He said nothing but just looked her over for a few seconds, as if he'd spoken before he'd thought. Then he shook his head. "No," he said. "No. Forget it."

"Oh, tell me, Stephen." Her face had begun to flush, and she clapped one powder-covered hand to her cheek, making a big white blotch.

"No. Sorry." He shook his head some more. "I forgot. They say it's not worth it once you're more than fifty pounds overweight." He smiled at me and back at her. "Guess you're stuck with that lard rump and the six chins."

Freddie's hand moved to her chin, making more white streaks along her jaw. Tears welled up in her eyes. Stephen's smile turned almost pleasant. "Just joking," he said to her. "Just joking."

"Oh, I know, Stephen, I know. Never mind."

I poured myself another cup of tea. This kind of meanness happened five times a week. The more she forgave his little cruelties, the more cruelties he spoke. And the more she gave him things—a pen that had been her father's, a silver letter opener—the more things he broke. It was as if her every kindness caused him pain.

Occasionally, when he wasn't bugging her, he talked about his work. He was forever hunting acting jobs. Life was that way for actors, I supposed. Television and stage, commercials when he couldn't get the other. He'd even work as an extra when someone made a movie in the city. He bartended too, in a Mackay Street pub. His hours were peculiar and sometimes quite long. I went to two plays he was in at a theatre near St-Denis. The audience sat on benches. Stephen, prowling up on the stage, speaking lines in his deep voice, seemed more believable and normal than he did in Freddie's house, even if the

plays—both of them set in ancient Greece—seemed to
be about some very strange brothers and sisters, and about
strange mothers and fathers too. Stephen got a good
deal of applause at the end, and afterwards when I met
him for a beer, he was as near to relaxed as I'd ever seen
him.

Later in the fall I saw him in another play, this time at
a theatre in the old quarter of the city. In this play he
acted the part of a lover. The play was not so interesting
as the others, the characters being quite silly and the lines
set up mainly for laughs, but once again he seemed, walking about on the stage and speaking words which were
not his own, more human than he did in my bed or in
Freddie's kitchen.

One night, while this play was still running and I had
worked the evening shift, I met him after his performance.
We went out for onion soup and tourtière, and he told
me that he felt better acting than at any other time, and
that other actors felt that way too. I'd hoped that night to
meet some of his actor friends, people from the cast, but
he'd come alone out a back door of the theatre and hustled us straight along the street. I realized then that he was
not willing to introduce me and supposed that I came
across as countryish, though I tried not to. I supposed, too,
that he had other girls, actresses perhaps, the ones who'd
played his mothers or sisters or lovers.

In December the big storms began to hit. Freezing rain
came first and then snow. Wind blew around the frames
of Freddie's old, warped storm windows. We couldn't sit

near an outside wall without a scarf and extra sweater, and even so our feet were always cold and the tips of our noses and fingers too. Snow piled up around the front and back of the house, and looking out my window I saw the houses across the lane begin to disappear like shy old ladies behind their veils of snow.

Another boarder moved into the third spare bedroom. She was an old friend of Freddie's and temporarily low on funds, since her husband had died and there was some delay about the will and winding up his estate. Mrs. Edgerly was her name. She was small and olive-skinned and quick in her movements though her hair was grey. She taught biology at a girls' academy high up the hill near Westmount Avenue. She came and went bearing sheaves of exams and homework assignments, all of them crammed into an old brown briefcase that was worn nearly to holes at the corners. And she called me Nancy Jean in a voice of such certainty that, around her, I felt like I was back in high school.

She prevailed on Stephen to shovel the short front walk whenever he was around. It was the only chore I ever saw him do at the house, and Freddie thanked him over and over until I thought he was going to stop doing it and we would find the shovel broken in pieces. Life was generally harder than it had been in the fall. I had thought being in the city would make winter barely count, but I had not figured how snow and ice could drag things down. Power lines fell. Sand and salt made everything filthy. Buses came late. On the mornings when new snow had fallen, getting to work took forever. Waiting at the bus stop, I stamped and shivered, and my feet froze and my legs chapped. In our various hotel rooms George rubbed oil into my skin and cringed over my legs. "Feels like you're going to crack," he told me.

"Not me," I said, but all the same he went out and bought me two pantsuits, one in dark green and one in a black-and-brown check. Both had matching gored skirts which I kept neatly folded in a drawer at work so I could change into them after I got there. At lunch hour I changed back into the pants and went out walking, just to be among the Christmas shoppers and have all around me the coloured lights and red and green and gold decorations. On every street corner I heard the ching-ching of Salvation Army bells, and in the store windows I caught my reflection, quick and dark, a city girl like any other.

The days right around Christmas, Cardiff's was open until nine every night, and we all worked overtime. They'd transferred me back downstairs, this time into Men's Ties and Shirts. No matter what, this would have been more exciting than Junior Dresses two floors up, but it being Christmas, the transfer was bliss. I didn't even care that most of my customers weren't men, but women buying presents. At least I was back on the ground floor. People were shopping like crazy, crowds of them shoving through the aisles like cows headed out to graze: young people, old people, women and men, every face a stranger's. I could smell the outdoors off their coats, see the snow melting on their shoulders. I'd wait on them, sometimes laughing inside but being nice too, telling them what they wanted, recommending ties to go with shirts. I was getting to be good at selling.

I guess George's wife kept him overtime these days as well. Maybe there were Christmas parties. Twice he took me to dinner without renting a room. He looked irritated

and distracted too, and he'd taken to watching me without saying anything, as if he was making up his mind to
some decision. It did cause me to wonder if one of these
days he was going to say "so long." But for my Christmas
present he gave me a heavy, gold-link bracelet that came
from a jeweller called Lucas, and he bought me a long,
long, tight-waisted black coat. This was a maxi-coat, in
style for several years and still extremely chic, although
the hem dragged in the salty slush on the bus steps and
once, for a few terrifying moments, got caught in the down
escalator at Cardiff's. He also bought me real leather boots
that had fur lining and kept my feet quite warm.

Over New Year's weekend, when I finally got some time
off, I took the bus back to Claudeville and had a visit
with my mum. I didn't call Albie. He'd sent me some
papers about a divorce, and I'd written him back from
Montreal to say a divorce was fine with me. My mum
looked the same as ever, worn-out skin and blue, distracted
eyes. She wandered about same as ever too, attended by
Mr. Pritchard and tolerant in her unobserving way of
my dad. He'd been busy with the church over Christmas.
Food collections and services for shut-ins and all manner
of carolling. You'd have thought he was the minister for
all he said he'd had to do. And he behaved all right with
me for the first day and a half, said I looked healthy and
asked if I still had my job. Then he had himself a glass of
whisky after supper and then another, and trouble was
on its way. We were sitting in the front room, my mother
with her gardening magazine and me and my dad with
the day's newspapers. (George had got me in the habit of
reading the paper on account of all his talk about politics

and other current events.) My dad seemed all right reading at first, but I could see his eyes narrow bit by bit and
his nostrils get tight, and I could hear him breathing hard
through his nose. Every time I looked over at him his face
had got more fearsome.

After a while he glanced over his newspaper at me.
"You know you're a shame to this family," he said. I stared
at him. "Wronging your husband like that, like you had
a right. Not a person for miles around doesn't know what
you are, off to the big city." Here the two white lines I
knew so well that I could see them sometimes with my
eyes shut appeared like old knife scars on either side of
his mouth. "Don't think I don't know what you're up to
there, leading a whore's life..." His voice was still low,
but my mum stood up at this point and wobbled out of
the room, carrying her gardening magazine in one hand
and her sherry glass in the other. "Never was a time you
weren't a stubborn, wilful brat..." (the words were coming faster now), "sluttish from the day you were born."

That was the line that pulled him to his feet. Things
about sex usually did. Adulterers and fornicators, not to
mention sodomists and rapists—they all galvanized him.
I'd wondered for years how it was he failed to notice Mum
and Mr. Pritchard mooning through the house and garden.

"...Time come, you'll pay for your sinning." He
made a broad gesture with the back of his hand, as if to
sweep away my sins and possibly me as well, and instead
swept a china lamp and an ashtray off the table beside
him. In that tiny, horrid speck of time while we waited
for the crash, I saw his face go blank as an empty plate.

The lamp shattered like glass, pieces flying everywhere. The crash, I understood, would be my fault. And

then he was moving around the coffee table towards me, his feet crunching through the debris. His face had recovered its rage. Back when I was a kid or even a teenager, this was the moment when the screaming and crying would begin. My screaming and crying, though the noise I made always seemed a space apart from me. I could still feel in one part of my brain my need for such a ruckus, the only way to hold my ground. But now, in another part of my head, my thinking had turned cool and clear, and this made me cool all over and clear in my sight instead of blind. As he came towards me, his eyes slitted, his mouth marked with the white lines, I stepped the other way around the table. Quick and cool as a fox was how I saw myself to be. I turned, still just as cool and quick, and left the room. Up the stairs I marched; I can remember every footfall smacking the hard wood of the treads, and how I listened for the sound of him following behind. But there came no footsteps besides my own. Up I went and passed along the hall. I went by my brother's little bedroom. Since he'd left, my mum had turned it into her sewing room, and she was in there now, snoozing in her sewing chair, her head lolled to one side, her magazine hung over her knee.

In my own room, I threw everything I'd brought into my suitcase, snapped it closed and carried it back to her room. She was still asleep. I took her by the shoulder and shook her. The magazine slid to the floor. "Wake up, Mum."

She blinked up at me. "Nancy Jean?" she said, as if she wasn't quite sure it was me. Then she saw the suitcase in my other hand and straightened up her head.

"You're walking downstairs with me," I said. "He won't get after me if you're there."

"Oh, I don't like—," she began.

"Get up," I said, my hand still on her shoulder. "It's time you helped me." She looked up at me then, really looked, and she got to her feet and came downstairs with me. As we passed the front-room door, I saw he'd sat down again in his chair. He glanced my way, grabbed the chair arms as if to rise, but seeing Mum with me sank back. That was all.

"Goodbye," I said to my mum, after I'd got on my coat and boots.

"Mind the ice on the stoop," she said, as if I were going to town for the groceries. And then I was outside in the dark and hearing the door shut behind me before I was halfway down the little walk.

I trekked about a quarter of a mile along the highway, thinking I'd hitch a ride to the bus depot in Claudeville, switching my suitcase from hand to hand, hearing the crunch of frozen snow under my feet. Our farm was out of sight by then, hidden behind the dark mound of the hill I had just marched up and down. But I could see in my mind the house and the horse barn and cedar hedge and my mum's garden lying ruined beneath the snow and the field behind running down to the pond, all of it receding from my view as though I were moving away at the speed of a jet plane. The stars were out, and I felt that this time, more than back in the fall, I was truly leaving. Staring up at the sky, I began to think about Stephen and how he was as out of reach as those points of light in the black sky and how that must be what drew me, the ice of him. Even the bits of cruelty he tossed off from time to time—though not at me, not so far—even they were icy cold.

My face felt frozen by the time a car stopped. At first I was glad that the man who picked me up was no one I knew. I didn't want to be explaining why I was hitching a ride this time of night. But on a long curve just past where the old schoolhouse stood, he reached across the seat and laid a heavy, gloved hand on my thigh. "Whyn't we stop for a little drink?" he said.

"Hey," I said, and swung my knees away from his grasp.

"Now, don't be like that, honey." He turned his head towards me and jerked the wheel so the car shimmied and skidded in its ruts. In the darkness I couldn't see what his look said, but his voice had gotten rough. "Listen, you want a nice ride to town, don't you, honey? You don't want to walk or nothing?"

I thought I could smell him then, a sharp, dirty smell, like old sweat. Ahead of us the road ran straight towards blackness. "Well," I said. "Well, a drink would be pretty nice, I guess." The cool, clear part of my brain took charge again and went on telling me what to do. I let us get closer to town before I started twisting around in my seat and staring like crazy out the back window. I did this every few seconds.

"You got a problem?" he finally said. A couple of miles ahead of us now was a roadside place I knew called Happy Hank's. Probably that was where he'd had in mind for our little drink. I could get away from him there, I supposed, but it was a joint for louts. The bands did drugs, and there were regular Saturday night fights on the dance floor. I didn't want to be stuck there, and besides, I would miss my bus.

"Oh, no," I said, twisting around again. "No, not a problem. It's just my husband. We had a fight, that's all.

Of course, he probably won't mind my taking a ride with you. Probably. It's just . . . " I paused and shook my head.

"Just what?" he said.

"Just, well, he's ever so jealous, see. If he catches me with a man in a bar . . . well, the last time, he got sent to jail."

"Jail?" The man's head turned again to look at me. The car veered towards the snowbank, and he righted it. "You shitting me or something?" he said.

"Well, you're right, I shouldn't complain," I said, more cheerful now but wagging my head too. "They did let him out pretty quick. It's just this time they might—"

"This time?" The man was staring into his rear-view mirror.

"Well, if he beat you up or something. He gets all crazy mad, see, all white around his mouth. He used to do boxing, see? He likes to hit people." I could see just around the next bend the low, ugly sprawl of Happy Hank's, lit up like a gas station by its parking-lot lights and its big neon sign, and now, turning to look back through the rear window of the car, I spotted a light-coloured car cresting the hill behind us. "Is that a white car?" I said, making my voice high and nervous-sounding.

I got no answer. Staring into his rear-view mirror, the man hunched forward over the wheel and stepped hard on the gas. We shot past Happy Hank's and aimed towards Claudeville at a scary speed. The man didn't speak to me again but drove straight on to the bus depot. When he let me out, he didn't even turn to look at me but kept revving the engine while I got my suitcase out of the back seat. He drove off before I could get the door properly shut.

With my suitcase in my hand, I walked into the depot. The big, square waiting room was warm and brightly lit, and altogether quiet too. The old wooden benches, scarred and scraped, sat empty except for one where a man lay sleeping, his coat over his head as if he were a dead man. The magazine and candy counter opposite was shut. Behind the ticket counter, the grumpy, bearded man, who'd worked there as long as I could remember, scowled at me.

Never in my life had I been so glad to be in such an ugly place. The cold calm was still running my head, but my hands, I now saw, were shaking, and I could barely pay my money to the man behind the window. "Cut it tight, didn't you?" he said to me. "Bus's already here. You haven't got but five minutes."

With my ticket in my pocket, I found the ladies' room and washed my hands and face. In the mirror over the sink, my eyes were huge and dark and my cheeks bright red. I nodded at myself as if to say, You made it through another time, Nancy Jean, and then I went outside and climbed up inside the bus to Montreal. During the trip, while the lights of the Eastern Townships' autoroute flashed past one by one, I thought of my brother, and I wondered where he was and what he might be doing.

PART 2

THE NEXT MORNING FREDDIE'S whole house smelled of baking and especially of cinnamon and other spices. "A few cookies just for tea time, don't you know," she said to me. She stood in the front hall wiping her hands on her apron. I'd just come downstairs and was sitting on the bottom step, hugging my knees and being glad I was here in her house. "You've got ever so many messages," she added, pointing out a little pile of them on the table.

There were five to be exact, one from a girl at work and the others from George. While I was in Claudeville, I hadn't thought of him once. Even Stephen I'd thought about only after I'd left the house and was walking down the road. In my parents' house the world shrank down.

"He must care for you, that young man. All those phone calls, don't you know." Her eager nodding told me how she hoped this was true.

I let her make me tea and toast while I ran back up to my room and then down to the basement to start my laundry. When I'd got her old tub machine churning away, I came up and sat with her in the big, white-painted kitchen. Despite the ice crusted round the rim of the back window, we were warm enough for once. Of course, I had a sweater on over my nightgown and a bathrobe over that and on my feet two pairs of socks. Sipping at my milky tea and looking across the table at her, I thought that she seemed calmer and that her clothes seemed properly middle-aged, a grey wool skirt and cardigan and only a little lipstick so that her jowly face looked not so massive around her tiny mouth.

"You know, dear," she said after a bit, "I had a beau once myself."

"A beau?" I said.

"Oh, yes, I did. He was around calling on me two and three times a week, having chats with my father, don't you know." Talking, she poured me more tea, refilled her own cup and set the teapot down again between us. "And then he up and married my friend. Sugar, dear?"

I shook my head. "Just the milk, please. Married your friend?"

"That's right, dear. The best one I had. They met at my house, of course, and more than once, him being my beau and her my best friend. It was her took his fancy away from me, though I don't suppose she realized that at first, and maybe he didn't either, and then of course they both did."

"Your best friend and your boyfriend," I said, awed. That had happened once in high school. The two girls had had a terrific cat fight in the cafeteria, knocking over a tray with someone's lunch on it and some chairs too, and pulling out one another's hair, just like in the movies. Of course they got themselves suspended for their trouble, and by the time they came back to school, they had got to be quite good friends again, having had nothing to do during their suspensions but see each other. And neither of them liked the boyfriend any more, though that might have been because he'd already got himself a new girl.

"But I couldn't be mad at her or at him," Freddie was saying. "He just didn't love me; that's all there was to that." Her face had gone pink. She stirred her tea extra hard, and I saw she had a brightness in her button eyes. "He had chestnut hair, rich-looking, like Stephen's when he's not dyeing it for one of those TV shows. He could have been Stephen's father, don't you know. He's the right age, and with that hair and all..."

"Stephen doesn't seem like anybody's son," I said.

"Poor boy." Freddie was shaking her head, which

made her cheeks and her curls quiver. "He never had a proper home, father up and left them, mother a menace to herself, so they tell me. My sister lived next door. She was the one sent him to me. Some trouble he'd got into there in Halifax, police and all, some money that went missing and gossip about some girls and another time about an old relative of the mother's. A handsome boy like that. You know how people will say things." Saying all this she got more and more breathless, as though there was some kind of strain in telling me.

I took one of her cookies just to give her time to say more about Stephen's past. The cookie was soft enough to chew for once, and I ate it slowly, but she didn't seem to have any more to tell, so when I'd finished I went down to the basement. It took me a while to pass my laundry through the wringer and get all my things hung up to dry. When I came up to the kitchen again, Freddie had gone upstairs and the telephone was ringing.

It was George, and I remembered then about the messages. He sounded excited, as if he'd escaped from somewhere, and I supposed that in one way or another he had. Hearing his voice made me feel I'd got back my Montreal life, as if Claudeville wasn't entirely real but something like a bad dream, one I didn't have to have again.

That evening though, in George's latest restaurant, with George staring at me across the table and not a trace of good humour on his face, I wasn't all that sure. Where was cheerful, amusing George? And what were we doing in this, the toniest part of downtown Montreal? The restaurant faced across Mountain Street towards the big side entrance to Holt Renfrew, which was the ritziest store I knew of.

The room where we sat must once have been the front parlour of an old mansion. Plaster flowers and leaves decorated the ceiling and a portion of the walls like frosting on a wedding cake. The wine glasses looked like my mum's sherry glasses. I could imagine old-fashioned, well-heeled people wandering about in here a century ago. I myself was wearing my green pantsuit and my gold bracelet and quite a lot of eye makeup, though I had stopped using the frosted, white-pink lipstick. I'd pulled my hair back and up off my face and had clipped it high with two big barrettes so that it fluffed down my back. This was rich-girl style, as I'd read in *Cosmopolitan* magazine, sexy and elegant and just the sort of hairdo to entice a man accustomed to debutantes and other society women. I had expected to have a good time, to have George tell me funny, wonderful stories that would make me forget Claudeville altogether.

Now, across the table from me, George's eyebrows slanted together like two black marks, crossing out the usual cheerfulness of his face. He'd hardly talked, and he kept staring at me so hard I felt as if there was something I should understand without being told. At nearly every table, people were eating and talking. They looked serious, some of them, and you could tell a lot of them were trying to impress someone, but nobody except George looked like they knew the secret of when World War III was going to start.

Swirling the pale wine in my glass the way George had taught me to do, I sniffed it, as he'd also taught me to do. Then I took a swallow and gave him a look over the rim of the glass. "I'm bored, George," I said. "Tell me a story, a good story."

He blinked at me a lot then, as if he was trying to get back to his normal self and was also thinking over what I'd asked. At last he smiled. "A story it is," he said. Then he nodded as if he was agreeing with his decision, drank some of his own wine and nodded again.

"This one's about a friend of mine," he said finally. "He's a lawyer, a new partner in one of the top firms, offices in Place Ville-Marie, branch offices in London and Paris, and he's set to run for Parliament sooner or later, whenever Trudeau calls an election. It's the guy's ambition. You know the type. He's been raised for it. He's educated and bright, fluently bilingual, talks well, likes the crowd scene. His wife's on board with the plan, connected as hell herself. Her father's head of a major brokerage. He's got the world's cutest kid too. My friend, I mean. A two-year-old boy." Here, George stopped as if his story had surprised him.

"Sounds like I'll be reading about him," I said.

"Well, you're right." George was nodding. "You will. I mean, you would have, except the guy's gone and done the damnedest, stupidest thing you could imagine." He took another swallow of his wine. "So stupid, so nuts you can't believe it. And the thing is, nobody can talk him out of it."

"Sir." The waiter had brought our menus and was trying to hand them to us. George waved him away.

"Hey, listen," I said, "I'm hungry." But the waiter had already turned away. "What do you mean?" I said, " 'Talk him out of it?' I thought you said the guy already did it?"

"He has, but he's going to do worse." Now George was leaning towards me, and I could see his face flush up. "What he's done, the stupid idiot, he's fallen in love with some girl two-thirds his age, a child if you get right down to it. He's nuts about her, nuts, like . . . " Here he drew a big breath and shook his head as though his friend was just now telling him the story and he, George, just couldn't believe his ears.

"He told you all this?" I said.

"He tells me everything. His friend has told him not to do it."

"Another friend said that?"

"No, my friend did. I mean, I did to my friend. Call him Charles. He's going to—"

"Charles?" I said. "Your friend's called Charles?"

George shook his head, then nodded it. "That's right," he said. He was looking around the room as if his own story had confused him and he couldn't figure how he'd gotten to where he was. Seeing him do this, the waiter headed for us again.

"Would you let that waiter give us the menus this time?" I said. I could feel that cool part of my brain taking over. "I'm truly and really starving," I said.

"Oh, right. Sorry." George took both menus from the waiter, flipped one open, then closed it. "We'll have the potage, whatever it is," he said to the waiter, "and the tournedos Rossini, rare. All right?" He glanced over at me. "That's a steak."

"Okay," I said, and shrugged.

"And a bottle of that claret you gave me last week, the one you import yourselves," he added, looking up at the waiter, who was writing things down and nodding vigorously, as if these orders were brilliance itself.

When the waiter had gone, I leaned back in my chair. The chair had arms and was almost as comfy as a real chair in a real front parlour. The wine in my glass was the same pale, greenish gold as the bracelet on my wrist. "So," I said, fingering the bracelet and lining up the links, "do you call him Charlie?" I glanced up to see George was back to staring at me. His face had flushed up again, and behind his glasses his eyes had gone all wild, and I could see he was thinking about going to bed with me. "Your friend," I said. "You call him Charlie?"

"Oh." He shook his head. "No, Charles. Only Charles."

I nodded. "Sounds high class. Charles. Like a minister in the government or whatever he has in mind for himself. Maybe he'll be the prime minister, your friend Charles." I shook my head. "If he doesn't screw it up, poor guy."

Over the steak George told me his friend Charles wanted to set up the girl in an apartment. He wanted to send her to university, have her quit her job. I ate my meat; it had bacon wrapped around it and, stuck on top of it, a piece of something black that George said was truffle, and also a slice of liver paste, which I didn't ordinarily like but which tasted much, much better than liver ordinarily did. I wasn't talking much, even between bites, because I wanted to hear everything George had to say and because I was still thinking, and one of the things I was thinking was that for a girl who'd lost her feelings, I had a lot of them roiling around in me right now.

Finally I sat back and wiped my mouth politely on my napkin and put it back in my lap. "Listen, George," I said then. "You know, it's amazing, but I just thought of something. This friend of yours, he wouldn't be R. Charles Weymouth by any chance?" George's mouth dropped open. "Because, you see, there's this remarkable thing..."

I paused and shook my head as though I was barely able to speak about such a remarkable thing. "Well you'd just hardly believe it, but I believe I know the girl he's so crazy about. Her name is Esmeralda." I smiled at him, ever so brightly. (When I was quite little, I'd used to imagine I was adopted and my true name was Esmeralda.) "She works at Cardiff's, right beside me in Men's Wallets and Belts. Can you believe that? She's still married in fact... to a loser guy that she's ditched back in whatever loser town she comes from. And she's told me that about the last thing she wants these days is some thirty-something guy with a wife and a kid, who by the way doesn't have the guts to use his own name with her, can you believe that, the last thing she wants is this guy to lock her up in an apartment so that she can study university books all day and all night except for the once in a dog's age when mister thirty-something can sneak away from his wife and kiddie. That's about the most deadly boring kind of life my friend can think of." I took a deep breath. "By the way, what's the R stand for?"

George had shut his mouth. His face was a deep purple-red. His eyes behind his glasses kept blinking as though they were seeing something they'd never expected to see. "You're married?" he said finally and knocked over his wine. We both watched it pour into the basket of bread. I remember thinking it was a good thing I'd already sopped up most of my steak juice.

The next Sunday, which was three days after the dinner on Mountain Street, George showed up at Freddie's. I'd left the restaurant right after the wine spilled. He hadn't been able to follow me on account of it and the bill, so I was able to pop outside and dash up to Sherbrooke Street, where I caught a bus. I had not returned his telephone call, and there had been only the one.

Now, standing in Freddie's hall, he looked like a bum and also like he hadn't slept in all the time since I'd seen him. His dark brown hair was sticking up in little points, and his glasses were held together at one corner with a safety pin.

He didn't talk like a bum though. Stamping the snow off his boots, he talked like someone in charge of a project. He'd organize my divorce, he said. His own would be a bit trickier. We would get married.

"Now see here," I said, staring at the safety pin. It was impossible not to.

"Wait, listen, I've got it figured out..." Holding up one hand like a traffic cop, he went on talking, so fast I missed some of his words. It was as though he was trying not to allow either of us to notice the earthquake-size upheaval that his words were concocting. The *R* in his name, he concluded, stood for Reginald. He never used it.

"That makes sense," I said. Above us I heard Freddie's ponderous footsteps, and for the second time since I'd lived at Freddie's, I dragged him into the parlour. For just a second I thought to wonder if it was here in this room that Freddie's best friend and her beau had told her how things stood. The afternoon sun was shining through the front window and making beams of golden light in the dusty air. Sunlit, the old plush sofa looked dustier than ever and the sunlit rugs did too. I took George by the forearms and backed him towards the sofa. When he was safely sitting, I went myself and half-sat, half-leaned on the arm of a chair far enough from the sofa that he couldn't reach me.

He started in again right away, going on about private bills in the Senate and how, thanks to Pierre Elliott Trudeau saying the state had no place in the bedrooms of the nation, such things were no longer required to get a divorce, and then he talked about his career plans and how he meant to alter them, and about his little boy and how he knew he wouldn't get custody but how he would still be a good father to him, teaching him to play hockey and squash, and making him study history and economics. Finally I stood up and walked back over to where he sat and put my hands on his shoulders. "Listen to me, George."

He put his hands around my hips, and for once his grabbing me was not full of ideas about sex. Instead, the clutch of his hands felt as though he was hanging onto me to save his life. I was looking down onto the thin spot on the top of his skull, and I could feel the desperation in his hands, and I found myself wondering if he could stand the strain of his own desires. I had never done that before, actually thought about what someone else was feeling, and it gave me an odd floating sensation for a second or two, as though I'd temporarily lost gravity.

"Now pay attention to me, George," I said to the top of his head. "Try to take this in. I just got myself free from my old life, see?" It was true: I had walked out the door of my parents' house not a week ago, and it had been an important door for me to walk out of, much more important than the door of Albie's and my apartment. "Free is what I want," I said. "Not your apartment. Not getting married. I'm twenty years old next month. I've got myself to myself for the first time ever. I'm in the city. I'm having fun. And I'm going to have more fun." I paused because it occurred to me that fun was not what I'd been having lately.

While I was trying to think about this, George let go of me and kind of collapsed back on the sofa. The dusty light from the window shone against the side of his face, so that I could see where the dark whiskers grew from his skin. He went on some more, mostly out of reflex, I guess, but I could see he'd got the message, because all the while he was talking and talking, he was looking up at me too, in a surprised way, like I was someone other than who he'd thought I was.

Finally, he got to his feet, and at that moment we heard the front door open and shut. Cold air blew into the parlour, rattling one of the lamps and the ornaments on Freddie's green plastic Christmas tree. It was stuck over in the corner where it wasn't much to notice. She herself preferred real trees, she said, but this was a tree her parents had got in their later years. "Decorated it up so beautifully every year. They'd got too old for the mess and fuss of a real one, don't you know."

For me this tree recalled my parents' own tree back in Claudeville, which for the last ten years had likewise been a plastic one. My brother and I had deplored it, but ever since the year our cut-down tree had burnt up in our front room the day before the New Year, my parents had refused to have a live one.

The fire happened when I was in the fifth grade. The flames had seemed to burst from nothing. One second, ordinary lamplight lit the room, and my brother was reading a book about dinosaurs that I hoped to snaffle from him as soon as possible. My mother was mending socks over a wooden form that she called a darning egg and that looked like a miniature bowling pin. And then in the next second, our front room was brilliant with orange light and full of the fiercest crackle and roar. I remember my brother shouting, "Fire, fire," in a voice so happy it didn't sound like his. My father roared something about us two children fetching a bucket. My mother shrieked that she had always hated Christmas. "Always, always..." I had never heard her voice like that, like it was torn out of her, and I can hear it still.

In the few seconds it took for those things to be said, flames had burnt up our entire tree and most of the curtain on the west window as well. My father, after shouting his order about the bucket, which each of us had ignored, managed to smother the burning windowsill and what remained of the tree fire with our hall rug. The fire, we then saw, had melted all the ornaments and turned the wall and ceiling black. The rug in question had been a square of flowered English carpet that my mother had brought with her from her own mother's house. The rug survived (though with its bottom side blackened and peculiarly crisped) until spring cleaning, when on a windy afternoon in early May, it disintegrated while being beaten on the clothesline.

These had all been dramatic, wonderful incidents— the tree, the curtain, my mother's and brother's remarks, my father's competent action, even the delayed demise of the carpet square—and each one well worth the happening, but it was the fire itself that had thrilled me above all, the amazing moment when the tree had burst, all at once it had seemed, into flame. As though real Christmas angels reaching down from heaven, their mission to destroy, had touched its every branch and twig with fingertips of fire.

"You could catch your death in this house." George was shaking his head. He must have interrupted himself from whatever he was saying in order to tell me this. "I mean, feel that draft. No insulation. You'll get pneumonia one of these days."

"No, I won't," I said, still thinking of that Christmas tree. "I'm a very healthy girl. There's always a draft when someone opens the door."

We walked out into the hall, and there was Stephen with snow on his boots. His suitcase stood beside him on the floor. He was stripping off a beautiful pair of brown leather gloves that I hadn't seen before, and he looked worse than George. He looked, in fact, like he had been through some dreadful illness. His skin was ashy and his eyes were all purple underneath. A red mark ran along one side of his jaw. Even his hair, which reached his shoulders now and had recently been bleached to the colour of brass, looked ruined and dirty. For all that, standing there, he was still a beautiful creature.

He raised his eyebrows at me. "So, Nancy Jean." He spoke in his deep, actor's voice. "Back from the country."

"That's right," I said. I introduced the two men and watched them shake hands—George, a head taller nearly, Stephen staring up, his face without expression. They grunted something manly at one another. Then Stephen stepped around us and headed for the kitchen, leaving his suitcase melting snow onto the hall rugs.

"Jesus," said George, gazing after him, "that's one weird-looking guy."

"He's an actor," I said.

"He doesn't look safe to have around," said George.

"Oh, Stephen's harmless," I said. "Besides, I can take care of myself." I picked George's coat off the stair railing where he'd tossed it, hours ago it seemed, and handed it to him.

"Taking care of you is my job," said George. He sounded so pompous I laughed. I let him kiss me, and, while he was putting on his coat, I promised to meet him after work in two days' time. At the door he grabbed both my hands. "Listen, just don't—," he began.

"By the way," I said, interrupting him, "You should get your glasses fixed."

After I got the door shut on him, I stood there watching through the pane of stained glass until his green and blue self had disappeared down the street. I felt tired then in a way that I almost never did, and for a second I laid my cheek against the varnished wood of the door. When I turned, Stephen was standing at the far end of the hall, his body silhouetted against the white light of the kitchen. I couldn't tell if he was facing me or the kitchen.

Then he came towards me, and I could see his face again and the look of sickness on it. "That a boyfriend?" he said.

"Sort of." I shrugged. "You look awful, by the way. Did someone try to poison you?"

"More or less." He came up close to me and took the flesh of my cheek between his thumb and forefinger. He didn't pinch hard, but I knew he wanted me to think how it would feel if he did. I remembered the rose-and-gold teacup, and he saw me remembering and smiled. Right after that we went upstairs.

It was the only time I ever had sex with Stephen in daylight, and afterwards I cried. I did not think the two facts were connected. As soon as the tears started down my face, Stephen got up and began to pull on his pants. These were black, tight around the hips and flared wide at the ankle. He wore with them a cream suede shirt, very full in the sleeves. Theatrical clothes. Expensive too, and I thought to wonder where he had got them.

"You going out with this Charles sometime soon?" He spoke without looking at me.

"Charles?" I sat up on the bed and rubbed my eyes, which were sore from the tears. My head had begun hurting too. And now I saw that my clothes were all over the floor; Stephen was standing on my sweater.

"What's-his-name, the guy who was just here," said Stephen.

"Oh, Charles. Yes, tomorrow, I guess . . . or rather—"

"Too bad," Stephen said, buckling his belt, which was several inches wide and had metal studs punched into the leather. "There's a party tomorrow night. Some actors from the play." He kicked my sweater aside.

"Oh," I said, thinking I did not much feel like a party. However, tomorrow was not today. I would take Aspirin, something to make me feel better. Actors, he had said. Actors were people who spoke sentences invented by other people, made fake lives look real. This, it seemed to me, might be the greatest freedom, to live an entirely made-up life, full of glamour and crisis, yet without consequences. "A party," I said. "Well, where should I meet you?" I saw contempt in his smile. No need to tell him he wasn't really breaking up a date between me and George. "I get off work at nine," I said.

"St-Denis metro, by the ticket booth." He forgot to make his voice deep and it twanged a bit. He turned and walked out of my room.

Later, when I was taking my laundry down to the basement, I could hear him in the kitchen teasing Freddie. He was speaking in the falsetto voice he used to mimic her. "Oh, heavens," I heard him say.

And then I heard her say it too, "Oh, heavens. My mother gave me that. Oh, heavens!" She sounded close to crying. Perhaps she already was. I've got to get out of here, I thought, and was immediately surprised at the notion.

The next evening, it had got near to ten o'clock by the time I met up with Stephen. I was feeling much better. Work had refreshed me, it being the month of big sales and the store consequently being full of bargain hunters, most of them in a mood to fight and buy. We'd moved almost all our Christmas stock, even including a few pink-and-yellow ties I'd thought no one would ever buy. I guessed the January thaw had brought out so many shoppers, there was bound to be someone among them who would choose the worst there was.

The night was still not perishing cold the way it had been at Christmas. Wrapped in my new coat I felt citified and clear-headed and on the verge of new adventure. Stephen and I walked up the hill from the metro, crossing Sherbrooke and Pine, climbing more and more gradually through the snowy air. The lights and the cars sloshing by on the salted street, the people alighting from cabs in front of restaurants or popping out of bars along the street, everyone bundled into coats and scarves and hats, all of it and all of them seemed to me wonderful. I had been so glad that whole day to be back at work. Now I was glad to be walking with beautiful Stephen at my side, his hair gleaming in the street lights.

Our destination, Stephen said, was a friend's apartment. Turning east off of St-Denis, we threaded through a narrow, snow-blocked street and then another. The friend's place was in a red stone house that, I supposed, had once been fine. A stone beast with claws and a monster's head crouched above the door. The lintel was wide and massive-looking, the floor of the foyer paved with squares of pale stone. If I hadn't immediately smelled garbage and, in the stairwell, bad plumbing as well, and if I hadn't, with every step, ground unswept grit beneath the soles of my boots, I might have thought the place quite splendid.

Lifting the long panels of my maxi-coat, so they wouldn't drag and trip me on the stairs, I climbed and at the same time listened for party sounds, but all I heard was Stephen's tread close behind me like an echo of my own. In all this tall, old house, it seemed, there was only the sad clatter of our footsteps.

At the fourth flight I was breathing hard and thinking of reasons for why I should leave, when I heard the click of a door opening above us. In the sudden wash of light, the hall and stairwell became empty and strange. "My, oh my," came a dry voice. "If it isn't pretty Stephen come to see his friend Del. And with a little chum. How jolly."

The man waiting to greet us as we reached the fifth level was taller than Stephen and more solidly built. He was also older. His long black hair had grey mixed in. "So. The country girl," he said to Stephen and shook my hand in an exaggerated way. Though he had sounded sarcastic, his eyes gazed at me and then at Stephen with what looked like reproach and maybe sadness too.

In his apartment there was no party, no people at all but us three, and, to tell the truth, the big front room looked not quite furnished. There were places to sit, but it was as if earlier in the evening a couple of broad-backed movers had lugged in the black leather couch and the small white and black rug, the metal floor lamps, the chair made of chrome and canvas. These were set at one end of the room like rocks in a river. The rest of the wood floor was bare and shiny. Along one wall, shelves held records and what looked like fancy stereo equipment. On the opposite wall hung a bunch of photographs. These were black and white and all, as far as I could see, of naked men and women arched or folded into dancer's poses.

While Stephen went out to the kitchen to find us something to drink, I walked over to look at these pictures and discovered the people in them were not in fact naked, but wearing leotards. I supposed that Del had something to do with dancing as well as acting.

"Got anything new?" That was Stephen's voice calling from the kitchen. "You lost out to Franz at the Tuppenny, didn't you?"

Del had dropped down onto his leather couch. The cushions had made a sound like a slow fart as his body sank into them. His eyes had been following my stroll along the wall, and now I saw them squeeze shut for a second, as though the mention of his losing out to whoever Franz might be was too much for him to bear. He drew a hand across his brow, like Camille dying in the old movie. "Oh, Stephen," he said, "don't remind me. You know the drill, mostly voice-overs . . . nausea first and last.

I did read for Gustav last week, but of course I haven't heard. It's just—"

"Are you sure you've got something decent to drink out here?" That was Stephen again.

"Of course, I do, Stephen, dear. Over the fridge. Just look. I had some grass too. Jean-François brought me a tot of Acapulco Gold last week. He buys it over at the université. But that's all gone bye-bye now." He glanced over at me then. I was still standing in my coat, more or less in the middle of the room. "Do sit down, Nancy Jean, darling, and do take off that long, long coat."

I slid out of my coat and then lowered myself into the chair. Del pulled out a pack of cigarettes and lit himself one. He sighed as he exhaled, and then, as if it was almost more than he could manage, he tossed the pack and his lighter to me. "Sorry, darling. I'm a beast when I'm not working."

I took a cigarette from his pack and lit it. The cigarette tasted dry and hot, as though the tobacco was old. I didn't much like to smoke in any case, but I persisted, taking big drags and exhaling as fiercely as I dared. I'd decided that I needed to do something in order to make my presence felt. Stephen came back with three glassfuls of a dark brown liquid that smelled of prunes but tasted worse than any prunes I'd ever been made to eat.

"Where do you get this stuff?" said Stephen. "It tastes like shit." I would have agreed if anyone had asked me. The drink had a kick though—it reminded me of the distilled cider we'd called white lightning back in Claudeville—and halfway through my glassful I could feel myself getting light-headed. I was getting bored too. If there was a party on its way, I saw no reliable signs of it.

Del had got up once to put a record on the stereo, a slow, husky voice sighing over lost girlfriends in a kind of French I'd never heard before. He and Stephen were talking about directors and other actors, especially one whose name was Porter. "The mental midget," Stephen called him, and Del said, "But he was in love with you, Stephen, dear."

The telephone rang twice, and Del talked for several minutes with one caller. When he'd hung up from the second call, I took another swallow of my ugly drink and asked him if I could have something to eat.

"You're hungry, darling?" he said, as if he'd never heard of something so peculiar.

"More or less," I said. The truth was that I was feeling a bit dizzy, but mainly I just wanted to do something. "I'll go get myself whatever you have," I added and stood up. Right then blackness flooded into my head. I felt myself sway and grabbed the back of my chair. The blackness filled my brain for another moment, with a kind of roar going on in my ears at the same time, and then both the blackness and the roar began to clear. I saw that Del had got to his feet and that both men were eyeing me. "I'm fine," I said, though they hadn't asked, and I thought to myself that I would not drink any more of the dark brown stuff.

"So, get her some food," Stephen said, as though his permission was required.

In the kitchen Del found me crackers and a wedge of Gouda cheese in its skin of red wax. My head still felt odd and my stomach hollow, though I had eaten supper in the cafeteria at work. He sliced the wedge in three and handed me a piece. I pulled off the wax and stuffed the cheese into my mouth along with a cracker.

My mouth was quite full still when he grabbed my wrist and leaned down into my face. "He's not for you. You leave him alone." His breath was warm and damp against my forehead, almost as though he'd spit on me. The knife he'd used to cut through the rind of the cheese lay between us on the cutting board.

I pointed with my free hand at my mouth to show I couldn't answer. In fact, I could think of nothing to say. He was still squeezing my wrist. "You're hurting me," I said finally, through the crackers and cheese.

He let go then. "You shouldn't have come. Nobody wants you here," he said to me, and he walked out of the kitchen. I saw him turn and head along the hall towards what must be the apartment's bedroom.

The crackers tasted stale, but I finished the other pieces of cheese and went back to the front room. Stephen, lounging on the couch, his fingers flipping the pages of a magazine, didn't glance up. From somewhere else in the apartment I heard a few bangs, like doors slamming or drawers shutting hard. My head still felt very strange, and now my stomach did too. I sat down again in the chair. That there was no party, never had been a party, I understood. What I didn't understand was why I was here at all.

I thought I would leave then, but my body did not move. The darkness from beyond the window at the far end of the room seemed to be flowing into me, filling my head again. The music on the hi-fi had changed to a song from *Sergeant Pepper*, angry sounding, though it seemed to be getting quieter and quieter, and I could not make out all the words.

"Don't pass out on me," Stephen's voice said, and I realized I had closed my eyes and begun to nod. He got up and came and hauled me to my feet and pushed me across the room. I kept losing my balance, and he shoved me quite hard so that I fell sideways onto the couch.

He began to unbutton my blouse and then, piece by piece, pulled off all my clothes, half-dragging me off the couch once or twice. After he had gotten everything off me, he made me drink what was left of the brown liquid in my glass, holding my hair so tight it hurt and pushing the rim against my lips. I meant to tell him to quit it, to say that I did not want to be treated like this, that I wanted to leave, but no words came out of my mouth. I hardly even seemed to be breathing. What happened next I could not afterwards remember too well, except that part of me seemed separate from the rest of me. He turned me over on my stomach, and some of what he did to me then hurt quite a lot, and that made for another strangeness which was that I couldn't seem to object to anything he did, though I heard a voice cry out in pain more than once and knew it for my own. A while later there was a loud thump somewhere nearby. I felt Stephen's weight lift off me, and I managed then to pull myself up to a kneeling position. Dizziness took my head for a moment but not so severe as it had been before.

A little ways away Stephen was standing naked with his arms folded, gazing down at me. I knew the look on his face, the shine of his grey eyes, the smile that was partly sneer. It was the look he wore when he'd done something really mean to Freddie. "So?" he said, and as if he had just finished some task and was showing it off, he snapped his fingers. "So, what do you think?"

I drew breath to say that I wanted to leave, and then I saw that Del was standing on the other side of the room.

He wore only underpants. They were black and the rest of him was a pale mushroom colour. He stood there sniffling and shaking his head. His cheeks, I saw, were wet. "Nobody can hurt like you, Stephen," he said.

"It's fun to hurt you," said Stephen. "I told you that."

"Oh, I know, I know." Del's gaze swung towards me. "Another one," he said. "She looks awful. What is that stuff you give them, Stephen, dear?"

"What stuff?" I said, and my voice sounded fuzzy and far away. "Who's 'them'?"

They both looked at me. "Tell her, Stephen." Del's voice scratched. "Tell her what you did to the others. Tell her what you told them."

Stephen laughed. "You stink, too," he said to Del. "Don't you know that?" He laughed again and, stepping over to me, poked the calf of my leg with his foot. "You want to try her? She won't say no now."

Del's sarcastic voice said, "I'm afraid I don't have your tastes, Stephen, dear."

In my head the cold part of my brain was taking over. Trying to get to my feet, I felt as if I weighed a thousand pounds, but I made it to a standing position. "All you are is a nasty little bastard," I said to Stephen.

A look I had never seen before came over his face. For a second his features twisted into something not human but more like a dragon's face. His skin flushed red. Then he raised his hand and slapped my face so hard my ears buzzed. "Don't call me that," he said.

Del laughed through his tears, "Oh, do hit her some more."

At that instant, nausea went all through me. "Bathroom," I mumbled and then said it louder. "Bathroom."

The two of them stared at me. I clapped a hand to my mouth and Del took a backward step. "Oh, Christ," he said. "Not here. Don't hit her again. Down the hall, darling, on the left."

As I rushed past, banging into the door frame and then the wall, I heard him call, "Do hurry," followed by Stephen's rasping laugh.

It took me a few minutes to throw up the brown drink and all the crackers and cheese and the sandwich I'd had earlier in the evening at work. I didn't bother being careful where all the mess landed. When my stomach had ceased to heave, I washed my face and hands and threw water on my cheeks until I stopped feeling dizzy. In the mirror my face looked back at me, as if to ask what the hell had I done getting myself into this place. I fingered the broad, red mark on my cheek. It hurt to touch, and it was right at that instant I began to feel a clutching in my gut. This was not nausea but something deeper down, and I knew it for fear.

I took a towel and wrapped it around myself and headed back into the front room. If they tried to keep me here, and if I screamed, would anybody hear? Had there been a line of light under any doors as we'd climbed the stairs? Had I seen any lit windows from the street?

The front room was deserted. I stood for a second, wondering whether I was in luck and they had gone out. I was trying also to remember what had happened to my clothes. Right then I heard a grunt, and at the same time something round and pale rose above the back of the couch like a blind face peering over a wall. As I slipped around the end of the couch, I saw the two of them on the cushions, Del kneeling, naked ass in the air, his broad back and dark head bowed low as if in worship, and stretched beneath him like some kind of prayer rug, Stephen's prostrate form.

Stephen lay on his back, his eyes closed, his bright hair spread over the black leather. Impaled there was my first thought. He looked like a sacrifice, and for a second I actually believed that in some way he was. A heap of what must have been their clothes lay in the chair, and I saw my own clothes piled on the floor. On top of them, a man's shoe rested. It had left a dust print of its sole on the front of my black maxi-coat.

How exactly I got out of there, I couldn't afterwards recall. I dressed in the dark stairwell, pulling my clothes on any way I could, and then I must have found my way down the flights of stairs, out onto the sidewalk, figured out what direction to walk. Days seemed to have passed since I'd arrived, though it couldn't have been all that late because I remember stumbling onto a bus at the top of Pine and St-Laurent. I didn't know how many blocks I'd come from Del's apartment, only that I hurt inside and my feet were numb, and the rest of me was so chilled I never expected to be warm again. And I knew, too, that I felt lost, the way you feel lost in a dream, without boundaries or light or any kind of necessary knowledge. Lost in my new city.

During the night my head began to hurt so cruelly I believed I might die there in my bed, without ever having another adventure or even getting old. I had no idea what Stephen had put into my drink, but I thought the bones of my skull would split. Only towards morning did the pain ease enough so I could feel a deeper ache down inside my body. I dozed for an hour or so, then got up, still with the feeling of fever. I had taken a bath the night before, but now I took another, scrubbing my body as hard as I could stand to. When I came back to my room, I saw that there was blood on my sheets, so I pulled them off my bed. Then I put on an extra sweater and my socks and bathrobe and went downstairs to the kitchen.

I told Freddie I was feeling not too well, and she made me tea while I called in sick to work. We were alone in the house, she and I. Stephen had not appeared, and Mrs. Edgerly had gone off to visit a friend in the village of Knowlton. Freddie said I did indeed look ill. Bustling around the kitchen while I sat at the table, she talked on, filling the space between us. She thought she would get a dog, maybe two. "It's just the walking them in winter I worry about..." A moment later she was telling me about a recipe for lamb stew she'd clipped out of *Chatelaine*. "It's the quality of meat makes all the difference. They don't tell you that."

After a few minutes, she got down the red cookie tin, and, when I refused, she set the tin still open on the table in front of me. The smell nearly made me gag. She sat down facing me. "You know, dear, there's good in everyone, I wouldn't say otherwise, but the truth is Stephen's not always nice to people." I stared at her and then at the cookie tin. Her hand had plunged into it. "Now me," she said, "I don't mind his little meannesses, don't you know. An older woman understands." Out came the hand clutching a huge, lumpy cookie.

As she went on, gnawing at the cookie now and talking about Stephen and how she understood him, I sat there sipping my tea and hoping I would feel better soon.

Crumbs dusted her lips and her double chins, and into my mind came a picture of her face becoming altogether covered in bits of cookie. While she talked, her little eyes were peering kindly at me, and also a bit nervously, and I understood that this was because she was telling me, in the nicest way she could, that Stephen was really hers. I also thought that she was sincere in meaning me to understand that Stephen could be dangerous.

"Now that George fellow," she said, after a minute or two more of telling how Stephen's mother had done bad things to him, "he's ever so sweet on you, I can tell." Her voice had gone all cheery.

Meantime the tea was not agreeing with me. I'd already begun to sweat while she'd been explaining how it was she who understood Stephen, and now my stomach gave a fearful heave. "I don't feel so good," I said and jumped from my chair and ran to the sink. All the tea I'd just drunk came gushing from my throat, followed by some shiny, phlegmy stuff that I spat after it into the sink. I heard an "Oh, heavens," and a good deal of rushing about behind me. My back was patted and a towel pushed into my hand.

Finally the heaving ceased. I waited for a moment, then, as I had the night before, splashed water on my face and washed the mess down the drain. A bitter taste stayed in my mouth, and I felt as though I was doomed to go on vomiting up every speck of substance inside me for all my life, until inside my skin I was nothing but bone.

"A touch of the tummy flu, I expect." Freddie's voice was aflutter with concern. I stood up and glanced around. Her bright button eyes were gazing at me. Her hands were clasped over her apron. "You must have been exposed downtown," she said. "A big store like Cardiff's, it's a terrible place for picking up a bug, don't you know."

I nodded. "Sure," I said, "downtown is where I must've got it."

I stayed for a while at the kitchen table. I could drink no more tea, but I kept taking sips of water to wash away the bitterness in my mouth and throat. I was thinking that since coming to Montreal I'd made some big mistakes. Sex wasn't the fun I'd meant it to be, and wickedness hadn't lived up to its promise either. Not one of the boys I'd picked up in the bars, not even the leanest and cutest, had turned out to be half as much fun as the idea of him had been. The fact was I couldn't exactly remember one from another. Only Stephen I could not forget.

I moved out of Freddie's house quite soon after that. George (as I'd gone on calling him) was glad enough to hear my plans. "Didn't like the look of that actor type," he said and went on to tell me he was looking for an apartment himself, whether I was ready to marry him or not. "Near the squash club," he said, making a weird slashing motion with his hand. Squash, it turned out, was not a vegetable, but some kind of game played with a racquet.

Stephen I'd seen only twice since the night at Del's. One time a man drove him to the house and waited in his sports car, which I thought was an Austin-Healey, while Stephen ran inside to fetch his mail and other things. Both times I saw him he was wearing a heavy gold chain and beautiful new clothes, a brown cashmere coat and then a handsome sheepskin jacket, and both times at the sight of him, my stomach curled into a tight snaky beast. "So, Nancy Jean," he said, passing me in the hall, breezy as could be, and I knew I was afraid of him.

I'd already heard of a share in a Côte-des-Neiges apartment with three other girls, one from work and the other two her friends. They were pleased when I said I'd move in. There was a small, extra bedroom, going more or less to waste (they kept the ironing board in there now), and with me in the picture, the rent would be split four ways instead of three.

The day I moved, Freddie came up to my room to bring me the two big, plastic garbage sacks I'd asked her for. I'd bought myself some towels and sheets at the white sale up in Linens. On account of all that and George's gifts too, I had more stuff than my suitcases could take. The garbage sacks would hold the rest.

While I shoved the last things into the sacks, she stood in the doorway just as she had that first day, clasping her hands over her stomach and talking in her baby voice.

"Oh, I do hate goodbyes," she told me. "It was ever so nice to have you. I could tell from the first you were a nice girl." When she said this, I surprised myself by being grateful. She was wearing her favourite outfit, the crimson blouse and red plaid skirt she'd worn the day I'd arrived at her door. This was unlikely to be in honour of me, and I wondered if she was expecting Stephen back that day.

Downstairs she said again that she was sorry to see me go, and while I was waiting for the taxi, she disappeared into the front parlour and came back carrying one of the small rugs. It was rolled up under her arm, but I could see from the corner its colours of faded brick and rose and knew it was one I'd admired.

"I've ever so many too many, don't you know, and it'll keep your tootsies warm over there in Côte-des-Neiges." Her fat cheeks and her curls quivered as she spoke. Her bright little eyes stared hopefully into my face.

The taxi was pulling up outside. "Well, thanks," I said. I wanted to do something nice, to give her a hug or a kiss, but something about her body, something ruined or nearly so, made me not want to touch her. I took the rug and made myself pat her shoulder and tip my cheeks to let her kiss them. And then I hauled my baggage down her shaky front stairs and out to the taxi. Getting into it, I called back to her, "Goodbye, Freddie."

"Goodbye. Goodbye, Nancy Jean." She waved and blew me a kiss.

As we drove away down the snowy street, I turned to look back in case she was still waving. And sure enough, there she stood, her head beside the panel of green-and-blue glass, her crimson arm flapping madly. The very picture of someone's mother bidding a fond goodbye. Not like my mother shutting the door while I was still on the front step and wandering back to her magazines and sherry, forgetting before she'd taken a dozen steps that her only daughter had just left home on a January night. I could have frozen to death for all she'd have noticed, I thought, and realized that one way or another this had always been true and that I had always known it. Beneath my feet now on the floor of the taxi, the thick, soft cylinder that was Freddie's rug lay like a cushion.

Freddie had been kind to me, and I'd believed her when she said she didn't like goodbyes. But still, I thought, leaning back against the seat, still, she hadn't minded all that much. For the truth was that, with the goodbyes said, and with me out of the way and Mrs. Edgerly soon moving on, Freddie would have Stephen to herself. And he would have her. The taxi was chugging up Atwater Avenue, towards the corner where it swings around by the greystone convent school, when I had the thought that if ever I should feel sorry for anyone (which I generally didn't), then I should feel sorry now for Freddie.

I got along fine with my new roommates. The one, of course, worked at Cardiff's. I'd known her since the Imported Sweater counter. She'd worked across the aisle in Notions, and we'd used to chat during the slow hours and had sometimes taken our coffee breaks together. Another worked in a furniture store down on Notre-Dame Street, where she was paid under the table. She was an American with a funny accent, which she said was just her Boston way of speaking. Originally she'd come up to Montreal with a draft dodger boyfriend. Then her brother had got himself killed in Vietnam, and that had caused trouble between her and her boyfriend, so after he'd moved on, she'd stayed. The other girl was a nurse who worked down the hill at the Montreal General Hospital. Her hours were odd, but she was quiet enough coming and going, and, snug in my little bedroom, I hardly heard her. Altogether I felt quite fine. Freddie's rug, once I'd got the dust vacuumed out of it, turned out to have a design of flowers in rose and dark, smoky blue inside its border of rose and brick. Evenings when I went to bed and mornings when I woke, I'd see it by my bed like a sunny little garden. And Freddie had been right, it did keep my feet warm. I slept better altogether in the apartment, except for sometimes in the evening or early in the morning when I woke before the alarm. Those were times I felt a bit deprived. As though something that had been there, some particular shine to my life, a bracing wickedness I might have said, was gone.

I had lost interest in the bars and found I was heading back up the hill to the apartment most times right after work. I borrowed the nurse's skates sometimes and went skating at Beaver Lake over on the mountain. My American roommate had got a couple of books for Christmas. She said they were strange, but I began to read them, first one and then the other. Both told stories about girls on their own in London, England, though a while back in time. There were bits about politics and religion in them as well and sadnesses and other kinds of emotion and sex too, and reading them gave me a feeling about all the lives in the world and how they were out there somewhere or had been, just waiting to be known. I began to think that maybe a course or two about books at one of the universities wouldn't be such a bad idea, though I had no intention of telling this to George. He came over as often as he could and sat in our square parlour, which my roommates all called the living room, so I began to call it that too. He told me everything about his divorce, which was more than I wanted to know, and he watched my roommates run around in hair curlers and bathrobes. He'd stopped talking so much about us getting married, and he was all smiles when one of the girls came in, especially if it was the nurse and she was wearing her white nurse's uniform, although usually she changed at the hospital. His glasses had been fixed, so he looked sensible again, and when he walked around the apartment staring out our windows and looking in our fridge and studying the posters pinned on the white walls, mostly Beatles and Stones and good old, fuzzy-haired Charlebois, I thought poor George was considering whether he could be young again.

Towards the end of February, the assistant manager of our section asked me to take over her job while she went on vacation. She and her husband had borrowed a cottage in St-Sauveur for a week in March; they were taking the kids. The job wouldn't be too difficult, she explained, although math was involved. I assured her I could add, and also subtract, multiply and divide. I could even derive a square root if it came to that. She gave me a look and said that square roots would not be necessary.

The week of being the substitute assistant section manager went three times faster than any week since I'd started working at Cardiff's. I already knew how to sell; now I found out I liked being in charge. It was like carrying a big picture in my mind. The picture stretched over the day and contained all the people who worked in the section and all our registers and every tie and shirt that was stored in our drawers or displayed in the glass-covered counters and the counters themselves, plus all the sales figures for the day minus the returns and multiplied by the right percentages for the discounts and for the commissions for the salespeople who were on commission. I knew the total of every column. I changed the hours of two of my saleswomen so that we had almost no times when we were standing around with nothing to do and during the busy periods no lines of angry customers elbowing each other and being snippy to the saleswomen. Sales for my section that week were the highest they'd been since Christmas and beat both the previous year and budget. The section manager learned my name, and on Saturday afternoon, when I was closing out the registers for the final time, she came out of her office and told me I'd done a good job and that she was going to put me on commission and recommend me for promotion the next time an opening came along.

Monday morning when I came up from the metro into Cardiff's, I already missed the previous week. Nothing was going through my head, no lists of figures, no picture of our section and how it would run that day. For something to do I undertook to clean out and sort the odd stock we kept in drawers. I'd just got going, with the bottommost drawer emptied out onto the floor behind the counter, when I saw Mrs. McPherson coming along the aisle from Men's Socks and Suspenders. Her black dress did not exactly manage to disguise the pillow of fat around her middle, and her string of pearls (the only jewellery we were allowed to wear) had got tangled with the chain of her spectacles. Bearing towards me she looked like one of those bulgy old Cadillacs that sometimes waited at the store's side entrance for the rich ladies who shopped the upper floors of Cardiff's.

"Nancy Jean! Nancy Jean!" Underneath her rouge I could see that her face had gone the colour of flour. Her eyes, too, looked peculiar, fixed and out of focus. It was clear she had something on her mind.

"Hi, Mrs. McPherson," I said.

"Nancy Jean." She spoke in a stage whisper. I stepped out around the counter, and she caught hold of my arm. Though there weren't any customers in sight, she dragged me along to the far corner of Men's Ties and Shirts. "I had to come and tell you, dear."

"Tell me what? What's the matter?" I said. She was still gripping my arm, and now I could feel her shaking.

"It's Freddie...they found her in the bathtub. Yesterday, after church." She was still speaking in the stage whisper.

"Freddie in the bathtub?" I said. "What do you mean?"

Mrs. McPherson's eyes shut then, and tears appeared between her squeezed lids and spilled down her cheeks. "She wasn't there you see. I'd have remarked on that myself. She was always so faithful...Such a shame she had no voice for singing; she'd have been the soul of loyalty in the choir, and so many of them, you know, skipping half the rehearsals—"

"Mrs. McPherson," I said. "I don't understand. What's happened to Freddie?"

"Well, she's dead, dear. She wasn't there in church, you see, so they came calling, her church friends did. They went all round the house looking for her. It was that boarder of hers found her..."

"Stephen found her?" I said. My knees had gone weak, and I leaned against the wall for a second.

"No, no. That dreadful boy had gone off somewhere for the weekend. It was the lady from Wilbourne's School found her in the bathtub. Had hysterics, they said, screaming and crying right there in the bathroom, though I suppose there's many would have done the same. They had to leave poor Freddie underwater while they hustled the lady out and called a doctor. Her body was all stiff, you see. Drowned, most likely. The doctor said so when he got there. Water in her lungs. He found a big lump on the back of her head. She might have slipped or fainted, he said, knocked herself out. He was the one made them call the police."

Here Mrs. McPherson took hold of my arm again. She began to cry and shake. Freeing my arm from her clutch, I stared around at the other counters and the marble columns and the huge chandeliers hanging above our heads. I felt as if I needed to remember where I was. Then I kind of guided and pushed Mrs. McPherson along past Ties and in behind the Belts counter where we kept a chair for times when it was quiet and one of us could sit a spell. I could feel the rolls of fat under her arms and across her back. She was really crying now—heavy, wretched sobs that made her head bob up and down and sounded as if they would rip the skin inside her throat—and I was trying to shush and comfort her both. I was trying to think too, for it didn't seem possible that Freddie could be dead. My grandmother had died, of course, but there had been that woman's complaint and she'd been very old. Not all peppy and full of talk like Freddie. Freddie with her pots of tea and tin of fossil cookies.

After a few minutes the floor manager came by. Someone must have called him. He helped me calm Mrs. McPherson, and then he took her to his office. A few customers had spotted the commotion and had their eye on us by this time, but after she'd been led away they drifted off too, and I went back to cleaning. All morning I did this until the job was done. By then it was noon with customers beginning to come in, and I sold them shirts and ties, normal as anything, except every so often I would remember, and for a half a minute or so the shock would take me hard enough I couldn't move at all or speak a word.

That night Mrs. McPherson called me at the apartment to say that Freddie's sister had arrived from Halifax. The funeral was to be at St. Michael's Church on Côte-St-Antoine. This was the street Freddie had called the Côte Road. The service would take place three days from now, this to allow for relatives travelling from Nova Scotia. Telling me all this, she sounded more like herself, being busy, as she said, with plans for all the relatives and the funeral.

The next night she telephoned again. I had just painted my toenails a colour called "femme sauvage" because George was taking me out the following night, and I was sitting on the floor with my feet under the hot part of the radiator and my toes separated by little wads of toilet paper.

My Cardiff's roommate answered the phone. "It's for you, Nancy Jean."

I had to crawl through the parlour with my feet in the air. "Hello," I said, when I'd got over to the phone.

Mrs. McPherson's voice came popping through the receiver as if she'd like to scream instead of speak. "And him not even family. It's a scandal, that's what I told—"

"What's a scandal?" I said.

"That faggy boy!" she said, and then she told me. The scandal was about the will. Freddie's will. Her sister had inquired. She had wept and finally had to be given brandy, but the lawyer said there was nothing to be done. The will was proper. The house and all the furniture in it went to Stephen.

"That faggy boy," Mrs. McPherson said again. "Her sister's fair beside herself. It was their parents' house, you know. And it was her that had the idea to send him down from Nova Scotia. She went and tried to adopt him, you know. That's the truth."

"The sister did?" I said.

"Well, no. It was Freddie, you see. She went and tried to adopt that faggy boy. They said she couldn't, the lawyer or the judge did. But she went and changed her will just the same."

"Oh, poor Freddie," I said, and I leaned back against the wall. There was more about the sister arguing with the lawyer, but I scarcely heard. I gazed at my scarlet toenails, and I thought how Freddie gave things away. The watch and the cufflinks. The things that had been her father's and mother's. The cup. My rug. I supposed that Stephen just asked her for it, the house and the furniture and whatever else she had, told her he'd feel like at last he had a home or something like that. All she had to do was change her will and he'd feel loved forever.

George went with me to Freddie's funeral. He'd moved out of his house by this time and was visiting his little boy twice a week. There had been tears, he said, his own included, and I found it hard to make him laugh sometimes, though on the occasion of the funeral I didn't have to bother. His air of gloom suited things quite well.

The sky was full of snow clouds, the kind that seem to

hum just beneath the general noise of things. We parked on a side street above the stone church and, with the March wind blowing through our hair, walked down the icy slope to St. Michael's Church.

Inside it everything at human level seemed made of dark wood, the vestry doors and the panelling along the lower walls and even the pews; walking down the aisle I thought of Freddie's parlour. The pews were half-full, a few men in suits and the rest middle-aged ladies, whispering over the moan of organ music. Mrs. McPherson nodded at me and so did Mrs. Edgerly and two of Freddie's other friends.

Through a wide, arched window set high above the altar, glass-stained light slanted down upon us. This window seemed the only source of light, and in its glittering design of red and blue and green and gold, I picked out kneeling figures and above them a trio of angels, their wings outspread and hands upraised as if to warn and bless not just the supplicants at their feet but all of us, the congregation.

Straight ahead, in the chancel, I saw the big, dark box, a wreath of daisies and some larger yellow flowers laid on top. Had they dressed her in the crimson blouse and red plaid skirt? Had they set her grey curls, closed her eyes with pennies, spread powder and rouge on her pudgy face, painted lipstick on her tiny lips? I could imagine all this like a scene in a play.

George and I slid into an empty pew, and a minute later Stephen walked by, looking neither left nor right, and took a seat on the other side of the aisle a few pews in front of us. I stared after him, my heart pounding against my chest. His hair shone a new and fiercer gold than I remembered; his features from the side were still and smooth as polished stone. And that is when I knew.

Sitting there in church, with mourners all around and my hymnal in my lap, I saw, as clear as if it had happened right in front of us, how he'd entered the bathroom, his face dead still like it was now. And I saw how she'd looked to him in her bath, walrus-naked, her rolls of flesh all sagged of their own weight like loaves of unbaked bread, her curls sodden against her cheeks, the pink rubber duck a-wobble between her knees. I saw how her face had flushed to instant pink. "Oh, goodness," she would have said, all horrified and thrilled, her baby voice atwitter. "Oh, goodness, Stephen dear. Oh, I don't think..." Did he lie to her, give her a last moment of pleasure? Did he say to her, "Freddie..." in one of his deep, seductive voices, as though he desired to see her naked in her bath? Or did he enter silent as a stone, close the door behind him fast, lest the latch slip and reveal to Mrs. Edgerly or any other visitor that he had returned to the house and what he was about to do? Did he cross to the tub in a few quick steps and with those strong and slender hands reach out to grip the wad of curls on either side of Freddie's head? Did he crack her skull against the curved rim of the tub, then hold her head underwater? (This was what I thought he had done.) And feeling the fiery blow did she stare up at him, not knowing for a second what it meant? Then, as she sank, still gazing up through water at his undulating face—a smile upon it now—did she know that her lovely angel boy was murdering her?

Beside me George took off his glasses and polished them. Resetting them on his solemn face, he glanced at me and gave my hand a squeeze, as though I must be mournful of the death. I thought then, eyeing his knotted, silk-striped tie, his glossy white collar and charcoal-grey lapel, that he would never know what I was thinking, not then, not ever, not from one minute to the next nor from year to year. No matter how long he knew me. This truth seemed to me a pleasant one, a space in which I could be always free, and it caused me to give his hand a quick squeeze back just before I glanced up the aisle at Stephen's gleaming head.

All through the prayers and the songs, the minister's bossy little talk about giving thanks for Freddie's life, I went on watching the side of that perfect face. Once or twice his eyes closed. In boredom, I imagined.

I thought about Freddie and about Stephen, and I thought about the desire he called up in me and how it came all mixed with fear. And I understood what sex with him had been about for me. I had wanted to be broken like Freddie's beautiful cup, the shiny rose and gold of me split asunder. To have for those few minutes all the devil's desire. But it was to Freddie he'd offered the ultimate sensation, and not to me. And she was the one who'd accepted it too. I, after all, had left Del's apartment; I'd moved from Freddie's house. The truth was, Freddie *had* won out over me.

Back when I'd moved out of her house, I had not missed her. But now I thought I would. I would miss her bright, baby eyes, like two raisins in the vast cookie of her face. I would miss those awful cookies too, her endless offerings of tea and her baby way of speaking.

George's manicured fingers were flipping through the pages of the hymnal, searching no doubt for the final song. He looked dedicated to his task and also somewhat bored;

probably he had been that way for all the time he could remember. He had needed me to escape his gentleman's life, those private schools and fraternity-boy parties, his marriage, maybe even the ambitions crafted for him by the ones who raised and taught him. And thinking of escape, I glanced towards the front of the church.

Four men in black suits had stepped out from a side pew. One of them plucked the wreath of flowers off the coffin, and then all four began to heft the big box from its stand. Behind me I heard the bleat of someone's weeping and some other snuffles from across the aisle. But as the organ struck its startled chords and we stood up to sing, and I saw the wave of Stephen's false gold hair swing forward across his cheek and jaw, what swept me then was longing pure and true.

For it was Stephen, and no other, who had known what I was. To have been with him crouched over the tub—I could almost feel that moment come, the dying eyes upon us both. And as the music swelled and the coffin swayed towards us down the aisle, my body began to shake. I could not stop it.

George slid his arm around my shoulders and held me steady while the coffin passed on by. And when it had gone and the air around us cleared and emptied of its spell, I felt myself warmed in his grasp. At the front of the chancel, in the space where the coffin had lain, the minister stepped forward now, beneath the angels' window. And raising up his hymnal in thick-palmed hands, he commenced to sing of death and grace, and then so did we all.

HERE IN THE MOUNTAINS

T HE CATS, PLUCKED FROM THE CAGES and the prospect of a gentle death at the animal shelter, arrived on a Sunday morning. The early fog had blown off, and Pete was frying eggs and trying to decide whether he would flip them, even though he usually preferred eggs sunny side up. He was also, with another part of his brain, thinking about a hike on the mountain that afternoon. The views would be clear, the trails dry by then.

Over at the kitchen table, Graham poured himself another cup of coffee. "Well, Diefenbaker's screwed it up yet again," he said. He reached for the carton of milk. "This wheat deal... What a mess."

Pete remembers the moment perfectly, how the door opened and sunlight leapt into the kitchen, and how Sonny, their new roommate, stood in the doorway, his glasses askew on his narrow face, his arms cradling a pile of fur.

"Hi, everybody," was what he said, as though he were arriving for a beer bash. "Breakfast time?"

Across the kitchen Graham glanced up. His forehead, which still bore a tinge of last summer's tan, creased into a frown. "Are those cats?" The pile, grey-striped on one side, a muddy caramel on the other, had begun to wriggle.

"Well, yes," said Sonny. He stepped inside and kicked the door shut behind him. In the restored dimness there was a furious mew and a pair of thumps.

"Now, just a minute," came Graham's deep monotone. "The shelter only keeps them for a week—"

"My mother had a cat," said Graham. "An ugly beast, half black, half brown. The thing was a bloody nuisance too. Crapped in the flowerpots." He took a swallow of his coffee. "It jumped on her head one time, when she was driving it to the vet's or someplace. She wiped out a parked car and a stop sign. My father damn near had a fit."

"They were going to put them to sleep," said Sonny.

The discussion went on for several minutes. Beneath the voices, the cats sat down rump to rump on the kitchen floor and fixed Pete, or maybe it was the stove itself, with their jack-o'-lantern eyes. He remembers flipping the eggs before he set the spatula beside the pan and squatted down. He'd meant to add his own voice to the exchange just then. Something to the effect that what they didn't need around this crummy rented cabin was cats, that cats made him sneeze. But at that moment an odd thing happened.

Squatting there with his fingers buried in the rough fur and the warmth of the small bodies creeping into his hands, Pete saw how things could have been—as if someone had shoved a snapshot in front of his face—the two creatures curled together, caramel fur and grey, lifeless in some shelter's gas chamber.

"Well, say, Graham," he said, glancing up. One of the cats had begun to purr; he could feel the throb against his fingertips. "Cats aren't so bad. Besides, they'd be outside a lot." His friends' faces stared down at him, Sonny's eyes unblinking behind his glasses. But it was Graham's expression that Pete has not forgotten, the exasperated flattening of his lips, the deep furrow in his brow.

That was six weeks ago. The cats, of course, are a nuisance. They steal food off the kitchen counters. They nap on newly typed pages of Pete's and Graham's theses. The tabby, whose stomach must have been ruined by years of scavenging, vomits onto their green shag rug. It's beyond any kind of washing or cleaning now. And speaking of cleaning, no matter how hard Sonny or sometimes Pete scours out the cats' box, it always reeks. Graham had things figured.

He and Pete have been friends since the beginning of their doctoral program. Something about him always puts Pete in mind of an English lord—Graham's deep, unhurried voice, for example, as though he expects idiocy from all quarters but is prepared to deal with it. Even his thinning, blond hair has a polished look. Of course, being from Canada, he can be expected to act and look a bit different. He and Pete have talked of starting an economics research firm together, of being their own bosses and of hiring a bunch of other hot young Ph.D.s like themselves. This would be in Toronto or New York. His family, it seems, has plans for him and his younger brother, Graham being destined for big business, while the brother, Charles (never Chuck or Charlie), is headed for law and politics. Graham has a girl back in Montreal whom he sometimes refers to as his fiancée. Her father, according to Graham, is big in venture capital. Graham's own father is a senator, although being a senator is different in Canada, apparently more an honour than a job.

Sonny, on the other hand, is in his first year at the Divinity School. Before coming west he spent something like ten years in Cambridge, Massachusetts, mainly writing poetry and driving a taxi, as far as they have been able to tell. "The saint in human form," Graham calls him. Or sometimes, "Jesus." As in, "Has Jesus taken out the garbage yet?" "Jesus" quite often fails to notice when the pail is full.

At the moment, Sonny is sprawled in his huge armchair. At his feet his cats are nosing through a cheese sandwich. Sonny himself is spouting one of his religious theories, something he does all the time, waving his arms and carrying on in his sweetly sincere voice.

"You remember in the garden at Gethsemane? When He's out there with all His people, and He's scolding them because they keep falling asleep, and in between He's praying and sweating and asking to get out of taking the fall for everyone?" Pete nods at intervals. Sonny's armchair looks like a giant nest, the shredded upholstery, the wads of stuffing that blossom from its arms. Next to it, their old couch and coffee table (the latter recently painted black after an exploding ashtray fire), even the woodstove, look like play furniture.

"So He assumes He can get out of it, see? And it's only after a while that He gives in and says to let it happen, which means He didn't have to." Sonny has rested his hands on the arms of his chair and is gazing up at Pete as though there's some obvious response to what he's just said. His pale hair has slid down over the tops of his glasses.

"Right," says Pete, "right. I've got a meeting by the way. My next chapter outline, my thesis advisor wants to see it."

The phone's ring is muffled. Sonny slips a hand under the stack of newspapers on the coffee table. As he extracts the phone, the top half of the stack slides to the floor.

Pete picks an apple core off his briefcase and drops it into an ashtray. "Oh, hi, Donna," he hears and then, "No...no, he's not here, but Pete's heading down to campus. He can—What was that?"

A moment later, Sonny hangs up the phone. Glancing over at Pete he shakes his head. "She called him a bastard," he says. "And she dropped a Coke or something; you could hear the crash."

"Yeah?" Pete jams the papers deeper into his briefcase and zips it shut. "She was angry?"

"I think she was crying," says Sonny. His hand reaches down and travels gently over the back of the caramel cat.

For a moment, Pete stands watching. Bits of bread and cheese and lettuce are stuck to the cats' whiskers, and more bits are sprinkled over the rug. He thinks about mentioning this, as he thought earlier about mentioning the newspapers. Graham hates a mess. Instead, he pushes open the screen door and steps out into their little front yard.

Across the yard, a wooden stairway climbs the rocky bluff to the road. The level plot of ground where Pete is standing, and which holds only this yard and the cabin, is no more than an outcropping of rock. It's like living on a platform fixed to the side of the mountain. When Pete gets in the mood for a hike, he climbs the stairs to the road and drives over into the next valley, where the descents are more gradual. Here, the slope is too steep for walking, though the view is spectacular; below them the valley, choked with tall, light-seeking redwoods, continues its plunge for something like two hundred feet. At the very bottom, according to their landlord, a stream bed winds its way in darkness between the walls of the valley. Next spring, when the rains have come, they may be able to hear the rush of water.

Compared to some of their old rentals down in Palo Alto, the cabin is rickety, a shack really. But it's cheap and quiet. Just times like now, when he emerges to smell the redwoods and the clear, chilly air from the mountain, he regrets ever having to go inside again.

Climbing the steep wooden steps to the road, he regrets as well yesterday's hour of tennis. Graham, who seems to have grown up playing squash and tennis and golf, has said that Pete should learn to play. "Listen, it's an entrée, old man" is what he said, and the lesson took place on a court behind the high school in town. Graham wore sweatbands around both wrists and a white knitted shirt with a club crest. His shorts were white too, and emerging from them his sinewy legs looked brown and purposeful. His forehead, with its incipient businessman's frown, looked purposeful too. "Like that," he said, time after time, taking a single step forward and angling the ball away from Pete. "Keep your balance . . . a quick stab. Try it again."

Pete, wearing chinos and a T-shirt with torn-out sleeves, did try it again. And again. Now his buttocks and calves ache. So does an odd, cold place somewhere inside his right shoulder. The pain reaches deep into him, momentarily piercing his stomach with a slight nausea and giving birth, as he reaches the final stair, to the unthinkable notion that he will someday no longer be young. The year is 1961. He's twenty-five.

At the top he pauses, rubbing his shoulder. (Is it possible that, along with his father's skill with numbers and a head of dark, scrupulously straight hair, he has inherited his bursitis?) Then he lights a cigarette. He turns and looks back; the view from up here, except for their yard and the roof of their cabin, is all treetops, a rough, green hammock strung between the ridged mountains. As he walks along the gravelled edge of the road to where his car is parked, he recalls that before the conversation with Sonny—if you could call it that—he'd meant to dash off a letter to his girlfriend's mother. It's already long overdue. A thank-you note for the week he spent at her house on a lake in northern Wisconsin.

That dwelling, too, was somewhat dilapidated. The floors of the house sloped under their covering of rag rugs; the walls met at corners that were not square. But the lake out back offered an expanse of clear, brown water, warm for the last week of August. He swam in it morning and night. And the woods smelled of pine trees and woodsmoke.

"A real small-towner," Marnie said, describing her mother. Her father has been dead for many years.

"Hey," Pete said. "My parents are small-town too." He did not add that they would have scorned Marnie's mother as frivolous. (They took a Calvinist view of things, his parents did. His father was a deacon of the local Presbyterian church. Sin was sin, hard work and success the evidence of virtue.)

Marnie's mother bustled through the house talking to one or another of her mongrel dogs, losing her glasses, lighting cigarettes and forgetting to smoke them. She baked—cakes and brownies and large, soft, raisin-stuffed cookies. Cookies like pillows. The house was full of the smell of them, and full of Marnie's mother's friends. That was another thing his parents would have frowned upon, these stout-waisted, cigarette-smoking women given to pouring measures of brandy into their teacups.

"Don't mind the house being so . . . all women," Marnie whispered the first evening, pressing against him in the hallway. Supper had long since ended, and a trio of these friends sat with her mother around the kitchen table. A cloud of cigarette smoke hovered, like the ghost of their shared past, inches above their heads. All four women seemed to be talking at once. On the table, within easy reach of their fleshy arms, sat the teapot and a half-pint bottle of brandy.

"It's okay," he whispered back. "They're nice. I like your mother. I like your house . . ." He paused, unsure what it was he liked, then put his arm around Marnie. Through the open door he could see the women passing round a pack of Lucky Strikes.

"They go home early," said Marnie, still whispering.

"Marnie, dear," her mother called in her smoke-roughened voice. "Could you bring me some more matches? There's a pack out there by the telephone."

"Coming, Mom," called Marnie, her voice turned childishly high and clear. She slipped out of Pete's embrace.

Her mother glanced up and smiled as the two of them entered the kitchen. "Oh, there you are, Pete dear. Come meet my friends." Her chair scraped across the linoleum as she pushed it back from the table and stood up to introduce him. Her round, smiling face, Pete saw suddenly, was a weathered version of Marnie's.

Marnie had been right. The friends consumed one more pot of tea. Then almost as quickly, they were standing out on the back porch, their goodbyes flitting through the darkness. A few moments later, Marnie's mother, her arms full of laundry and knitting, called good night from the living-room door. "Don't forget, Marnie, dear...the dogs out...the screen in front of the fire..." She was already out of sight.

She did not come back down to check on Marnie and Pete, not on that night or any other. Nor did she appear to notice which rooms they slept in. He had never felt so unnervingly free in a parent's house.

Saying goodbye to Marnie at the end of the week, he wrapped his arms around her, breathing in her hair (it smelled of her mother's baking). His plans were set. This was to be the year of the thesis; by next summer he would be in New York. Yet, standing there in the clearing beside the house, with the sturdy warmth of her in his arms, he felt for just a moment that this was all he wanted, a summer job, a late-August tan, a girlfriend in a sleeveless blouse and pink Bermuda shorts.

"Next year," Marnie was saying. She meant when she had graduated, he knew, when he was back from the West Coast. She too would find a job in New York "in advertising maybe, or publishing." She considered herself to be artistic and possibly literary. She had wept over Hemingway's suicide earlier in the summer. "An apartment over in the Village," she said now, her voice bubbling up between them, "those funny old houses . . ."

Gradually his lethargy gave way to awareness. What was it he heard in her voice? Doors clicking shut, curtains swishing closed? His scalp tingled, and he lifted his face out of the warm aroma of her hair. Off in the distance— quite far away, it now seemed—the lake glimmered at him through the grove of pines and spindly birches. "I've got a fair drive ahead," he told the top of her head. "I said I'd be on the road before noon."

Here in the mountains, the sun sets early, taking with it a good deal of what heat remains in the autumn air. As Pete lopes down the wooden stairway, he can see below him the smoke rising from their chimney. It winds slowly upward into the remote brightness of the sky. The house itself already lies enfolded in shadow.

Indoors, evening has begun. An oblong of flame swarms in the stove's belly, casting an oily glow over the three seated people. The tableau is typical—Sonny sunk deep in his chair, Graham looking athletically broad of shoulder as he lounges on the couch, beer in hand, his other arm resting across the shoulders of the girl curled beside him.

Graham raises his beer bottle now. "*Salut*, Pete, old man. Grab yourself a brew. Got the usual gang coming by later."

The girl is Donna. As Pete drops his briefcase on a chair, she glances up, and her hair, bleached to albino white, makes a sudden halo around her head. Whatever her problem this morning, she looks fine now. Her small, heavily made-up face reminds him, as it has on other occasions, of the children who've rapped on their various rented doors at Halloween, their faces garish yet vulnerable under the startling makeup of clowns and fairy princesses and witches.

"Hiya, Pete. Cooler's by the door there." Her crimsoned lips kiss the words at him, Marilyn Monroe style. She would be delicious in bed. The thought sends a stab of envy through his gut and makes him vaguely ashamed.

He smiles at her. "Hi, Donna."

Only now does Sonny glance up. With his floppy hair and round, bespectacled eyes, he looks like an attenuated child himself. "I've been explaining," he says. His voice is sweetly earnest, what Graham calls his "Jesus voice." "About Gethsemane. There's Simon Peter denying Him and then afterwards Pontius Pilate deciding which one to hand over to the mob."

Graham grins at Pete. He's gotten so most of the time he's amused by Sonny. Pete grins back. The beer is icy in his throat and gradually warmer as it sinks down his gullet. These friends of Graham's, "the usual gang," are older. They play tennis, most of them. And they seem, with their knowledgeable talk of business and their contacts in this or that company, miles ahead of the game. Certainly miles ahead of Pete.

"Otherwise people couldn't have been saved," says Sonny.

Graham turns to Sonny and shakes his head. "Listen, as a thesis topic I'm afraid it's a zero, old man. Out of style." Pete shakes his head too. He's had the same thought. Sonny sounds like the aging minister at his parents' church.

"Well, I think it's sort of interesting! About Jesus and all." Speaking, Donna tosses back her hair. Then she shrugs off Graham's arm and sits up. Both Pete and Graham stare at her. Her big hoop earrings flash as she turns her head towards Sonny.

Donna is a teller in the local bank. On occasion she also subs as the receptionist, and she was seated at the front desk, doing her nails beneath the bank's annual report, when Graham walked in to open a chequing account. More than once, in Pete's presence, she has marvelled aloud over that day. Leaning her head on Graham's shoulder, she speaks as though she and he met against heavy odds and are a remarkable couple. Above her head Graham merely smiles.

"He could have saved Himself," Sonny says nodding at Donna, "but the real issue, even from the time He was a baby..."

Donna, who has been nodding back, abruptly shakes her head. Her hands flop down hard into her lap; her eyes swing round to Graham. But Graham is getting to his feet. "Dinner!" he announces, as though it has just marched in the door. He reaches down and, without looking at Donna, briefly lays his hand on her cottony hair. She closes her eyes.

Compelled by something raw in their faces, Pete stands up. "I picked up the hamburger this morning," he says quickly. "And the buns. They're out in the refrigerator, on top of the grapes."

"It explains everything. It frees you. If you look at it right," Sonny says. The others ignore him.

In the kitchen light, Graham's eyes look strained. He rubs his lips with the tips of his fingers, then jerks his head in the direction of the living room. "We seem to be pregnant," he says.

Pete stares at him. His mind rolls back to the lake house. Though he and Marnie have been careful enough, he has always felt uneasy making love to her. As if someone, God or his own parents, was watching them. Now a similar, though less intense sensation sweeps him, as if watchers hover nearby, as if they cast a shadow across himself and Graham and the chipped enamel table that stands between them.

"Tough," he says, making his voice deep and, he hopes, man-of-the-world.

Graham dumps the bagful of buns out onto the table and starts separating the tops from the bottoms. "It's the second fucking time," he says.

Pete rises to get the package of hamburger from the refrigerator. Returning, he plants himself in a chair on the other side of the table and begins to scoop up mounds of meat and slap them into patties. He prepares himself to say something sympathetic, even to reach across the table and put his hand on Graham's shoulder, man to man. But Graham seems somehow unneedful of such a gesture, though he does not seem altogether unneedful. "I told her," he says now, "I'll handle it just like the other time, drive her down to the clinic in Tijuana, pay the whole shot. I told her all that."

The first set of Graham's friends arrives with cases of beer. The next set brings more beer and a pile of records. Pete, himself, downs several bottles and tells a girl he hasn't met before tonight that he was engaged to a girl from his hometown but that he has broken up with her. None of it is true, but it seems to him that it is. "We don't think the same way about things," he says, wagging his head.

"Who does?" says the girl. She has long, sand-coloured hair that she keeps pushing back behind her ears. "I'm not ever marrying," she adds. "All those dirty socks."

He hears himself arguing with her. "Marriage is an act of bravery, the high point of civilization." His voice goes on and on. Once or twice, the girl puts her fingers on his arm, lightly but insistently, as though there is a distant bark or bird call she wants him to hear. It doesn't occur to him that he might be boring her, but he does have the odd sense he occasionally has with women, women of various ages, that he is being indulged for a purpose beyond his understanding. He thinks of dancing with her. A Johnny Mathis record is warbling away at one end of the room. Then he remembers that he doesn't like to dance.

Hours into the evening, the stove begins to smoke. It has a tendency to do this if the wind turns and blows down the mountain. Someone opens a window. The house grows chilly, and smoky again after someone shuts the window.

Graham and Donna have been sitting together in the huge old armchair. From across the room, Pete sees her scramble out of the chair, then whirl and stand, hands on her hips, looking down at Graham. Her skirt is tight, and it reveals perfectly the swell of her hips and buttocks, the matched curves of her thighs. Her voice comes in aggrieved spurts. "You got all the answers." From within the chair, Graham's measured reply: "Listen, I told you before..."And Donna's voice again, quieter in the quieting room: "Graham, you're always telling me. I don't want to hear you telling me nothing. It hurt me last time, Graham. Doing that. Like someone shoved broken glass into me."

At the lake, Pete wakened Marnie before dawn on the second to last day. "We have to go fishing," he told her, running his fingers through her curly hair. Her scalp was warm, and damp where her head had rested against the pillow. "Your lake is supposed to be a fisherman's paradise. They've all told me that." When she was awake enough to understand, she got up and pulled on a pair of shorts and a T-shirt.

They dragged the old rowboat down the slide of pine needles and shoved it into the water. On the far shore a mist obscured the other cabins and docks, and as they pushed away, the water dripping off the oars made a series of notes like a bird's trill.

Out in the middle of the lake, the fishing rod jerked lightly in his hands and bent like a divining rod towards the water. He played out his line once and began to reel it in. A whitefish, he guessed, spotting the quick gleam in the water.

A few minutes later he swung the writhing creature into the boat. It was a whitefish and barely big enough to keep. It would make a nice breakfast though, fried in butter. His mouth watered. "At least," he told Marnie, "we won't come in with nothing."

The fish was flipping around his feet, slapping itself against the ribs of the boat. Marnie stared at him and then down at the fish, her brown eyes wide and stunned. Abruptly, while he was still trying to get a grip on the frantic body, she bowed her head and covered her face with her hands.

Seeing her hunched in the bow of the boat as if she would never come nearer to him, he unhooked the hapless fish, probably already beyond recall, and tossed it back. The wet body slid from his hands and landed on its side in the water. For a second it lay there. Then flicking its tail, in silent rebuke, he felt, it sank through the brown water and disappeared.

Shaken by the unfairness of it all—hadn't she come along without a word of protest?—he said nothing to her, did not, in any case, know what to say. Across the lake the mist was fading, and, while he rowed them back, the first needles of sunlight pierced the trees. A moment later, she shocked him further by dropping to her knees and carefully crawling the length of the leaky old boat. As she laid her head in his lap, her hair, soft as feathers, fanned out over his thigh.

The party ends in a fist fight. Donna has been dancing with one of Graham's friends, while Graham himself has gone to sleep in the chair. He only wakens when the combatants fall on him. As the two are being pulled apart, someone turns off the music, and eventually the entire group spills out into the blackness of the yard.

In the icy air, Pete feels his skin tighten, the components of his brain click into place. Couples walk by him, some laughing, some complaining. Most carry flashlights, and above him pools of light move up the stairway. Briskly, as though he too is leaving the party, he crosses the yard. It's only at the far side, with his hand on the stair railing, that he turns to look back. Stragglers, some clutching bottles of beer, still emerge from the rectangle of light that is the doorway. Last comes Donna. Her hair has frizzed out around her face, and she shakes it slowly from side to side as if trying to restore her equilibrium. In the next instant, her silhouette has sagged against the door frame.

"Graham!" Pete shouts. But it is Sonny who steps into the doorway, as if he has been there the whole time, waiting at the edge of the darkness. Awkwardly, looking like a crane or a stork, he bends down towards Donna. As he steadies her, she leans her head against his chest, and for a second they stand like that, framed in the doorway, set similarly aglow by the light that shines round their heads.

With his arm around her, he escorts her across the yard. As they reach the stairs and pass by Pete, she's already talking. "So there's this hum, see, in my head, and everything goes black, just like they say, and, being in my condition..." Her whispery voice drifts down to him as the couple disappears into the upper darkness.

A moment later Graham comes out of the cabin. He pauses for a second and passes a hand over his hair, as if he is preparing to deal with some new idiocy. Then he heads towards Pete.

"It's the usual mess in there," he says. "Has she gone up to the road already?"

Pete nods. "She got a little woozy when she hit the cold air. Sonny was giving her a hand."

"Ah." Grinning, Graham glances towards the stairs. "The saint in human form. See you later, old man." He slaps Pete on the shoulder and heads up the stairs. Pete hears more voices from above and the slam of car doors.

He has just started back towards the cabin when a shout explodes somewhere above him. Another fight? For a second he imagines another pair of Graham's friends rolling around in the gravel parking area up by the edge of the road. Then comes crashing in the bushes and a second, louder cry.

"Look out," someone calls uselessly. But the crashing has stopped already. In the sudden hollow of silence, there is only the snick of small rocks striking one another.

"Sonny!" The name bursts from Pete's mouth.

Suddenly, everyone is calling, "Sonny? Sonny?"

From up at roadside, Donna's voice sings out, "The lights, Graham. Where's the lights?" A second later headlights beam out across the valley, illuminating with pointless clarity the forest on the far side. Here, on the near side, the absence of light seems the more profound. "Sonny," they go on shouting, "Sonny!"

The voice coming out of the blackness is thin as a child's. "Hey? Somebody?"

"Don't move," Pete calls. Even as he runs for their biggest flashlight, the one they keep under the sink in the kitchen, the extent of his relief shocks him. Most likely

Sonny fell from the edge of the road farther along where the cars are parked. And if he did, he could easily have gone on sliding down the steep slope, past the cabin and its little yard, all the way down into the trees. That's what could have happened—Sonny hung around a tree fifty or more feet below them, his long unmuscled body insensate now and bleeding, or dead, even dead.

Taking a stance halfway up the stairs, Pete begins to swing the big flashlight in long arcs up and down the side of the mountain. It takes just a moment to fix Sonny in the beam. He lies on his back nearly level with Pete, some thirty feet from the stairway, among the rocks and bushes. The slope is so steep out there that he's nearly upside down. If he starts to slide, there'll be no stopping him until he hits the trees.

"Now, how the hell did Jesus manage that?" Graham has come back down from the parking lot and stands just above Pete on the stairs. In his thick white sweater he seems bulky and solid.

"The police, I should think. Let them deal with it," Graham says now. "They must have equipment—slings, ropes, that sort of thing. He's too far out. No sense in one of us ending up somewhere halfway down the mountain." Dusting off his hands as if they have got dirt or grit on them, he gives Pete a brief clap on the shoulder, then steps around him and heads down the stairs.

Gazing after him, Pete feels the summons in his gut. He could follow Graham, and the two of them would cross the yard, re-enter the shabby little house together. A telephone call or two, to the state police most likely, and someone else would come and deal with the fallen Sonny.

He swings the flashlight away from Sonny's out-stretched body and lets it point down towards their little yard. Light rains onto the half-dozen or so people stand-ing there. The top of Graham's head is visible passing through the group; a second later his broad back fills the lit doorway.

In the group below, faces have tilted up, eyes are being shaded by cupped hands. "What gives?" someone calls. "You figure out what to do?"

Pete casts a glance towards the now empty doorway. Directly beneath, the faces gaze up at him like so many children's. "Right," he calls down. The sound of his own voice surprises him, as if someone else has taken charge. "Right," he calls again. "Could one of you guys come up here, give me a hand?"

In the end it is one of Graham's tennis partners who stands on the steps holding the flashlight while Pete works his way on his stomach across the side of the steep slope, testing each rock and bush with his hand or knee, creeping like a beetle into his own shadow. Twice he dislodges a rock; the clatter descends into darkness and disappears.

As he nears the upside-down body, his shadow crosses Sonny's chest. Sonny turns his head and squints into the beam of the flashlight. "That you, Pete?" His glasses, Pete sees then, have been jammed against his forehead, the lenses smashed. Beneath them, a network of black streaks spans Sonny's forehead.

"Yeah," says Pete. "It's me."

He is stretching forward to take hold of Sonny's shoulder when he starts to slip. "Hey, careful!" someone shouts from the stairs. Grabbing at the ground he feels something gouge the palm of his hand. His legs slide into the roots of a bush.

"Pete? You okay, Pete?" Sonny twists his head around. The streaks on his forehead have begun to slither like thin black snakes down the side of his temple.

"Yeah, I think so," says Pete. "Sorry." The roots of the bush seem to be holding him, but what is he doing out here? He can feel it now beneath them, the dense, squeezed-in darkness of the valley, the fatal drag. They could fall, both of them, like the rocks, skidding and bouncing down and down.

"Pete. Pete." Sonny's arm reaches through the beam of light. "Your hand, Pete. Give me your hand. I can shove myself along on my back . . . with my heels . . . I just can't see where to go."

Pete grasps the groping hand. The palm of his own hand stings. Another rock skitters out from under his elbow. "Right," he says against the chatter of the rock's descent. "Right." Sonny's hand is surprisingly strong.

It takes them a quarter of an hour or more, working their way bit by bit back towards the stairway. Below them showers of pebbles and small rocks clatter away into darkness.

"That's the way," someone calls, as though all along people have been advocating this action.

Every few feet they stop for a moment until finally Pete's shoe bumps up against the wooden stair. By then Sonny is breathing in gasps. His face and neck are wet; his forehead, with the smashed glass embedded in his skin, is dark with blood. His pale hair, too, is streaked and matted with it.

Even after each of them has been hauled to safety on the steps, and Sonny has then been carried up to Pete's car, no one dares to try removing or even touching the glasses.

In the hospital the three of them—Pete, Graham and Donna—wait for what feels like hours, extracting paper cupfuls of bitter, brown liquid from the coffee machine in the corner, leafing through a cache of ancient magazines that smell like dirty hair. A bank of fluorescent tubes paints their faces in a livid, shadow-erasing glare.

At one point Pete tries briefly to sleep, stretched out on one of the ripped leatherette couches, but his heart is beating too fast, his skin feels dry and hot. A little later, Sonny is wheeled through the swinging door marked Emergency and trundled off down the corridor. His hand and forehead are now wrapped round with gauze through which a brownish-yellow stain has oozed. He doesn't speak but looks over at them and lifts his unbandaged hand in a sort of salute.

On his return, his head has turned to one side and his eyes are closed. His long body bounces slightly as the orderly wheels him along. Across his chest, like the day's mail, lies a large brown envelope.

Donna flips her coffee cup into the waste bin and gets to her feet. She falls into step beside the rolling bed. "So what d'you think?" she says to the orderly. "He okay?"

The orderly drags the bed to a halt. There is a dark smear across the front of his shirt. "You Donna?" he says.

"That's me," says Donna.

"Yeah, he said that name a little while ago. You his girlfriend?"

"That's right," says Donna. "That blood on your shirt?"

The orderly looks pleased. "Part of the job." He nods at Sonny's inert figure and more vigorously at Donna. "He's okay. They give him a shot of something is all. You should see some of them as comes in here."

When he has pushed Sonny back through the swinging door, Donna returns to the couch. Sinking down onto it, she closes her eyes and leans her head back against the wall. A patina of sweat appears on her face. After a moment, her eyes open and swivel towards Graham. "I want to go home," she says. "Not your place. Home."

"Sure," says Graham. He glances at Pete.

"I'll stay," Pete tells him.

Graham nods and gets to his feet. Holding open the door he lets Donna's platinum head pass under his arm before he glances back. "Listen, it's getting light out. Might as well sack out at her place." He winks at Pete. "Catch up with you later, old man."

Pete nods. "Right."

"You want to hang around my place, I don't care," says Donna, her voice coming from beyond the door sounds snappish, "just you're on the couch, Graham."

For a second, even as he is still nodding at Graham, Pete sees his roommate's face as it will someday look, the eyes permanently narrowed and the cheeks gone to meat, the dominant forehead stamped with deep parallel lines.

Keeping his expression neutral, Pete raises his voice. "'Night, Donna," he calls. "I'll swing by when I leave. Let you know what happens."

Graham's forehead furrows deeper, and he stares at Pete as if he's not sure he heard right. "Swing by?" he says. "I hardly think—"

From behind him comes Donna's voice, still sounding irritated. "That's a real good idea, Pete. I'll make us a cup of coffee when you get there." The big door clunks shut.

The doctor, who they'd all thought at first was the nurse, emerges a quarter of an hour later to explain that more X-rays will be needed. "Your friend's all right," she tells Pete. "We got most of the glass out of his forehead, cleaned him up, but he'll be here for a while. There are a couple of fractures in his hand, the shoulder we can't tell about yet, probably ligament damage. You might as well go home and get some sleep, call back about eleven." Speaking, she passes her hand over her eyes. Her glossy, dark hair is tied up in a ponytail, and if she didn't look so tired, more tired than any girl Pete has ever seen, she might be pretty. He wonders how many cracked bones she's dealt with that night.

The visit to Donna's apartment is brief. When he gets there, he finds the morning paper on the doormat. The door is unlocked, and he enters to silence. Graham, still in his thick sweater, is stretched out like a toppled statue on the couch. At the far end of the room, an open doorway leads to what must be the kitchen. Pete can see a refrigerator door and the corner of a sink. A second doorway is partly closed off by a canvas curtain.

For a moment Pete stands gazing around the little sitting room. Graham's body remains motionless, his eyes closed, his breathing heavy and phlegmatic. In sleep his slackened face looks emptied and smooth. Next to the couch a plastic-wood coffee table holds a glass, a bottle of gin and several copies of *Photoplay* and *Modern Screen*.

Over in the corner a small television set, rabbit ears flared, sits on a metal stand.

While he is wondering what to do next, Donna pokes her head around the curtain. Grinning she blows a kiss at Pete and disappears again. A moment later she reappears wearing a pink bathrobe and pink fuzzy bedroom slippers. Most of her makeup is gone, though the shiny hoop earrings still dangle from her ear lobes.

In her tiny kitchen he waits while she makes him a cup of instant coffee, then drinks it down as fast as he can stand to. The space is so narrow he has to flatten himself against the refrigerator each time she scuffs past him in her slippers. This might be the minute he could take her in his arms, tell her he wants to see what lies on the other side of the canvas curtain. Yet he makes no move to do so.

As he is leaving, she follows him through the sitting room, both of them tiptoeing past the body on the couch and out into the hallway of the building.

As they stand facing one another under the hall ceiling light, he can see the darkness at the roots of her whitened hair. She glances towards the open door, then back at him. "He told you? About me?"

Pete nods. "Yeah. That's rough."

"He keeps saying about that same clinic down in Tijuana. It's the way to go, he says, but it's me that has to have that metal thing stuck up inside me again. And all what comes after, the bleeding and the mess. Him, he goes out for a tequila or three and after a while he comes back. He doesn't..." She pauses, blinking, and lays a hand on Pete's forearm. "I told Sonny, right there before he took his crash. He'll help me, he says. There's better places to go, he says. And he says if Graham..." Again she pauses.

"You didn't have any trouble with him tonight?" says Pete.

She shakes her head. Her earrings swing back and forth against her neck. "Not when he knew you were coming over, Pete. That was real nice of you."

As if on cue, from inside the apartment comes the rumble of a full-fledged snore. They both glance towards the door and then grin at one another. "Any time," he tells her. "Pete's world-famous, night and day rescue service."

From the parking lot beside the road, he can see the beer bottles and potato chip bags scattered over the weedy grass of their yard. The screen door to the cabin hangs open. Descending the stairs, he stops to pick up a windbreaker lying crumpled on the step. In fact, the mess seems no worse than the usual residue left after a Friday night beer bash. At least the door isn't off its hinges the way it was the last time.

In the living room the lamps are still burning, their light all but invisible in the sharp sunlight that slants through the dusty windows. As he walks around turning out the lamps, the cats emerge from Graham's bedroom. Mewing and rubbing up against Pete's ankles, they follow him as he carries the glasses and bottles and the paper plates and the brimming ashtrays to the kitchen. There is a smashed beer bottle in the sink. He gazes at it for a moment, then dumps the contents of the ashtrays into the garbage pail and the remains of the hamburgers into the cats' dishes. Abruptly the mewing ceases. Leaning against the sink he lights a cigarette.

His clothes, even his skin and hair, reek of wood-smoke. The palm of his hand has scabbed over, but it's still sore and grit is embedded in the deepest scratch. He should have a shower and scrub it out, change clothes. Instead, he walks into the living room and sits down in Sonny's chair. The tufts of cotton stuffing make soft bumps under his forearms. After a while he tosses the cigarette into the stove and gets up again. He searches about in his desk until he finds fresh paper and a pen. Returning to the chair, he begins to compose a letter to Marnie. While he's scribbling, first the caramel cat and then the tabby wander back into the living room and settle at his feet.

He writes Marnie not one, but two letters. "You're still young," he announces in the first, as though he is now decades older, adding that, although he does not intend to marry for any number of years, when that time comes she is the girl he would like to marry. Nonetheless, he says, he does not want her to feel tied down.

In the second letter he writes that he misses her and that he thinks of her as she was in her mother's house at the lake. He says he felt love for her when she cried over the fish. "I wanted to put my arms around you," he writes, "everything I had to put around you." The sentences, ambling in crooked progression down the page, surprise him as he reads back through the letter, as though not he, but the cats strolling across the forbidden territory of his papers have somehow left, in the imprint of their paws, these improbable words of love.

Both letters he puts into a single envelope. Somewhere in his desk he's got the number of Marnie's postbox at college, probably in the middle drawer; his address book would be under his box of typewriter ribbons. But he does not get up. Instead he sits with the envelope in his hand. After a while he addresses it, in his clear, slanted and somewhat childish handwriting, to Marnie in care of her mother at the lake house. There beside the lake, with the coppery water lapping at the shore and the woods shot through with autumn sunlight, Marnie will read the letters. Perhaps she will make more sense of them than he can.

He walks out into the bright morning—a squirrel carrying part of a hamburger bun in its mouth stops to watch him from the edge of the littered yard—and then he climbs the steps. His calf and buttock muscles still hurt. Up at road level, he places the envelope inside their metal mailbox and sets the red flag upright.

As he returns the way he came, step by hazardous step down to the little dirty house, he begins to feel sleepy at last. At the same time he begins to feel more cheerful and more normal and to lose, though not altogether, his sense of what exactly it was that happened during the night.

AMERICAN
TRAGEDY

I N THE SUMMER OF 1963, John Kennedy came to
Boston. The roommates hung out of their apartment
window, staring down over Commonwealth Avenue.
It was Willa who spotted him first. She had come to envy
the Americans this glamorous leader. Handsomer than
the men in movies. And now there he was for real, the
thick hair and short, straight nose, the gestures so intent
and youthfully brisk. How much did she or any of them
really see that day from five floors up, how much remember from a thousand magazine and television images?
Afterwards none of them could say.

That day, certainly, he was grim, barely acknowledging
the groups of people turned to wave at the passing motor-
cade. His wife, the wide-faced Jacqueline, had lain in pre-
mature childbirth out on the Cape, and now the baby lay
in his own travail at the Children's Hospital, crippled by a
hyaline membrane, penalty for being born too soon.

All that week Willa and her roommates went to work
through the grey heat. Their hair (cut in the latest "swinging

hair" style) hung in limp curtains around their faces. Their blouses and their cotton skirts wrinkled in the subway on the way to work. Come evening, they returned to their apartment, climbing the stairs with weary feet, the light dimming and the air growing warmer floor by floor until at their own landing they could scarcely breathe it in. Kennedy was staying at the Ritz. The girls tied up their hair and took showers and, turning their faces to the spray, thought longingly of the Ritz, its cool, marble lobby and air-conditioned bar, only two blocks down the street. After their showers they sat around in towels drinking gin and tonic and doing their nails while they sighed for the weekend.

The prettiest hoped to be invited to the New Hampshire shore. Her name was Abigail, and she was inclined to optimism. "I met him right at the beginning; you'd think it was meant to be. He stepped on my foot. Lawrence of Arabia eyes, blue as blue . . . Everyone at the party loved him." The invitation was, however, by no means a certain thing. The man with the Lawrence of Arabia eyes was a friend of the man who'd been her date at the party. Thus the invitation had been circumspect; sneakily delivered, Abigail had to admit. The other roommates nodded. Such complications were not rare. Nor were men reliable in such matters. Tossing off invitations in a burst of competitive zeal, then rethinking them or, worse, forgetting altogether to follow up. You never quite knew where you were.

"There's a beach," said Abigail, splaying out her fingers as though to span a stretch of sand, though in truth she meant merely to examine her newly lacquered nails. "Fire 'n' Ice"—the sexiest shade, the girl at the makeup counter had assured her. Meanwhile, up through the open window wafted the sounds of the city—sirens, horns, the brutal revving of car engines—but no breeze, never a breeze.

The baby died. *The Boston Globe* announced the death in headlines two inches high. Patrick Bouvier Kennedy died without leaving the Children's Hospital. The whole city felt the failure. In the subway, on the street corner, from desk to desk across their offices, the girls heard people wrapping up the event. Poor Jacqueline, two out of four lost, all that money doing no good. Still, there was John-John (idiot nickname), and Caroline too, of course, which was more than some had. And it was different for the Kennedys anyway. Things were different if you were very rich. But the baby, wealth was no help to him; four days of life and all of it a misery.

Beset with the futility of it all, not to mention the heat, Willa decided to break her engagement to David. Mornings at the Elvira Whittemore Business and Secretarial College made her want to run screaming into the middle of downtown Boylston Street. And afternoons were scant improvement. Her boss at the dry-cleaning company where she worked part-time had taken to pressing unpleasantly close while he showed her how to balance his monthly accounts. Moreover, her period was late, as usual, and she was aware of a rigidity to her skin, a vague stuffiness in her head (not quite a headache).

There were other, less ephemeral reasons to off-load David. An inattentiveness on his part that was not gentlemanly. He interrupted her little speeches saying, "Right, right, got it," well before the end. Other times he didn't listen at all. And then there were his table manners. The way he stabbed his food as if each bite were a small, wiggly beast on his plate. She had doubts, too, if the truth were told, about marrying an American. Americans, as her parents had pointed out, were so noisy, so uncertain of their ancestry, above all so irritatingly pleased to be Americans.

Mummy and Daddy were English to the core. Brought to Montreal as children, they had been raised, a street apart, in the south shore village of Ste-Marie-Madeleine, directly across the river from, but in no way contiguous with, popish Montreal. Neither could speak a coherent sentence of French. Her mother's favourite human being was the Queen Mother, her father's his colonel from the old regiment. Mummy and Daddy would be less than thrilled with an American fiancé.

Willa's year in Boston, in fact, represented a compromise. Her parents had wanted London; there was a secretarial course at Mummy's old school, and Aunt Fiona, leasing now in a Kensington mews, was ideally positioned to look after her Canadian niece. Willa herself had longed for New York.

The choice of Boston had been somewhat ameliorated by the envy of her friends. No French to struggle with, as they'd all said wistfully, and the Americans so with-it, even, presumably, in Boston. But now—now with this heat and secretarial school and her boss's accounts, not to mention the weight of tragedy in the air—what was so "with-it" about a stifling walk-up, a boyfriend with no manners? Perhaps it would be better to return home to the shores of the St. Lawrence unencumbered.

Two days after the death of baby Patrick, Willa stubbed out her suppertime cigarette and leaned forward on both elbows. Her pink-cheeked, rather broad face assumed an expression of what she hoped was pained gravity. "David and I have come to the end of the road."

She had rehearsed this sentence, but still it was gratifying to say it and to see the three pairs of startled eyes lift to hers. "David is simply too immature," she told the eyes, "too self-centred, too . . . too . . . " Dropping her gaze abruptly she began to fumble for a fresh cigarette; they kept a pack on the table, propped between the salt and the jar of instant coffee. She had been going to say "too American."

But the roommates were already nodding. "So, what'd he say?" demanded Charlotte. She was tall with fine, impossibly straight blonde hair and a habit of asking the questions that were on everybody's mind. "So, what'd he do? Did you tell him?"

"Not yet." Willa lit the cigarette and went on. David: always cracking open a beer as though he lived here, plunking himself down in the centre of the chesterfield and grabbing up the sports section of their paper, never noticing if she was wearing a new blouse or had got her hair cut. In his own apartment he did nothing but watch baseball and try to get her into bed. (She did not mention that he usually succeeded.) Nor was his apartment strictly clean. It smelled quite often of running shoes. Dustballs accumulated under his bed; grey, smeary things grew in his refrigerator.

"You're sure?" asked Betsy. She was short and round-eyed and generally called bouncy when she wasn't called cute. She was also the kindest of the four. Currently without a boyfriend, she had been eyeing a third-year Harvard medical student. A future obstetrician. He'd confided this plan to Betsy during the fireworks at a Fourth of July party, then asked her if she was a nurse. She looked like one, he'd said and kissed her on the cheek before weaving off beneath the exploding pink and green stars to get himself and her another gin. Obstetrics, she'd decided while waiting to see if he would find his way back to her, was a good sign. He had indeed eventually woven his way back, emerging out of the crowd with a smile on his face and half her drink sloshed over his sleeve.

"Of course, I'm sure," Willa was saying in her most positive voice. She nodded vigorously now, as if concurring with her own statement. "I've given it," she said, "a great deal of thought."

The roommates began murmuring approval. The summer, except for the Kennedy baby, had been notably short of event. Willa's announcement would mean whispered confessions, late night conversations and possibly (if Dave should turn out to be adequately heartbroken), even frantic, pleading phone calls. And when she had run the course of her explanations, they agreed to go out for the remainder of the evening.

In Dave's apartment the telephone rang through the din of the television. He answered it without turning down the sound. The Sox had just about blown it at this point, but you never knew.

"You have to come..." Willa's voice piercing the noise of the game sounded its usual insistent self. "The others are going to be out."

Imagining she wanted a quick hop into bed, this despite her previous refusals to do it in her apartment, he gave in more quickly than he might have done. The last month or so, he'd begun to wonder about himself and Willa. Flaws like the bump on her nose, the bossy, almost English inflection to her voice, her habit of finishing his sentences, had begun to attract his attention. At work he had flirted with and then surreptitiously begun to take out another girl. However, Whitey Ford was still pitching, the Sox were already behind by five, and now, in the bottom of the eighth, while Willa was still talking, a third Yankee got on base; it was game over. A fast run to Commonwealth Avenue wouldn't take that long.

Willa turned down the lights, just a lamp here and there. She stuffed someone's laundry bag under the chesterfield and emptied the various ashtrays. In the shaded light the green canvas chairs looked almost substantial. Even the slant of the chesterfield was less noticeable, though she must get David to prop it up; the leg had broken, and people were always sliding off that end. But, no, she could hardly ask him that now. Doubt stirred in her stomach, disturbing the macaroni she had ingested at supper. Was it wise, to fling him out like a sweater the moths had got at? A sure Saturday night date. With uncertain fingers she straightened the copies of *Glamour* and *Mademoiselle* and *Chatelaine*. (Mummy posted down her own copy each month, its cover scored and dented, its recipe section a frail mosaic of rectangular holes.) What if Betsy was right and she did miss him? There were six months left on her visa. What if there was no one else to go out with?

The squawk of the buzzer sent her dashing to press the latch button. And then, while David's footsteps sounded in the stairwell, she began to feel all around her the gathering drama, as if cameras were approaching, the director opening his script. From grade school came a memory. A play—"Princess Margaret"—yes, that was it. They had made up a play, Willa and her Ste-Marie-Madeleine friends—Princess Margaret, in a long tulle dress and jewelled crown, renouncing Townsend. Willa could see him still, the comely English flyer with his dark, too-long hair, his thin-lipped, hero's smile. She had forgotten the reason for the renunciation; it had been something Mummy had understood, to do with divorce and the archbishop and Margaret being a princess.

Ten minutes later, Willa was still striding about the living room in full voice. David, slouched on the chesterfield, his hazel eyes adrift, had spoken not a word since the beginning of her speech. He'd arrived panting slightly and, in the middle of her sombre greeting, had thrust a hand up the front of her sweater. She'd quelled him with a barrage of words.

Now, as she spun around in mid-sentence, she registered his bored expression just as her fingers smacked against something hard. Beside her the floor lamp teetered, and in the same instant here was David leaping to his feet and his hand shooting out to steady the lamp.

He remained standing, lamp in hand, while she stared up at him. Really, didn't he look exactly like a soldier with a spear? Now, where was she? Something about the engagement, their marriage . . . oh, yes. She took a deep breath and began again. "And as for our marriage, David.

I simply don't see how it could endure such inconsiderate, selfish . . . " Now what was he doing?

For David had taken a sharp backward step, dragging the lamp with him. His hazel eyes had gone wide with what looked like shock. His lips formed the words "our marriage," as if he was trying to mimic her, though, curiously enough, only a deep, strangled sound emerged from his mouth. Now he had let go the lamp and was backing up again.

"Where are you going?" she said.

"Got to head back." This time his voice came out thick, and he swallowed. She could see in his throat the tiny volcano of his Adam's apple. His hand reached behind him and twisted the door knob. "Okay," he said as if agreeing with something he or she had said. If she hadn't known better, she'd have sworn he was terrified. His hand pulled open the door. "Okay," he said again. "Call you."

And then he was gone, his footsteps reverberating faster and faster, it seemed, from the hollow of the stairwell until they were abruptly silenced by a thudding slam.

The roommates returned as soon as they dared, salivating for details, each secretly hoping Dave might still be in the apartment. Entering, they cast swift glances around the living room. But Willa, dry-eyed and silent, was standing alone by the window. She had her hairbrush in her hand, and she was staring down into the street as if she expected some interesting event to occur there shortly.

"You okay?" said Charlotte, shaking back her blonde hair. She'd pinned it into a French twist, using all her bobby pins, before they'd headed out to the piano bar at the Copely Plaza. Might not there have been some man there, elbows on the bar, a lit Marlboro afloat between his fingers, a man who preferred the sophisticated, Grace Kelly look? But no such man had appeared and just as well, for the French twist had betrayed her, unravelling strand by strand until she'd been forced to retire to the ladies' room and undo the whole mess. "Did he show up?" she added, wondering suddenly if this could be the cause of Willa's apparent gloom.

"Of course he did," Willa said now, speaking over her shoulder. "He was devastated." She had not moved from this spot where half an hour earlier she'd watched David lope across the strip of park that bisected Commonwealth Avenue, his long unruly legs dodging people and leashed dogs and park benches, his pace increasing as he reached the corner and headed into Berkeley Street.

Now, in the avenue below, a taxi was disgorging a couple. The woman stepped up onto the sidewalk, did something with her purse and patted her hair while the man leaned back into the taxi. They looked like a married couple. Not so old as her parents, nor so stodgy—the woman had on a bright green dress; the man's movements were crisp—but they looked settled nonetheless. Impossible that she, Willa, would ever be such an age.

At least, she told herself as she turned to face the roommates, at least now that he was gone, there would no longer be the monthly terror. The waiting, like a dog for its dinner, longing for her period. Of all things, her period—the nuisance of it eclipsed by the joy of reprieve when at last the first pink spot appeared and sent her flying to the linen closet. And what had David ever cared about her worry, always wanting to "do it," merrily assuming she would take care of what he called "that stuff."

"So? What'd he say? What happened?" All the roommates were now staring at her.

Willa shook her head. "I don't want to talk about it." And she began to brush her hair with furious slashes.

The roommates glanced at one another. This was hardly fair. Then they all shrugged. They would get it out of her eventually. Willa always talked. And with one motion they turned and headed for the gin bottle.

Soothed by the icy liquid, they sprawled on the chairs and the slanting sofa and began to chat. Their voices, breathy and solemn in the humid air, floated back and forth across the fierce silence that emanated from Willa. The lamps gave off heat, and one by one the girls turned them out until only the floor lamp was left to illumine the room.

"What about the weekend?" asked Charlotte. "Is the heat supposed to end by then?"

Would it ever end? Each of them felt that it might not, so heavy and immovable was the night, so flaccid their bodies, their white, soft skin in the lamplight. How they missed the tans of earlier summers. The suburban parks and beaches. Their lost freedom. Surely this heat would be pressing upon them forever.

"Well," they said to each other, blotting the sweat from their foreheads. "Well then. Who's for more gin? Who's for more ice?"

Exactly when Willa began to cry they weren't sure. Just gradually her snuffly weeping grew louder until they all knew what they were hearing and stared at each other in dismay.

"Oh, Willa, you didn't love him?" cried Betsy.

Rising to cross the room all three roommates clucked and mewed like the fussy, sympathetic mothers they would someday become. "Don't cry. Don't cry. You'll feel better soon. You won't miss him at all . . ." And, staring at one another across the top of Willa's bowed head, they all wondered. A boyfriend, after all, was a valuable commodity. Dave was a bit of a clod, it was true, but on the whole an okay type and for sure better than no boyfriend at all. Why ever had she done it?

The baby was buried. This surprised the girls, who hadn't thought of babies being buried. Dutifully they pictured a country graveyard, the old-fashioned kind with trees bent low over the rough grass and a profusion of tiny stone crosses flanking the bigger monuments with their half-rubbed-out dates and peculiar names (Ezekiels and Jeremiahs, Josephinas and Hesters and Hattie Maes). Whether Patrick Bouvier Kennedy had a little cross, or any marker at all, was not mentioned in the newspapers, only that he was buried beside the body of his sister, a baby girl, stillborn, no given name.

The following night the apartment was, if anything, hotter. Since supper, Willa had remained hunched in one corner of the sofa, uncharacteristically silent, the shadows under her eyes seeping like a fog through the room. The roommates were beginning to wonder about her. She was of course Canadian, but still . . . That morning she had refused breakfast altogether, declaring herself after the first few bites too upset to eat, then rising and proceeding with dignified steps to the bathroom. The bitter sound of her retching had reached them only slightly muffled. Eyeing one another, the roommates had taken large swallows of their sugar-laden coffee and shaken their heads.

Dave, sweating in his own apartment, pried the cap off a bottle of Molson Export. The last one in the refrigerator. He had failed on the previous evening to hook into the supply in Willa's apartment. Her speech had gone on too long, the final portion been too big a shocker.

Changing into T-shirt and shorts (he still had not got used to the confinement of a business suit), he recalled that Willa had been remarkably good about stocking a supply of beer for him, sometimes even making a special trip on the subway to Cambridge, where she could buy the Canadian ale to which she had introduced him and which he now greatly preferred. She had, of course, told him about each one of these trips, her tone of martyrdom so self-satisfied that he generally couldn't bring himself to thank her.

Further rumination brought to mind the fact that he had left his sweater in her apartment some weeks earlier, before the weather had got so stinking hot. The sweater was an old one, baggy and worn at the elbows, his favourite in fact. Gulping his beer, the final beer, he tried to consider the entire business in a rational, executive manner. He and Willa got along well enough, except when she was in her lecturing mood. (The girl in his office was a passing thing.) Girls like Willa just needed to stir things up once in a while. That last speech of hers had been sort of stirring actually. Was she that crazy about him? She'd looked kind of cute pacing around her living room, all pink and damp around the edges. The bump on her nose wasn't that big. Canadians were nice people, no different from Americans really.

He dug his sneakers out of the closet and jammed his feet into them. Besides, wasn't she going back to wherever in another four or five months anyway? (He could never remember the name of the place she was from up in Canada. Saint something, a French name, near the big river.) The whole engagement fuss would blow over. Where she'd got that idea, he couldn't imagine. Anyway, nothing could *make* him get married. And besides, he needed his sweater. Knocking back the last of the beer, he set the bottle by the telephone and dialed her number.

When the telephone rang in the dimness of the living room, Willa scarcely lifted her head. Charlotte, who answered the phone, recognized the dangerous voice of Dave immediately. It was she who shared a bedroom with Willa, and the chance for a more central role in the drama threw her into full alert. What to do? Deliver a dignified rebuke? Refuse in a haughty voice to permit him access to Willa?

"Who is it?" called Betsy, noticing the silence.

"Just a moment," Charlotte said severely into the receiver and made a meaningful face at the others. "Willa," she hissed. "Willa! It's him! What'll I do, tell him you're out?"

"It's *he*," corrected Willa from her slump, and then her head snapped up. "David?"

"Do I tell him where to go?" Charlotte said.

"On the phone?" yelped Willa.

"Yes!" Charlotte jerked the receiver, causing the telephone to jingle angrily.

Now Willa was on her feet, springing through the solicitous huddle. Just short of the telephone, she got hold of herself and reduced her rush to a saunter.

"I'll speak to him," she allowed. Her hand closed around the receiver.

"Hello," she said, and they all three admired how her voice came out flat and indifferent. In the minute of silence that followed, no one could see her face. Just once a shrill "You do?" escaped from her. Then more silence, and finally a calm "Very well, David. If you really want to," that was barely spoiled by her eager "Okay, g'bye!"

Bang. She had hung up, and here she was spinning around to face them, the smile unfurling across her face like a victory flag. Got him! Even in the dusk they could see the triumphant gleam of her large, imperfectly straightened teeth. Though what she had got, or got back, no one could yet guess.

Willa was fingering the forwardmost lock of her swinging hair. "My face," she said now. "My hair. I'm out of spray net."

"Use mine," said Betsy. "It's superhold." The others nodded.

As Willa headed for the bathroom, the roommates gazed around their living room. Flies circled the single illuminated lamp. Their supply of ice, dumped earlier into a bowl on the coffee table, had melted into a single glossy lump. Across the hall, noises of restoration gurgled through the thin panels of the bathroom door.

Abigail knelt at the coffee table and began to chip ice from the lump in the bowl. The other two moved to refill their glasses, scooping up the chips of ice, then sloshing

gin and tonic over the whitened fragments. In the final
moments before the squawk of the buzzer, they sat sipping their gin and contemplating their finger marks on
the misted glass. Abigail decided that if the man with the
New Hampshire beach house called before Friday, she
would buy a new bathing suit. Betsy concocted a plan to
telephone the medical student. If he showed signs of remembering their encounter, recognized her name for
example, she would ask advice about a mythical friend's
medical problem. Charlotte, shaking back her slippery
hair, made up her mind, come fall, to grow it long. The
new assistant vice-president in Consumer Loans, quite
tall and rumoured to be unmarried, had just that morning
remarked in her hearing that he had a thing for long-
haired blondes.

Willa emerged from the bathroom; the crown of her
hair was teased into a dome, the ends loose and properly
curved forward across her cheeks. "How does it look?"
She made smoothing motions all around her hair.

"Perfect," they assured her. "You look just perfect,"
although in the dim light they could hardly see her face
as she passed through the room.

In fact they could hardly see one another. Tomorrow
they would perk up of course, buy more gin and more
magazines, choose brighter shades of lipstick. But the
truth was, they had no zest for the hunt. Not now. Not
tonight. In the pliant, indifferent night, in Willa's eager
capitulation, they had felt the untextured folds of their
future lives: the husbands, as yet unflushed from cover,
the square suburban houses full of sagging furniture and
casserole-encrusted dishes and children—ah, yes, the
children yet to be born and agonized over, raised and lost.

Apparent in everything around them was the absence of glamour. Dave would be back, fixing the sofa, cadging beers. And what would sustain them in all this heat? What drama? What crisis to sharpen the edge of their days? (Kennedy come back? Bombs to fall?) How would they ever get through the summer? How would they ever get through their lives?

KNOWING

AROUND THE TIME MY BROTHER Kevin got his driver's licence and began to shave once or even twice a week, my mother fell in love with him. Kevin was older than I was and something of a star. At our high school, he ran pep rallies for the football games and sock hops on Saturday nights, and in the spring he played catcher on the baseball team—he wasn't big enough for football—and he bestowed on people a quirky, optimistic smile that made them happy.

He made my mother happy too. She was the kind of woman who brightened around men, and her face would flush and her eyes go shiny when he came into the room. At such times I could imagine how she had looked when she was young, a flirty little Irish girl with a snappy tongue and quick eyes. After dinner, when my father was reading in the living room and she and I were doing the dishes, Kevin would sit on the big, white kitchen table talking and swinging his legs back and forth. He knocked bits of paint off the table legs doing this, but my mother never complained. Swathed like a nurse in apron and rubber gloves, she whisked around him bearing leftovers to the refrigerator and dishes to the sink, all the while providing little nods and mm-hmms and clickings of her tongue. She asked him questions about football scores and baseball statistics. "What about Koufax?" she would say, touching his arm with the tips of her rubbered fingers as if she really longed to know. "What about our Red Sox?" Boy things, things I knew she didn't care about.

Other times she just watched him—he had a shambly, loose-kneed way of moving—and her eyes would follow him while he was loping up the stairs or slapping together a sandwich or ambling out the door to pick up a date. Of course, she didn't like any of his girlfriends.

After graduation Kevin went to Boston College. He lasted until the fall of his third year, until one Friday afternoon to be exact. I'd just finished my homework when the doorbell rang—Kevin could never find his key—and there he was on the front stoop. All around his feet sat stuffed laundry bags and cartons of records and another carton piled high with baseball things. A fine wind was blowing up from the harbour, and it riffled his dark hair as he stood there.

I was wearing my own hair in a ponytail at that time, and he reached around behind my head and pulled it, not hard so it would hurt but just to say hello in a big brother way. "Hi" was all he said.

"Hi," I said back. I could see, poking out of the one carton, his chest protector and his bats and, in another, sitting on top of his transistor, the big leather saucer that was his catcher's mitt. These were his most precious possessions, and I understood that he wasn't going back to Boston College. The friend who had delivered him and his worldly goods must have known too because his battered Plymouth was already backing down the driveway at a speed that would have earned him a lecture from my mother had she appeared at the front door in time to apprehend him. She wasn't shy about such things, and our friends were wary of her.

She did walk out from the kitchen a moment later while Kevin and I were dragging his stuff indoors. Her hands, which had something white stuck to the knuckles, dropped to her sides. "Darling!" I can still hear the joy in her brilliant, high-pitched voice. Her face went crimson, then, as she registered his news, slowly emptied. Tired of studying, tired of books, his explanations were offered with baffled good cheer. He didn't himself seem to know why he'd wanted out. My mother began to look as if she might cry, though I knew she wouldn't.

"Tired of books?" my father said to him that night and shook his head, rejecting this incredible notion. "Only a cretin gets tired of books."

It would turn out to be everything he had to say on the subject. They were standing in the living room at the time. My father, who'd been heading towards his favourite chair, was holding a book, his forefinger inserted in the pages. I remember the smile curling up Kevin's face as he noticed, and the way he draped an arm over my father's shoulder, indulgently, as though he understood my father and forgave him his abstraction, his will to live his life apart from us. They were the same height standing there, but my father was nearly twice the thickness (he was a bulky man), and Kevin's arms and legs were longer, as though he might still grow another inch.

My mother remained profoundly disappointed. "All those smart Jesuits, and the college right over there in Chestnut Hill. . ." But unlike my father she didn't give up. "What about Fordham? Did you think of writing them? Or Notre Dame? Indiana's not the farthest place. . ." In the bright snap of her voice, I heard how much she hated those potential miles between herself and him. "Or that other one. Georgetown. What about Georgetown?" She had a new suggestion every day. I think Kevin was not sorry to get his draft notice.

The year and a half while he was in Vietnam must have caused her agony, though she never spoke of it. We both wrote him, even my father wrote once or twice a month, and his girlfriends did too, though at first they had trouble getting his address from my mother. She kept saying she'd mislaid it, or that he was about to get a new one.

By then I had graduated from high school. My boyfriend had another view of the draft and of a good many other things as well, and after my stint at the Elvira Whittemore Business and Secretarial College in downtown Boston, I followed him north, over the Canadian border to the shore of the St. Lawrence River. There, in a city I knew only from travel posters, I found a job typing and filing invoices in the office of a furniture store. I spoke no French, but another girl answered the telephones, and my boss didn't care what I spoke as long as

my letters were neat and quickly done and he could pay
me less than minimum wage under the table.

Around the corner from the store, the greystone parish
church loomed, solemn and paternal, over the neighbourhood, its stone towers strangely hollow in appear-
ance, though from them at various hours, bells rang out.
St-François Xavier the church was called, and at lunch
hour, or sometimes after work, I used to creep into its
dim and rather damp interior to say a prayer for Kevin.
My mother did not question what I was doing in Canada.
A boyfriend was a boyfriend, and following him was a
reasonable thing for a girl to do. Getting married, after all,
was a girl's business. (I did not press upon her the information that I was actually living with him.) She wrote me
that she lit a candle each day in our church for my brother
and that she knew he would be fine because he was
Kevin. In nearly every letter she wrote this, as though it
would be traitorous to think otherwise. And I believed
her, as I believed her about most things.

The way my mother told it afterwards, she was sitting
at the telephone. In those days telephones didn't travel
around from room to room. There weren't very many of
them in a house either, one for the ground floor, maybe
one upstairs (if there was an upstairs), placed on the table
between the parents' twin beds. Our phone resided in
the front hall. A shiny, black pyramid set like an icon on
a little mahogany table. The table was meant for this purpose. It had spindly legs and a shelf underneath for the
telephone book. It also had a matching, upright chair
of comparable spindliness. It was on this chair that my
mother was perched. She was a short woman with a flat,

girdled fanny, and she would have been wearing stockings and high-heeled shoes and a straight tweed skirt (the matching tweed jacket would have been hanging in her closet). This was what she wore for an ordinary day. The jacket was added if she had to go out to the grocery store or the dry cleaner's or sometimes to a Catholic Daughters meeting. I do not remember ever seeing her in pants.

That particular day, she was chatting with a friend when she saw the grey Chevrolet pull up outside. The marine officer driving it was in full dress uniform. Since my brother had joined the marines, she had learned the officers' uniforms, and she could see this one clearly through the windows on either side of the door. He had just started up the walk, this officer, when she said to her friend—in a voice as calm, the friend told us later, as if the milkman, bottles clinking in his metal basket, were arriving at the door—"I've got to go now, dear. Kevin's been killed."

Kevin died on the jungle floor in the company of a second lieutenant. This lieutenant wrote us about it, how Kevin lay in his arms, and how he said nothing, but after a while died. A helicopter had dropped them into a clearing that had turned out to be an ambush, and I guess another helicopter took them out, as they then were: some living; others, like Kevin, merely bodies.

It wasn't clear to us from reading Kevin's letters, or the ones we got afterwards from his marine friends, what their mission was. He and his platoon seemed to be dropped into one part of the jungle or another to fight each day, then collected at the end of the afternoon like a remote work crew. Perhaps in some fragmented way he enjoyed these outings. He had written that he loved being out of doors, that he thought he could never live an indoor life again. He did not speak of fighting in his letters—the last three came after his death—but of friends, of the past, recalling the time he and my father painted the garage, the time he found a library book, missing for years, under his bed. He wrote other times of the future, making plans for how he would study forestry or agriculture, live on a mountain in Oregon or in Maine.

We three were Catholics, my mother, Kevin and I. All through my childhood, we'd eaten fish on Friday night and gone weekly to mass, my mother and I with scarves in our coat pockets to tie over our heads, my brother galloping on ahead like an unleashed dog. I remember even as a child praying for my father, unredeemed as he was. Not only had he never converted, despite long years of good Catholic influence, but he was unperturbed by this failure. I can still see him glancing over his reading glasses as we fidgeted about in the front hall getting ready to leave. His smile, crooked like Kevin's, flashed over us with amusement.

My mother, spotting this, bristled. Her gaze swivelled towards Kevin, and I could see the anger growing in her eyes. "You might come with us once in a while, make a decent example."

I'd been folding my head scarf into a careful square since my mother was likely to scold me if I got it wrinkled. Now I poked the scarf into my pocket and stared at my father. He was leaning back in his reading chair, and his expression as he gazed at my mother evinced a complete, though amiable, lack of interest. It occurred to me that he didn't really care what my mother thought, and this knowledge gave me a peculiar sensation in my stomach, as if I had recently eaten something that was not likely to stay down. Far better, I decided then, if he would behave like other fathers, pound the chair arm, shout orders at her.

"Now, Rosie," he was saying in his flat, unconcerned voice, "we can't all be saved at once." He'd gone back to reading a book called *Their Finest Hour* before we got out the door.

Perhaps it was in compensation that my mother had always hoped for Kevin's faith to increase in strength. The Church was what she'd had in mind for him, and if Kevin's departure from Boston College took her by surprise, the diversion of war must have been a raging shock, the marines not being remotely in keeping with her plans. A Jesuit for a son, that was what she'd had in mind, a son backed up by that ultimate bossy male, God himself.

"And why not? A priest can go anywhere," she would say with a pointed glance at my father, who was generally deep in his book. "Look at that Father Drinan, gone down to be in the Congress..."

Usually my father would glance up and shake his head, as if he could think of better futures for my brother but wasn't going to push it. Once he said to her, "Well, Drinan's an interesting fellow. I'll grant you that," but after a second he shook his head as if to suggest that Father Drinan, too, might have done something more worthwhile with his life.

"A priest counts for more than anyone," my mother said then, her voice so sharp it hurt my ears.

We held the funeral on a bright, windy day in April. I'd taken a bus down from Montreal. My boyfriend, being a draft dodger, couldn't come with me, of course. And arriving with my parents at the church, I felt I had returned to an earlier, more daughterly time. In the crowd milling around outside, I saw the people I'd grown up with, our old neighbours, my parents' friends, a lot of Kevin's school friends, too, and some of mine from high school. I even spotted a pair of Kevin's old girlfriends. As we walked by them, my mother frowned beneath her veil. But then she surprised me by stopping abruptly, as though she'd just remembered they would no longer be a vexation to her. She addressed each girl by name, saying that it was kind of her to come. Both girls looked startled, and one began to cry, but my mother seemed not to think anything of this. She just nodded once or twice and gave each girl a glance before moving on.

Following her and my father up the church steps, I began to imagine that somewhere just ahead Kevin was waiting. He would quite naturally have got a bit in front of us. Or perhaps he had not come with us at all today but was off on a school trip, or maybe he had gone to early mass and was now out sailing.

At the top of the stairs I paused for a minute, not wanting to go inside. Our church was built quite high on the hill, and it was possible from here to see the rock promontory for which our town was named and the long, narrow wash of blue where the harbour penetrated the land. My mother had always been proud that our town was an old fishing village, with its fleet and its proper historical past, but she feared the water as much as she admired its presence. As far as I know, she never swam a stroke.

My father and Kevin, on the other hand, loved to sail. They'd gone out weekends and sometimes after supper in the long light of early summer. April was too early in the year for sailing, of course, but as I stood there, the wind caught my veil and blew it off my face, and for a second I felt as though, from my post up there on the steps, I should be watching for their dinghy to come sliding around the rock, leaning from the wind as it headed towards home and my mother and me. Then my father's hand tapped my arm and my mother's tongue clicked its familiar summons, and pulling my veil back across my face, I turned and followed my parents into our church.

After the mass was over, I could recall almost nothing of what had transpired, not a word that was said, none of the music, none of the prayers. Only the end stayed in my memory. Kevin's body had been sent back to us in a military casket, and what I remember is the final moment when the marines bore it out, treading the aisle of the church with stiff-legged precision, and how my mother began to shake. The entire congregation was on its feet, waiting for us to follow the casket, and for a second I couldn't think what to do. Then I put my arm around her waist, and at the same time my father took her elbow, and we walked out like that behind the long, grey box that contained the debris of my brother.

Afterwards, I left the Church. I'd found I couldn't stand to go inside and smell the old, damp wood and stone. I couldn't stand to see the priests up at the altar during mass, their backs to us while they turned the wine into blood. Even the littlest sounds at mass, the sighs and coughs around me, the clinks and shuffles, the tinkling bells, I couldn't bear to hear.

I left my boyfriend too, for reasons that had something to do with his habit of always telling me what was what. I'd had enough of priests and men just then, I guess; though later I changed my mind about the latter.

My mother fussed over the boyfriend, but she surprised me by making little protest about the Church. For a time I assumed that, for her too, Kevin's death had sucked from the cavernous, candlelit interior the very spirit of male domination in which she'd believed and had taught me to believe. It was only after a longer while that I realized she'd kept to her ways with the priests and weekly mass and other parish doings, and I understood that to her it didn't matter so much what faith claimed her female child. Faith in the grander sense not being a female issue.

My mother lived for three more decades, and other sorrows befell her. She lost a breast to the surgeon's knife and my father to a massive stroke. And she garnered some triumphs too. My little Canadian son loved her above all other creatures, and she bore him off on special granny trips to the seashore and the mountains and, when he was a teenager, to Rome. Once or twice he complained to me that she watched him too intently. He could feel her eyes on him, he said. But mostly he basked in her attention. She even learned the names of some of the hockey players and would ask him questions about the Montreal Canadiens, mispronouncing the French names in hilarious ways, but sounding for all the world as if she cared.

In our town she retained, long after the war, the crown of a martyr-mother, triumphant as much in her refusal to mourn as in her unrequitable loss. Though she intermittently waxed snappish about the Church, she remained a stalwart there too, the way she'd remained with my father, I suppose, out of habit and social need. Priests came often to her home. They made, as she said in that vivacious, slightly angry voice of hers, admirable dinner guests.

I went quite often to visit her, driving my own car now through the flat fields of southern Quebec, then angling east and south across Vermont and New Hampshire, down to the outer edge of Boston. There, with a line of miniature skyscrapers pricking the horizon, I turned north and followed the old road around to the sea. Our town remained familiar to my eyes; the changes as they came seemed small. My mother sold our house on the side of the hill and bought a condo down near the harbour. The view, of boats and the temperamental water, suited her, she said.

The commotion of moving suited her too. Most of the organizing she managed herself, choosing paint colours and ordering new slipcovers for the chairs and sofa, and shipping off our big, mahogany sideboard and too-large dining-room table to the church's second-hand furniture sale. She refused my offer to come down for the move. "You'll only get yourself in the way," she said. And when I arrived a month afterwards for a visit, I found her standing, quick-eyed and impatient as ever, in the doorway of a brand new, two-bedroom apartment.

She showed me around the whole of it in five minutes, dismissive of my interest, yet pleased with herself too. "Now then," she said, shutting the door on her perfectly arranged linen closet, "a cup of tea would do quite nicely."

She made the tea while I opened a package of ginger-snaps and arranged them as instructed on a pewter plate that she'd kept because it had been her aunt's. We had our tea in her new living room with its broad picture window and view of the harbour.

"That ocean's a menace, up over the rocks last week. They had to take out the boats early this year." There was pride in her voice. "Mind you don't spill," she added, handing over a full teacup with her shaky hands. She'd poured in a small tot of rum and did the same now for her own cup, then added a second splash. The rum was in a little white pitcher.

Catching my surprise, she became brisk. "Quiets my hand, you know. That stupid tremor the doctors can't get rid of." I nodded but knew better than to smile.

My mother had become a peppy, bright-eyed and occasionally mean old lady, and she could still make her displeasure felt. She still wore her tweed suits too. She was wearing one now as we sat in her living room sur-rounded by furniture from our old house. My father's

chair had been slipcovered in a flowered cotton, as though
my mother had meant to disguise its intransigent bulk,
and behind it on a shelf stood the framed photographs I
knew so well—of Kevin in his uniform; of me in my
white organdy confirmation dress; and another of herself
and my dark-haired son standing in bright sunlight just
outside one of the long colonnades that flank the Vatican.

"The Church is useful to a woman, you know." She
spoke as if this were apropos of something I'd just said.

I put my teacup down on the little piecrust table beside my chair and peered at her wrinkled face, trying to
read what she was after. "It didn't seem so to me," I said
finally, and then I surprised myself by adding something I
hadn't intended to say. "The Church didn't save Kevin
for you."

"Oh, not useful for that," my mother said sharply, as
though I was being a bit thick. "It's priests I'm talking
about. They're always there. They always know."

"The priests?" I said. "They just think they know."

But my mother shook her head. I was being thick
again. "Knowing is knowing," she said. "It doesn't matter if they're wrong."

Through her picture window, I could see the choppy,
grey water of the harbour. It was you, I said speaking to
her in my mind, though more truly to myself. The reason
I had to leave. Not that boyfriend, not the war, not even
the Church so much as it was you. I heard her voice begin
again, "Why, when my friend Mrs. Fitzwilliam lost her
husband—his third heart attack, they're always fatal—
it was that Father Torrence came and told her what to
do. Right then and there, all about the death notice and
the funeral."

I drank my tea—the rum was aromatic as perfume—while she went on telling me the tale of her widowed friend, and I thought how certain my mother always was and how wilful, about small things and large, about men most of all (even if these days the men were mostly priests), and yet it seemed to me that not any of them nor anything she had willed around us here, not the afternoon tea nor the harbour view nor the new condo itself, was for her anything more than an after-act, an epilogue. All about us, like a brighter-lit scene, I could feel that long ago moment in our front hall on that long ago morning. That, it seemed to me, was the quintessential moment of my mother's existence. The centre of her life.

Even nowadays when I think of her, I think of her there. I think of that instant when she knew, absolutely knew, Kevin was dead, and she sat clear and apart in the hallway while her friend's voice rattled in her ear and the marine officer came up the walk—that instant, before sorrow struck, when she knew that she would never lose her son to another woman.

WINDWARD BEACH

THAT NIGHT, WHEN SHE ROLLED against him in bed, Geoff turned away. It was the last thing he'd meant to do. But in the dark their trip across the bay had come back to him and with it the swell of nausea in his stomach. The storm had caught them just outside the harbour. If he shut his eyes, he could see the spray flashing again and again over the salt-smeared windows, feel the lurch and plunge of the ferry.

Beside him now, the bundle of silence that was Kit shifted. Guiltily he waited, staring into darkness for what seemed a long time until finally her breathing deepened and slowed. Then he got up and walked into the living room.

Carpet squished between his toes as he felt his way about, bumping into first one and then another piece of furniture. The condo belonged to a friend from work. The friend was in the midst of a divorce. His wife had decided that she preferred women, more recently that she merely wished for no more men. Neither her husband, she announced, nor even she herself had ever had an inkling what she was really about.

"Hell," Geoff's friend had said, reporting this to him over a series of beers, "what's anyone about? I just wanted to sail on weekends; I wanted *her*."

Earlier Geoff hadn't thought the living room anything special. When he and Kit had arrived, soaked and laden with suitcases and groceries, the place had seemed no more than a refuge. But now, as his fingers found a lamp switch, the sudden light laid a sheen of glamour over the pine liquor cabinet and leather chairs, the painting of a square-rigger afloat on a cerulean sea. Blinking, he stared around. Whatever her sins, the ex-wife must have had style.

The painting, framed in gilded wood, hung slightly askew above the cabinet. He righted it and poured himself a Scotch from his friend's supply. The whisky warmed his throat, then sank reassuringly into the pit of his stomach. His nausea began to abate.

Drink in hand, he wandered across the room. The armchairs looked comfortable, and dropping into the nearest one, he breathed in its rich, meaty smell. There had been a fat, red-faced man on the ferry. For some reason Geoff thought of him now. The man had spent the entire trip alternately shouting drink orders and one-liners, the latter for the benefit of everyone in the bar. The woman with him, a wobbly blonde with rounded shoulders and big breasts, had hung on his arm and laughed at all his jokes. Some of the jokes had been pretty funny actually, the woman's devotion kind of touching. Probably in calmer weather the trip would have been fun. He took another swallow of the whisky. Maybe it wasn't such a bad idea, a condo out here on the island. There were pills for seasickness. If he avoided any deep commitments, and if he managed a couple more big sales, he could think about buying such a place for weekends, not necessarily on this part of the island (the nearby beach club was reputed to be snooty, hard to join), but in a place like it, with a beach and a view of the sea.

Marriage to Kit seemed unlikely. She attracted him, but when he thought about marrying, about having a wife, he found he had in mind a different sort of woman, stable and self-possessed, a solid presence. Not that Kit was timid or unreliable, but there was a fly-away quality about her. He was never quite sure where she was heading.

He glanced over at the big window. It offered the glassed-out image of a man in a chair, his solitary shape slumped beneath the yellow cone of a lamp. The scene hovered in darkness, just beyond the rain-streaked window, and staring at it he thought, as he sometimes did late at night, of his father's death the previous year and of the irrelevant but surprising fact that he himself would be thirty that fall.

His father had gotten divorced from his mother the year Geoff turned thirteen, and Geoff had not seen him all that often. A man with hopeful eyes and gradually thinning hair, his demeanour one of manic good cheer, Geoff's father had sold medical supplies. His territory was large, and criss-crossing it he would, as he used to put it, blow into town at random moments. He usually bought Geoff dinner, schmoozing optimistically with the waitress and, as the evening grew late, reminiscing with increasing inaccuracy about vacations they had taken as a family. Geoff remembered these trips as a hodgepodge of broken tent poles and lost sleeping bags, mysterious engine break-downs, sunburns that turned his clothes into sandpaper, and he remembered too, through all of this, like an absence of oxygen in the atmosphere, his mother's in-tensifying silence.

In the morning the living-room window revealed a bal-cony and a view of the beach. A tree blocked off part of the scene, but he could see waves washing up the sand and a skyful of grey-edged clouds. In the distance a line of tiny sails nicked the horizon.

He had slept well after all (the Scotch had been a good idea), and the view seemed confirmation that things had turned around. In the kitchen he located the coffee maker and made a full pot. He was drinking this and buttering a muffin when Kit appeared in the doorway.

She was dressed in jeans and a sweatshirt. In the mask of her small, tanned face, her eyes glittered at him like a pair of aquamarines. The tan came from lunch hours spent on the roof of the hospital where she worked. Without speaking she poured herself a cup of coffee, spilling a good deal of it into the saucer, and then dropped two slices of bread into the toaster.

He left her peering into the refrigerator while he ran down to the lobby of the building to pick up his friend's newspaper. The newspaper—delivered, the friend had assured him, every Saturday without fail—was not there. A woman in a man's plaid bathrobe slammed her mailbox shut and turned to wag her head at him. "Every damn weekend," she said, "there's some damn storm and then no papers." She sounded grimly triumphant.

When he got back upstairs, the kitchen reeked of burnt toast. Kit stood gazing down at the two blackened slabs on the plate she was holding. Her dark hair had slid forward across her cheeks. She spoke without looking up. "You don't love me."

He took the plate from her hand. "These are burnt. You burned the toast last weekend too."

"You don't, do you? I thought about it while I was sleeping."

"I don't know," he said.

"If you don't know, that means you don't."

"That means I don't know," he said. "Besides, nobody thinks in their sleep."

"I do. Sometimes I wake up and know something's wrong in one of the experiments." Kit was a laboratory chemist. "Sometimes I know what's wrong."

"Nothing's wrong. I was in a lousy mood last night; boats don't agree with me. I'm sorry." He tossed the toast into the sink and pointed at the package of muffins. "Have one of those. They're not bad. There're no papers, by the way."

She tipped the coffee from her saucer back into her cup and then, with what seemed to him a flourish, poured the whole cupful into the sink. "You make watery coffee," she said accusingly. For a second he could see only her nose and her unsmiling mouth. Then she pushed back her hair, and the curve of her cheek appeared, naked and specific.

He took the coffee pot from the stand. "Here. If it's that bad, I'll dump it."

"I hate being on the pill," she said abruptly. She touched the tip of her finger to her cheek.

She had voiced this complaint before, and it was true that several months on the pill had produced a small circle of pigmentation on each of her cheeks, like thumbprints. These were scarcely visible beneath her summer tan; Geoff had told her so more than once. But every so often she stroked her cheek, as now, frowning slightly.

He set the coffee down again. "Listen," he said, "it's not that I don't care about you. I do. It's just that right now, I'm not looking for any—"

"Just don't," she said. The curtain of hair slid forward again. He waited for a moment, then poured himself another coffee. Sipping it—his coffee wasn't so bad—he turned and glanced out the window. The sand along the rim of beach looked damp. From the rain? Or was the tide going out?

That afternoon she stooped to pick up a pink-fleshed doll discarded on the beach. They had used the membership card lent them by his friend and were walking the shore in front of the beach club. This stretch of sand—from here all the way to the point—was called Windward Beach. The sand was a medium brown, paling to tan whenever the sun shone. The beach was nearly empty despite the fact that, since noon, the sun had begun to make cameo appearances, sidling through gaps in the clouds often enough that the skin on Geoff's shoulders was starting to prickle. He hated the show of putting on sun cream, but the truth was his starkly freckled skin had a tendency to burn with embarrassing ease.

Beyond the club's property the land curved out to the point. Along this shore stood the original summer houses. Built of clapboard and stone, shingled and turreted and girdled with porches, the houses loomed like benevolent, aging parents above the wind-stunted trees. On the other side of the point, invisible from here, the upstart condos had mushroomed, cluster after cluster, invading and then eliminating most of what apparently had been a grove of red pine and larch. The condos were selling briskly and, according to his friend, had become a considerable sore point with the house owners.

Did he love her? He had moved back to the East Coast from Montreal more than a year ago, not long after his Montreal girlfriend had dumped him (to his partial relief) for a motorcycle importer who, as she'd said, "addressed her needs." Though Geoff had occasional doubts (in the past he had been accused of being staid and socially ambitious; "selfish" was another word that had been used), he thought he knew what at least some of those "needs" were. The motorcycle importer was an easygoing fellow, exceptionally fond of his motorcycles and of himself; it was possible he hadn't minded Amy's volatility or her dependence on her brother. Whenever she and Geoff had battled—and the explosions had been frequent—she'd headed straight for her brother's apartment, as if only he could rescue her. Even in times of peace, she and the brother had held frequent, hour-long telephone conversations; Geoff had more than once found her asleep on the couch cradling the dead telephone receiver.

Amy had also been fiery and unpredictable in bed, and for a while after her departure his body had ached in memory of hers. There had been something about the way she could abandon herself to the moment, and to him—though no longer, of course.

Kit was an altogether different character. Calm and rather quiet, even a bit unaware. Yet there were times when they were together that he was quite sure she saw and understood more of their surroundings than he did, as if her eyes, aimed at the world or sometimes up at him, could see through solid objects, discern invisible spectra of light. Other times, their blue glitter dimmed, Kit herself seemed to cling, and he was sharply aware of her physical smallness. She did not, however, so far as he could tell, need rescuing from anything.

"The tide's going to wash this away." She was holding out the doll. Her expression was grave, as though the doll were evidence of some flaw in the nature of things.

He nodded. "Toss it up above the tide line. That way they'll find it."

"I guess so, if they come to look for it . . . " But she carried it all the way up to the lifeguard's shelter and left it there on the bench.

Waiting for her, he noticed that the undertow warning had been erased from the blackboard outside the shelter. It was also true that large patches of blue had appeared in the sky. Yet the wind did not seem to have let up; waves still broke almost as far out as the point.

When she returned he called her attention to this. "Those look big enough to try bodysurfing."

He'd thought she might demur, but her face brightened. "Really? But what about the undertow? That sign?"

"The sign's gone." He indicated the blackboard. "Besides, we won't go out far." She was already nodding.

In the end they waded out perhaps fifty feet into the surf. He had swum with her before and knew that she was an excellent swimmer, strong of shoulder, very light despite her complaints about gaining weight since she'd gone on the pill. In university she had raced at under a hundred pounds; her preference had been for distance events.

Now she easily outdid him at the tricky business of catching a wave. Here in the surf his broad chest and thick-muscled, rather short legs seemed to weigh him down. Time after time she gauged the exact second to fling herself onto the crest, while he, becalmed and futilely paddling in the shallow aftermath of a missed wave, watched her body go flying into shore. Curved over the avalanche of water, she looked like a creature of the sea, a dolphin or a seabird.

In bed, she curved like that beneath him. The thought burst over him, as if the ocean had risen up and engulfed him in its salty, green-blue water, and he watched her pick herself out of the wash of surf.

He now noticed what she evidently had not, that the lifeguard was walking down the beach towards her. The man's tan was even darker than Kit's, and the shine of his teeth was visible as he halted a few feet from the water's edge and stood grinning down at her. Small in his shadow, Kit appeared to listen attentively. At one point she raised both hands and pushed the hair back off her forehead. It was a gesture Geoff had not seen her make before. Graceful, almost flaunting. At the same instant, a slight, ominous hum made him turn his head. A wall of water loomed over him. He whirled and dove sideways into it.

When he emerged, ears and nasal passages aching, Kit was waving him in. The lifeguard had turned and was walking away.

"He says there's still too much undertow," she explained a moment later, as Geoff clambered to his feet in the shallow surf. "The sign shouldn't have been erased." Her hair, bright with water, lay flat along her skull. Beads of water stood on her shoulders.

The lifeguard had moved along the beach and was picking up bits of driftwood. Coughing, Geoff drew himself up. "So where's he been for the last half-hour?"

"He says he's been watching us. But now that the tide's turned, it's more dangerous." A smile hovered at the corners of her mouth. The water foamed and licked around her knees. She looked, he thought, batting his engorged ear, completely in her element.

Earlier, on their way through the club grounds (as beach guests they were not allowed to enter the clubhouse itself), they had passed, just behind the clubhouse, a large terrace marked off by a hedge and a stone balustrade. Almost the entire width of the terrace had been shaded by a green-and-white awning.

Now, as they climbed the path from the beach, they saw that this awning had been drawn back and the terrace populated: men in dinner jackets and women in flower-coloured dresses, their faces variously framed by pastel hats—it was like a scene from a movie. People clustered in little groups while others moved down the stone steps and onto the lawn. Maroon-jacketed waiters slid among them, some bearing trays, others carrying bottles wrapped in white napkins.

"What do you suppose that's about?" he said with sudden irritation. They were standing by this time at the top of the path.

Kit's head had just disappeared into the folds of the sweatshirt she was pulling on. Her voice came up muffled. "It's got to be a wedding. All those hats."

"How the hell are we going to walk through it?" Something, the glamorous swoop of awning, the bright dresses blooming on the lawn, had spawned envy in his gut. He could almost hear the champagne bubbling into the glasses.

At the far end of the terrace now, a bride emerged through French doors, her white skirts billowing as if to embrace the crowd. Behind her, in a new surge of guests, came the fat man from the ferry. There was no question of not recognizing the man—his bald head, the bulge of his cheeks (they swelled directly from his collar)—and besides, he had his hand under the elbow of the blonde woman. A large, salmon-pink hat balanced like an upside-down canoe on her head. The hat and her equally pink dress bobbed along beside his black-clad bulk as they crossed the terrace.

"That's the guy from the boat. The fat, noisy one. There, with the blonde." Geoff gestured in the direction of the terrace.

But Kit wasn't listening. She had turned and was gazing back at the sea. All at once he felt this unconcern of hers viscerally, as he felt the sand in his shoes and the dampness of his bathing suit beneath his shorts. She didn't care about this party they weren't invited to. Nor did she

care that they would have to march, sandy and dishev-
elled, through the fringes of it. She went on staring sea-
ward, as though she had not come in to shore at all but
was still out there riding the waves. Reluctantly he turned
and followed her gaze.

As far out as the horizon, white caps exploded in broken rows across the dark swaying surface of the ocean.
Before it knelt the silent beach, powdery and pale except
along its dampened edge. (Was this how she saw it?)

A gust hit them. Kit's shirt flapped against her thighs,
and she rose on tiptoe as if the wind had lifted her. He
reached out and put his hand on the back of her neck; her
skin was warm and sandy. "You were great out there," he
said. She glanced around, her narrow eyes full of milky
light from the sea. He heard himself go on. "If we come
back tomorrow morning, early, around nine when the tide
starts coming in, maybe you can show me how you do it?"

She nodded. "Sure." Her eyes lingered on his face as if
she'd thought of something else she might say to him. But
she merely smiled and then bent to brush the sand from
the soles of her feet. As she straightened up, he cast a final
glance at the beach. Directly below them, on the bench
next to the lifeguard's shelter, lay the flesh-coloured blob
that was her rescued doll.

His mother had not loved the sea. She had not loved much
of anything, so far as Geoff could remember, not their
little house in a rundown section of town nor the trips
his father was always conceiving with his usual untrust-
worthy enthusiasm. The three of them had constituted a

socially uncertain family. His mother's own father had made and then lost a considerable amount of money before a heart attack had swept him from her life. She had been to Europe once, and to New York and Florida too, before circumstances had returned her to the little town, and, presumably, to the purview of Geoff's father. Both had been nearly forty by the time they married.

When Geoff was a boy, his mother had worked in the registrar's office of the local college. He remembered the dark sweaters she had worn to work, and, in summer, the dark sleeveless blouses. Emerging from these, her arms, freckled like his own, had looked thick and soft and sad, matching the distracted sadness of her face. He had never guessed or even tried to imagine what had made her this way, noting only that she had in a sense achieved her desired withdrawal. Her last years were spent in a nursing home that specialized in senile dementia. There, in an orderly backtrack through time, she had proceeded to unlearn her entire life.

His father had paid regular visits to the place. Neither he nor Geoff's mother had remarried, and she had gone on receiving her former husband with something like recognition for almost a year after she had ceased to know her son. For a time, too, she had mistaken the doctor for her father. Then came a period when she stared at them all with eyes clouded by loss, as if not merely faces but even shape and light itself had ceased to convey meaning. In the end, her jaw hanging open like a dead person's, she mostly slept.

Nowadays, Geoff seldom thought of those years, which had been his early twenties. They had not disappeared from his memory—how could he forget the eyes of his own mother gazing at him without comprehension?—but still he was surprised that second night on the island to dream of his father and his mother and one of their camping trips. He woke in the middle of the night sweating, convinced that something had escaped him, a piece of knowledge that would knit together his life, save them all. The bedroom, even the pillows and duvet, smelled of damp, a smell that reminded him of his mother's nursing home.

The storm had returned. Or perhaps it was a new storm. Gusts of wind and water were lashing the window as if at any moment they would breach the glass. Beside him Kit's breathing rose and fell in placid rhythm; he could hear it between gusts.

Odd how they seemed, she and he, on this occasion bound together not so much by passion as by old habit. As if they'd been together for some time. Dinner too, now that he thought of it, had offered the pleasing yet unmemorable comfort of an oft-repeated ritual. The wine, a Sancerre recommended by the owner of the liquor store, had been right, the lobsters sweet and luxurious, yet simple. They had bought them on the village pier. Kit knew a way of rendering the creatures comatose, plunging them into a sinkful of water, then gradually warming it, so that going to their deaths they did not beat against the side of the pot but sank without a twitch into the boiling water.

Drifting once again towards sleep, he thought of this careful mercy and then of how strange and distant he had felt the previous night. At his side, Kit stirred and then sighed into stillness once more.

The next morning, clouds still chuffed across the sky. The beach club, as Geoff and Kit walked through its grounds, appeared deserted. Tables and chairs had been shoved to one side of the terrace. The edges of the folded-up awning snapped irritably in the wind. Partway across the lawn, Kit shivered and pulled up the hood of her sweatshirt. She was still tying its drawstrings when they reached the top of the path.

Windward Beach, empty and pristine after the nocturnal sweep of tide—the scene had been so clear in Geoff's mind that for a second he could not believe what he was seeing. Directly beneath them on the beach, a crowd of people milled about on the brown sand. There were forty or fifty of them at least. And they wore street clothes, these people, windbreakers and even raincoats.

He glanced at his watch. "It's quarter to nine," he said helplessly. Kit was shaking her hooded head as if she, too, did not believe what she was seeing.

As they descended the path, he began to feel conspicuous. Had some special event been scheduled? For members only? He patted his shorts pocket. Yes, the borrowed membership card was there. Beneath his bare feet, the sand slid and ground, and then, as they neared the groups of people, grew damp and solid. Ahead of them, through a gap in the crowd, he saw waves foaming and spitting. Surfing would be difficult.

The body lay on its back in a trough of wet sand. Bald head, fat, pale shoulder—it was hard to see between the people. Only when the woman directly in front of them stepped aside did they see the stomach. It had swelled into a giant mound, the skin so distended that it shone in the silvery morning light. Geoff swallowed. At his side Kit made a sound that might have been a whimper. Her hand, cool as a fish, slipped into his, and he gripped her fingers. On the far side of the stomach, a pair of splayed-out feet protruded from the sand.

Earlier, perhaps during their breakfast—he could taste at the back of his throat the coffee and muffins, the ripe local strawberries that had stained their fingers—yes, back then, while he and Kit were eating, the retreating tide would have eddied and swirled around the body, scooping sand away from its sides, hollowing out this trough. Perhaps, too, this amoeba-shaped crowd was already gathering, standing slightly higher on the beach, staring in disbelief, and then horror, as the mound of gleaming flesh emerged like a giant pearl from the sea.

"Geoff." Kit was pulling on his hand. He looked down at her. The spots on her cheeks stood out like pennies. "We should go," she said.

With an effort he nodded. Somewhere in the distance, a siren was keening. He became aware of the rumble and slosh of the waves, voices catching around him like strands of seaweed.

"Must've gone swimming after that big party...took off all his clothes."

"They swell up like that in the water."

"Bunch of crazy people."

"Shh," said another. "It was a wedding."

At that moment Geoff spotted the blonde woman. She stood a ways off from the crowd, between two men, one of whom might have been the lifeguard. Both were talking to her. She herself gazed straight ahead. Her blonde head was bare, and the skirts of her pink dress puffed out from beneath the man's dinner jacket that was draped over her shoulders. Among the rain-coats and sweaters and windbreakers, she looked like a flamingo. In her arms she held a pile of black and white clothes; over the crook of her elbow dangled black suspenders.

When his mother died, his father returned to town. Other-wise acquiescent to all the arrangements, he had first insisted, then begged that she be placed in an open coffin. The idea had appalled Geoff, although in the end he gave way. His father's right seemed beyond denying.

Coiffed and made up by the mortician, his mother had looked healthier than she had in life, and Geoff had been shocked to see in her face a certain prettiness. The softened curves of her mouth, the peachy tint to her skin suggested a girl whom he had never known. "She never was much for talk," his father had said rumina-tively, gazing down at this face. "Times she put her arms around me even, I never was sure." He shook his head, humming slightly to himself, and Geoff had the impres-sion that he didn't know he had spoken. He himself had turned away, filled with an intense pain. Had there been something about her life that might have been otherwise? Had someone, he or his father, or his mother herself perhaps, missed some crucial information, a sign, the interpretation of which might have made all the difference?

"He looked pregnant." Kit's voice flitted across the room.

In the hour since they'd returned to the condo, the day had cleared and turned hot. The sky outside the window was lapis, the surface of the sea almost equally blue. It was as if a switch had been thrown. Wind to calm, grey to blue. All the way to the horizon, the water shone glassy and impenetrable, yielding up no whitecaps, no accessible swells and hollows. They were cleaning up the kitchen, planning to catch the midday ferry. "That's what I thought right away," Kit went on in the same light, not quite pleasant voice, "his stomach all swollen like that." She touched the tips of her fingers to her cheek.

Geoff stared at her. She had cried after they got back, steady, nearly soundless weeping that had shaken her small frame. He stopped wiping the stove top and crossed to her side. She had been washing glasses, and a row of them stood dripping on a folded towel. Her shoulder beneath his hand felt oddly complex, composed of an infinite number of bones and sinews. "Hey, it was a bad scene there this morning," he said. "I know you—"

Still in the circle of his arm, she shook her head. Her dark hair caught a gleam of sunlight from the window. "You don't," she said. "I couldn't stand it, I should have felt sorry for him, poor man. But all that fat and meat—I thought I was going to throw up right there on the beach."

Without warning the shine of her hair flashed through him. He heard her words, but it was her hair, and the curve of her hip against his thigh, the shoulder cupped in the palm of his hand that spoke to him. He had the sense they had just arrived. Everything that had happened up to this point had been a mistake. The discrepancy made the room rock. Plans needed to be made, plans to fend off chaos. He stood staring down at the top of her head. "Maybe I do love you," he said.

Placing the last glass on the towel, she turned and looked up at him. Her smile came slowly. And when it did, it was fond and possibly even constituted acceptance, but it made him feel, though he couldn't have said why, that for the moment, for the hour and the day as it had turned, he and his love were beside the point. "Maybe you do," she said.

Eschewing the damp bedroom, they spread a beach towel and pillows on the living-room rug. As he lowered himself onto the jut of her hip bone, then buried his face in her hair, he felt himself in new territory. Even the smell of her was different. Her body beneath his was taut and quick. Unwomanly. Exciting. From beginning to end, she did not speak.

Afterwards they packed swiftly, still without conversation. He stood in the bedroom doorway as she stuffed a last pair of shorts into her bag, then snapped it shut and shouldered it. "It's funny," she said, "but I used to think that if you loved me, I would feel lighter."

"Lighter?" He stared at her.

"I had this idea it would lift me up, or you would . . . something. That wasn't fair was it?" She sounded vaguely sorry.

At the door she brushed past him, bumping him slightly with her bag. As if she'd mistaken him for the furniture. And, turning to follow her, he almost missed her next words. "It's just that I'm tired of being a woman."

He caught up with her as she swung through the living room. Putting his arms around her, he pulled her back against him, flattening her breasts with his hands. Her bag slid to the ground, and he pushed it aside with his foot. "Don't," he said, speaking to the top of her head. "What are you talking about? I'll take care of you." Words that couldn't be true. *I'll take care of you. I love you.* He heard himself say them. Her hair smelled like the beach—salt-wind, seagrass.

But she was shaking her head. Her shoulder blades had gone flat and resistant against his chest. At the same time he could feel how, in the next moment when he dropped his arms (as he knew he must), she would fly up and out of his grasp. As if she had caught the crest of another wave. And he could feel how he would stand and watch, mired in the sand, while she was swept away from him down the long wash of water into the beach.

It would be, he understood, the story of their life to-gether. Perhaps it was the story of any paired life. These inviolable separations born in the spin of a moment, sepa-rations as absolute as they were impermanent. When she turned a moment later, her eyes had filled with that bright, blind light of her own creation, as though she had been where she'd wanted or maybe needed to go.

"You know," she said, and she was shaking her head again, as if at her own notion, "I was so skinny back at university, my collarbones stuck out. But I loved it all the same, being ninety-seven pounds. In the water, I felt like I could fly."

"You still can," he told her. "I watched you."

Again she shook her head. "There's so much weight to things now. I feel it in myself. Even love feels heavy." Her finger went to her cheek. "You know what I mean?"

He bent to pick up her bag. "Not exactly."

She took the bag from him, hooked the strap over her shoulder and stood for a second looking up at him. "Of course, I'm the one who brought up love in the first place, aren't I?"

"I'm glad you remembered that," he said.

Reaching up then, she touched her hand to the side of his face. He felt her fingers, cool against his skin. "It's okay, you know." Her voice, too, was cool, and clear, and it went through him like rain. "It's not so much to do with you and me. I'm just mourning my youth, or something."

He stood there for a second, gazing down at her blue eyes and sun-browned skin. He could almost have sworn she was standing in a swirl of surf. "There's always something to mourn," he told her.

She nodded. "So don't mind me."

He smiled at her then. "I'll try not to."

THE OTHER
SIDE OF
THE WORLD

OUTSIDE, THE SKY FILLS from moment to moment
with a deep ruby light. Like alien gas, Phil thinks
staring out the window. Beautiful. Poisonous. The
sun, tumbling backwards into it, has blurred to a glow.

There's a similar blur in his head. The first flight, Seoul
to Tokyo, lasted two hours; this one began less than an
hour ago. "Water, please," he says to the attendant as she
slips past, meek in her flowered kimono. His voice, which
he hasn't used except to order the two, or is it three, mar-
tinis, comes out a rasp.

She turns. Her eyes, outlined in black like an actress's
eyes, blink down on him with what he thinks may be
complete incomprehension. "Water, yes," she says, her
accent no more than a mild clipping of the words.

When she returns bearing a tray of misted tumblers,
he is absurdly grateful. His life will be saved. He takes a
glass—icy against his fingers—and sees, at the level of his

eyes, the sudden uptilt of the tray. The remaining glasses pitch sideways, away from him. In the same instant there is a mew of dismay from the woman across the aisle, a muted crash. "Ah, I'm so sorry, so sorry," cries the attendant in the flowered kimono. As she whirls and rushes for the galley, the glasses go rolling and clinking backwards down the aisle.

After she has returned, bearing towels and more apologies, and while the woman across the aisle is being mopped and soothed, Phil guiltily drinks his water and turns to the window. Last week, flying the northern route (Montreal to Seoul, via New York), he wakened to an afternoon view of Mount McKinley, its gleaming hood thrust into the sky like a white menhir. Now, with nothing beneath save the amorphous stir of air and ocean, he thinks almost longingly of mountains. The sheer walls of rock, the snow-filled crevasses. His stepfather, that most unkillable of men, is dead. This truth, imparted to him by satellite and telephone wire, seems unreal just now, an uncontextual bit of news. But he can feel it in the night ahead, rushing to meet him.

Last night in the blackness of his hotel room, his sister's voice offered no such apprehension. "Just like that, Philly. His heart, the blood vessels or something." Her words, shot halfway round the planet, popped in his ear like so many bubbles. It was morning where she was, the death a few hours old. Only after several minutes did he understand she was calling not from Montreal but from their stepfather's house in Florida.

In darkness he wakens to a meal. Bits of pastel sushi, followed by the flesh of a white fish. There are movies, something about horses and a waterfall and another about missing treasure. The next time he wakens, dawn tinges the sky ahead. The smell of coffee fills the cabin.

The big plane makes land's edge to the north of San Francisco. He's conscious of a sudden infusion of light and colour into the cabin. As though they've flown out of the void. In front of him a man stretches up his arms, flexing his fingers with audible cracks. Across the aisle the woman who was doused, in another lifetime it seems, clips on a pair of black-and-gold earrings.

Phil's tray is pulled out of the arm of his chair by the attendant with the kohl-rimmed eyes. A glass of orange juice and then an omelette appear in front of him, the Japanese cuisine of the previous evening transmuted evidently by the miles they have travelled. Between mouthfuls he gazes down on the coastal range sliding beneath them, the inland valleys, the long, sandy tongue of desert. When the plane dips its starboard wing and swings south, he discovers he can still see, off in the distance, the white-laced Pacific and the coastline that is the bevelled edge of California.

Only once does he think again of the old man. Not dead of a heart attack, but ripped and spurting blood, a barely stilled corpse sprawled by the side of a road. The vision is embarrassing, as if he has caught a maverick version of himself slavering over some massacre on network news.

After Los Angeles, his memory ceases to record. Meals are served. Hours pass. The rusted earth of Atlanta rises to meet them, then recedes once more. Another ocean appears. Another wave-striped coastline. They are slicing down towards the small Florida airport when it occurs to him that, despite the intervening night, yesterday and the day lying in wait below are one and the same.

He spots Amy at the far end of the terminal. She stands like a diffident boy, hands shoved into her pockets. In the crowd her darkness—her skin like his own is olive, her hair bluish black—seems a kind of reticence. Between them, whole tribes appear to have gathered. The humid air is thick with voices. Parents, children, grandparents. He shifts the suit bag to his other shoulder, edges around the man in front of him.

She would be good-looking, his sister (this thought jumps into his mind, not for the first time), if there weren't that something about her face, a twist to the corner of her mouth, an asymmetry that must worry people when they meet her, as if they are seeing evidence of a disease or accident of childhood that cannot now be spoken of. In the Middle East and some other parts of the world, when he sees such faces, he imagines a history of pain endured, of battle or prison and torture. With Amy this cannot, of course, apply. The twist is just a tic, left over from one bad experience.

"It was me." She says this to Phil as they are sitting in the rented car, a white four-door that smells vaguely of old cigarette smoke. Outside, sunlight glints off the windows of the car ahead of them. They are lined up waiting to exit the parking lot. She speaks in her light, rather child-ish voice. "My fault. I fell asleep. The nurse left pills for him to take. If I'd been awake and given them to him ..."

"Hey," he says, "you're not a one-woman intensive care unit."

"When it got light," she goes on as though he hasn't spoken, "I woke up and went out into the hall. He was lying almost in front of my door." Her lips twist. "In his nightshirt. His . . . his mouth was open. I knew right away."

He reaches across the armrest to ruffle her hair. In the dampness it has curled into tight coils. Her scalp is warm. Her eyes flow towards him. He has already noticed how the skin beneath them is stained a deeper shade than the rest of her face, as if the brown of her eyes spills over from time to time, breaching the integrity of her features.

When they were children, her face used to make him think of muffins or little cakes, round and soft, the features gracefully delineated like whorls of frosting. She used to follow him around, run errands for him, and he remembers her upturned gaze, eyes dark with pleasure, as she handed him his hockey cards, his fielder's mitt, the book he'd misplaced. In return he spent more time with her than an older brother normally might, playing games, sometimes reading to her. She was crazy about stories of magic, triumph through spells and counter-spells.

Around the time he was twelve or thirteen, their reading sessions came to an abrupt end. He'd fashioned them a hideaway in a far corner of the attic, piling up old chair cushions and corrugated paper boxes into a fort, and it was there on a Sunday afternoon that their stepfather found them, hunkered down shoulder to shoulder, munching on potato chips as they worked their way through an illustrated version of *Grimm's Fairy Tales*.

Phil can still remember the blast of light as the walls of their hiding place flew apart. The next instant, he himself was flying backwards, the iron taste of blood in his mouth.

"Creep, little bastard! What the fuck do you think you're doing with her?" He can still hear the words, still see the spray of chips fan out across the floor, the angry arch of his sister's body as she is borne from the room, the curve of the hand she beats against the old man's shoulder.

Her hand is angular now, sinewy and bold as it reels down the car window. "You understand?" she says. "The pills were for his heart. Cardiac arrest, that's what they said he died of." They have reached the exit booth. "Hand me my purse, Philly?"

He passes over cash from his own wallet. "I changed my Korean money for American before I left Seoul. I was supposed to be there for another week."

She pays the attendant and shuts the window. "You didn't know I was going to do him in."

"Give me a break," he says.

"I'm just telling you." She sounds irritated. Her hands yank the steering wheel.

"Look," he says, as they gun out onto the main road, "you didn't give him a heart attack."

"I took a sleeping pill," she says. "Two of them."

"Sleeping pills?" He hears his own voice, too high, foolish. A series of gas stations is flashing past on the left; farther ahead, a mall, banners flying, comes into view.

"They knock me out. Dom gets them somewhere in Europe." Dom is her latest boyfriend, a motorcycle importer. There is always some man or other in her life. As there is always, he would have to admit, a woman in his. With their mother's darkness and light-boned frame, their large and (many have said) beautiful eyes, both he and Amy attract attention from the opposite sex. A man notices her in the shop where she works, at a bar or a party. Things begin easily enough, but they don't last. She finds herself, as she puts it, floating away. The man's outlines become indistinct. She can't picture his face, doesn't recognize his voice. Phil hears these confessions with a certain elation. He wants her to be happy, of course. But the fact is he cannot imagine either of them married, himself fathering or her bearing children. Such sweaty, mundane attachments, moment by moment, breakfast to breakfast—the thought makes him queasy.

"I take them when I can't sleep," she says, "but only at the beginning of the night. I can't get myself to work the next day if I take them too near getting up."

"You shouldn't go around saying this."

"Philly, I'm not going around saying this. It's just you."

On the next corner, she shaves the curb; the car jerks and shimmies. "Jesus, Amy," he says involuntarily and adds, in the most decisive voice he can muster, "you're not a doctor. Even if you could have done something, given him something, if he was that close to death's door, he should have been in a hospital." He stops himself and takes a deep breath. "Look," he says, "just don't go announcing this. Okay? People love stuff like this. All his cronies, they'll talk and talk."

"That's not what I...," she begins and then shakes her head.

At the red light he reaches over and lays a hand on her shoulder. "Sorry," he tells her, uncertain what he's apologizing for. Ahead of them he can see the high arch of the bridge, the sheds and docks that line the river. Out on the water, gulls and herons and the ubiquitous pelicans perch on every available post and piling. It's nothing, he thinks as she guides the car up onto the bridge, nothing at all. Besides, he deserved it.

Their stepfather's house crouches behind a clump of bushes, its overhanging roof humped and scoriaceous in the sunlight. Getting out of the car, Phil shades his eyes. Above his head, the palm fronds droop like dead fingers, as though the sunlight shimmering through the hot afternoon has filtered all motion from the air. He has to force himself to breathe. And suddenly he feels the way he felt on the flight over the Pacific. As if the stillness that surrounds them is an irresistible emptiness into which a storm is being drawn.

Shouldering his suit bag, he follows Amy up the front walk. "Place looks kind of run down." He points at the patches of mildew darkening the stucco above the door.

Amy nods and pulls a key from her pocket. "It is," she says. She fits the key into the lock, then pauses. Her features, as she glances back at him, twist into ugliness. "I can't help it," she says. "I keep thinking he's in there."

In the living room the floor tiles are scratched and chipped. Leaves from a dozen scrappy-looking plants dapple the dust-thickened light streaming in through the window. "It's not very clean," Amy says. She flicks at a lampshade, shakes some shards of tobacco off a magazine. Her movements are apologetic. As if the mess is her fault. Her leg bumps the bamboo coffee table, and she leans down to rub her shin. He has always protected her. Always loved her. It's the one certainty he possesses about himself, the one truth he would never mention.

He remembers the day he first saw her, more than three decades ago. In a big oval basket, his mother and a neighbour woman making cooing and hushing sounds above her, the little face, all cheek and frown, the eyes like nuggets of black glass peering out from the blankets. He remembers, too, the tug of grown-up hands on his arms, the baby's thin yet surprisingly commanding cry, his own unshakable certainty even as he was pulled away that here was a creature for him.

Their relationship is very different now, of course, he thinks as he watches her crossing the room, though there are still moments. The way she runs a thin-fingered hand through her hair, then pauses in front of him. The way she offers him her sudden and still trustful smile. "Hey," she says, "it's you." He feels himself smile back and knows she has given it to him once again, this ability to rescue her, to make her happy.

During his second year in university, he came home for Christmas to find her metamorphosed. In August her chest had been flat as a boy's. Now, only four months later, her nipples had popped and a curve of breast had begun to swell against her sweatshirt. Her legs had elongated, too, into near boniness, as if the new breasts in their rush to bloom were drawing substance from the rest of her body. But it was the way the corner of her mouth twisted when she spoke, or sometimes when she did not, that truly changed her, pulling her lips and the tip of her nose sideways, dragging her eyes sideways too so that she seemed lost in some secret exasperation.

Applying a university man's solution, he sneaked a heel of vodka from the old man's liquor cabinet. Hers was

the room over the garage, attic-like with its dormer windows and slanted ceiling, and sitting beside her on the
bare floor, his back propped against her bed, he felt a
resurgence of big brother power. As though he might
once again thrill her with a reading lesson.

"Come on, Amy," he said. "What's the big funk?"

She glanced at her drink—he had cut the vodka with
Coke—and then, still holding the glass, she scrambled to
her feet. The foamy, brown liquid sloshed over her hand
and dripped onto the floor.

He stared up at her. Wiping her hand on her jeans, she
set the glass on her dresser and moved to shut the door.
Then she turned and gazed straight at him. Her curly hair
was pulled back by a headband, and he had a second to
think how closed and small her face looked, like an un-
opened flower atop the stem of her neck, before she
began to speak. Her lips moved out of sync with the
words that broke over his head. "It was a Saturday, Philly,
just after I got back from the movies. He came down the
hall, in that yellow nightshirt he wears. I wasn't going to
tell you. He was drunk, I guess, laughing. I could see
his... his thing sticking out."

He remembers trying to draw in air. His entire stomach threatened to emerge through his mouth. He must
have got to his feet and hugged her because he recalls
that over her shoulder he could see the dolls laid out
along the edge of her pillow like a row of miniature
corpses. Against his chest her breasts, bright young be-
trayers, pressed their secret. "I'll kill him," he told the top
of her head, the boyish futility of the words embarrassing even as he spoke them.

The "old" man was barely fifty and superior to Phil

by many degrees in weight and strength. A gun? The old-fashioned spanner that sat propped against the garage wall? A baseball bat even? His stepfather had taken a baseball bat once to a man who had stolen his space in an underground parking garage. The bat had belonged to Phil. The man's screams had echoed through the vast, cement-walled space until eventually a squad car came screeching down the ramp; the attendant in the garage must have called the police. Though he wasn't sure what had happened next, Phil could still see the man, the thief of the parking space, kneeling on the concrete, arms wrapped over his head, his shirt sleeves limp with blood. And his stepfather climbing into the squad car, his back broader than either of the policemen's. The person Phil couldn't recall was his mother. Whenever he tried, he saw only darkness. Though she had been there, he knew, sitting silent in the car from beginning to end.

The whole of Christmas vacation, he considered what he might do. The thickness of his stepfather's shoulders, the rumbling weight of his step and voice, seemed to take up entire rooms. He shouted rather than spoke, and laughter poured from him, laughter that was like anger, rolling down the hallways, crashing through doors.

"Too much," said their mother one night when he'd been roaring over the kitchen phone at one of the men who worked for him at the garage. Phil glanced at her in surprise. She never spoke against the old man.

She was seated at the kitchen table. Her black hair, uncut for the weeks of her recent stay in hospital, dangled like seaweed around her face. She'd been cleaning a silver pitcher; the kitchen smelled of polish and the reheated coffee she drank all day. Now she pushed her hair back with polish-smeared hands, and Phil saw that she was gazing at her reflection, distorted though it must have been, in the pitcher's bulbous contours. "Too much," she repeated. She was not, he now realized, speaking to either of them.

His stepfather hung up the phone and turned to look at her. His features sagged, and an expression that might have been defeat appeared on his face. He did not at that moment seem especially large.

That evening, he left the house as usual right after supper. He would come home later, drunk or semi-drunk. They would hear him banging around on the front porch. For now, the house was quiet. Amy was at a friend's. Phil made himself a couple of cheese sandwiches. He had skipped supper. He could not bear to eat with his stepfather, to watch him chew and swallow.

The sandwiches were dry; there was no margarine or mayonnaise in the refrigerator. Phil ate them while the news was on. Then he climbed the stairs and knocked on his mother's door. The room was hers alone; the old man now slept on a pull-out sofa in the spare room.

The door opened so quickly, Phil almost lost his balance. His mother's face glimmered in the doorway, all planes and hollows. The room behind her was dark, but she was still dressed and her cheeks were still streaked with polish. "Mother?" Her face did not move. "Mother," his voice sounded choked, as though the sandwiches had clogged his throat, "why can't he stay in his room at night?" Her head reared back as though he had struck her. "Mother?" But she was dissolving backwards into the darkness.

Her door swung shut across the space between them, and he stood gazing at his own shadow laid against the flat panels of the door. He was almost sure his mother stood, equally frozen, on the other side. After a few minutes of silence, he turned and headed for the stairs. As he started down, he heard the click of her lock.

Sitting now in the Florida church, he thinks of that moment and the click of his mother's lock and how he understood then what he must do. At his side, Amy, solemn in a garnet-coloured dress, is leafing through the hymnal and humming to herself in a low monotone. Her presence seems slight, like a child's. In fact everyone in the church seems child-sized, diminished by the echoing shale floors and high, unreachable ceilings, the minister's sonorous voice. Across the aisle a lizard scampers out from under the pew. Bunches of purple and white flowers sit, like offerings, on the broad steps that lead into the chancel. The place reminds him of university buildings, stone and glass soaring above human dimension. That was what he'd loved most at university, the institutional spaciousness of the place, the benign indifference that constituted a kind of freedom. And that, he understood standing there facing his mother's shut door, that was what he would have to give up.

After the Christmas holiday he phoned his Academic Dean, told an elaborate story about family illness. His grades were transferred to McGill, and from then on he lived at home, finishing out his degree by commuting to the downtown university. The solution, once it had occurred to him, seemed a decree of fate. How could he have done otherwise?

The service consists of two prayers, three hymns and a very short sermon about celebrating life (as opposed to what, the minister does not say). Afterwards, everyone shuffles back out to the narthex of the church. Phil shakes hands with all his stepfather's cronies, speaks politely to the leather-skinned, improbably golden-haired women who are their wives.

The doctor introduces himself and motions Phil aside. He is a stocky man with close-cut brown hair, most likely no older than Phil. His face glistens with sweat. "No question," he says. "Two previous infarctions at least. I'll send you the full autopsy report. Scarring on both ventricles." He shrugs, then shakes his head. "It's a wonder he could do all that stuff he did, airboat hunting, from what I'm told, deep-sea fishing."

Phil stares down at him. "My sister was worried he hadn't taken all the pills he was supposed to."

The doctor shakes his head again. "Most of that was to make him sleep. If he'd taken it, she'd have found him dead in bed instead of on the floor." He extracts a pack of cigarettes from his breast pocket. "If I'd known about the previous attacks, I'd have put him in the hospital, but it wouldn't have made any difference. Complete occlusion."

Taxis are called for several of the people milling around the church courtyard. The minister, still in his robes, shakes hands as people leave. His palm is wet, his tone biblical. "I understand your mother is not well?" he says to Phil and Amy.

"That's right," says Phil. Amy merely closes her eyes. Their mother has been variously diagnosed as clinically depressed, as schizophrenic, as borderline psychotic. She lives or, to put it more accurately, is housed in a chronic care hospital north of Montreal.

"Well," says the minister, "your father certainly was a man who left his mark."

"That's true," says Phil. He has discovered somewhere in his head, behind the solid bone of his brow, a fund of disappointment. An ordinary old man's disease? To fell the giant who snatched writhing creatures from the sea and clambered up the sides of mountains, who broke bones and fortress walls? No cataclysm? No blood-drenched patricide? No Furies to honour their liberation?

The feeling is still with him hours later as he slides open the glass door and steps out onto the veranda. The lamps are not yet lit. Amy is sitting, bare legs crossed at the knee, in one of the frayed rattan chairs. The bridge of her nose and her rounded cheeks gleam faintly as she glances up. Across the road, the setting sun has turned the sky and the surface of the bayou scarlet. Against the glow, the tall pines stand in silent witness.

"So. To celebrate the good news." He hands her a sherry glass brimming with what he's confident is a superbly made martini. "Found some vermouth in with all the gin and whisky. We might as well enjoy the old man's supply. Kind of a legacy."

"Good news?" She frowns at the glass as if its contents are in doubt.

A moment ago he had the thought that she looked girlish, almost pretty in the waning light. Now, in the grip of the frown, her features twist. "I mean," he says comfortingly, "the doctor was categorical. No pills could have saved him. You didn't—"

The snap of the glass stem is sharp. Like a neck being broken, he thinks, owls swooping on the small lizards that scamper up the stucco walls, the smack of death in the darkening air. "I meant to!" she says. He stands motionless as her silhouette rises, moves towards him. There is a chink of glass striking the mat-covered floor. "I understood, Philly. You wanted him dead. But he'd have killed you." Her hand brushes his cheek, travels around to the back of his neck. "I could hear him coming, you know, times when you were out. Down the hall, thump, thump . . ."

I should have killed him, he thinks of saying, but the thought has no ending, the deed was not possible. Only now is possible.

"And every time, Philly," her voice has gone liquid, a child's murmur against the side of his face, "every time I imagined it was you, Philly."

So this is how it feels, the moment before the cyclone crashes in. He hears his own voice like taped instructions, brotherly, reassuring. "I'll take care of you. I can do that now." He slides an arm around her shoulders, turning her torso away from his own.

She nods, sinking slightly into the circle of his arm. A light wind puffs through the screen, ruffling the lampshades. He feels the swirl of inrushing air, the universe collapsing back on itself.

Yet here at the centre nothing has changed. Nor will it again. Soon he will turn on the lights, pick up the pieces of glass. He will fix her another drink, a milder one maybe, with ice. They will sit facing one another on the old man's rattan chairs, their voices adrift on the perpetual current between them, while outside the colour drains from the sky until beyond the shaded glow of the lamps, the rest of the world has folded into darkness.

THE STEADY
STATE THEORY OF
THE UNIVERSE

T HE NIGHT I MET TERESA, it was snowing, big fat
flakes that went splat and made wet spots where they
landed. Strange how a thing begins, like you don't
know it, but it's been waiting for you. I remember I
wasn't in the mood for anything new that night, or for
any sort of thinking either. Franco's was what I wanted,
and that's where I headed. I'd taken the bus from the
garage, gotten out at Sherbrooke and walked all the way
up the Main just to stretch my legs.

The plows were out with their big yellow lights like
dinosaur eyes, and there were walls of slush along the
parked cars. When I came into Franco's, everybody was
laughing and swearing, the way people do in Montreal
when the weather goes crazy, and the ones that came in
after me were the same. The place stank of wet wool
along with the beer that had got spilled year after year and
was soaked so deep into the floor it was part of the wood.

Franco's was farther north than where I usually hung out. Back then it was a drinking man's place, not a tavern but the nearest thing to it, except they let in women. You could get big meat sandwiches there and fries to soak up some of the beer. That was the theory, so you'd drink more, but the food never did you much good. The smoke and the boozy light were what made you drunk. And the noise made you tough. I got into fights sometimes in Franco's. I liked the feeling of my fist sinking into the side of some guy's face, the soft crunch of flesh against the hardness of his jaw and the way his head would jerk back or sideways and his eyes would go slack. I picked up women a lot easier there, too. I wasn't a handsome guy. Face like a ham, my dad used to say. But I was thick and strong, and walking into Franco's I felt like I could do what I wanted, which is a good feeling for a man to have.

That night I made myself a place at the bar—you had to do some elbowing—and I ordered a beer while I looked around. I'd already spotted Teresa. First off, she was an overgrown kind of girl, close to tall as I was, and thin as spaghetti. I could have knocked her over with a flick of my hand. And I could see she wasn't the bar type. She looked polite, not snooty exactly, but high class. She wasn't what you'd call a pretty girl; her face was too much bone. What took hold of me was her eyes. Eyes so dark I didn't think of colour when I looked at them. They reminded me of somewhere or some place, but I couldn't think where. Her mouth had a wounded look, the lips full and soft and sad at the corners. Just looking, I wanted to fuck her, thought if I did I'd go right through her. I wanted to fuck her looking into those eyes. I would fuck her and I would protect her, from everyone but me, and that was how it should be.

When I worked my way down the bar to where she was standing, even the air around me got different. The wool smell and the beer stink were gone. I swear when I got up close to her, I could breathe her in, the smell that came out of her skin, grassy and cool but with a sweetness, like something you could get high on.

She had a woman with her—a cousin, as I found out. They were meeting the cousin's boyfriend, or looking for him anyway. The cousin was dark and thin too, but more of a talker, and when she got going with someone along the bar, I moved in on Teresa. Got so close to her she had to notice.

"You want something," I said to her, not making it a question. She turned towards me then, her eyes sliding past my face like she wasn't too sure it was me that had spoken. I thought maybe she was going to ask me to move away from her, but right then a guy came shoving past us, and I put my arm out so he couldn't touch her. She held herself still in the space my arm made for her.

"Come on," I said to her after the guy had passed and was shoving his way through someone else's space farther down the bar. "My name's Gil. The bartender's a friend of mine." She looked at me straight then. "What do you drink?" I said, this time asking. All the time I was breathing her in. "I'll get it for you," I said.

She put her hand to her throat. "I don't really... well, Cinzano, I guess."

She made it sound Italian when she said it, "Chin-zah-no." Her voice was light and a little raspy, like she was getting over a cold. She liked the sweet, yellow kind, she said. She generally liked sweet things, marzipan and brown-sugar candy and chocolate. The Cinzano she drank on ice. Never more than two glasses. I learned all that afterwards, during that time when you're learning things about a woman: her old affairs, the way she butters her toast—from corner to corner or just in the middle—the kind of food she likes, the kind of beer or wine.

When the bartender gave her the glass, she said thank you to him and, in the same polite voice, to me.

"Sure," I said. "Any time. Drink up. There's more where that came from."

She took a couple of sips and set the glass down. Her long, thin fingers made it look like some kind of fancy crystal. I told her who I was and all the stuff you say at a bar. Like did she come there often because I hadn't seen her before, and weren't we in for a hell of a winter, and did she know she had beautiful eyes. After a while I asked her what kind of work she did. All the time I'd been talking, her eyes stayed on me, somewhere between polite and nervous, but now her face relaxed. "Do you like flowers?" she asked.

"You mean like daisies and roses and stuff? Sure."

She nodded, almost smiling at me. "Daisies and roses, yes. And other flowers too. It depends on the season." And then she really did smile. Her teeth were nice, shiny and white-looking with her dark skin. "Anyway, that's what I do," she said. "Sell flowers."

"Oh, yeah? Flowers like in a florist place?"

She nodded. "Sometimes we do weddings, but mostly it's just selling flowers." The barman handed me the cheque just then, and I paid him with enough extra he'd be keeping an eye out. I didn't know the guy from Adam in spite of what I'd told Teresa. Then I turned to look at her some more. "It's called Jardin de Sylvie," she was saying. "Sylvie's the owner's daughter. He named the store for her when she was a baby. It's on Bernard near St-Urbain. Do you know it?"

"Not exactly," I said. "I don't live too far from there though. I guess I just never noticed the place. Flowers I don't buy much."

"No? People mostly don't, I guess." She took a sip from her glass and set it down on the counter again. "I think I like flowers more than anything." She said it slowly, more to herself than to me, and then looked away as if there wasn't any more that was possible to say.

"Yeah?" I said. "With me it used to be the big bikes. Or riding them anyway. Now I don't know. I guess I'm ready for something different." She didn't bite on that, didn't even look at me, and it took a few minutes to get her talking again.

How she got into the flowers business was because her father had been in the truck-farming business before he retired. They'd had land up in Laval, he and a couple of his brothers, good river-bottom soil. Their business was supplying markets and landscaping companies, but what he cared about was gardens. Growing stuff. It was from him she knew about plants. And she knew about other stuff too. She read books and went to concerts. She'd been to the Université de Montréal for a couple of years before she decided university wasn't for her. And there was something off-centre about her. It wasn't just that she was thin and shy or too much of a lady for a place like Franco's. I could tell, even there in the bar that first time, how something was missing, or could go missing at any moment, and how she needed a protector, and how she would be to fuck.

I wasn't far wrong as it turned out, but I didn't find out anywhere near as soon as I was thinking I would. That night her cousin's boyfriend showed up, and I stuck around as if I was already Teresa's boyfriend, and the four of us sat together at one end of the bar. Teresa didn't talk much after the boyfriend came, and when she did it was kind of like she felt she should make the effort. Her lips would press together first, and the words would come out so forced you lost the sense of them. Even though you'd heard her fine, you had to think a second about what she'd said to get the meaning. The one thing I remember was she said how she liked working on Saturday afternoon when people came in for the half-price cut flowers. The old ladies were her favourite. "They hardly have any money, most of them, but they buy a lily or one or two freesia, for the scent, and you know they care about each flower."

She nodded and smiled right while she was talking, like she was in the middle of serving one of the old ladies, and for a moment, while her black hair was slipping forward over her forehead and she was smiling at the old ladies, her face got somewhere close to beautiful. After that though, she mostly kept her mouth shut and her eyes flowing from one face to the other like she was just hoping to follow what was going on from what one of us was saying. In a while the other two left for somewhere, and I took her around the corner for a hamburger and walked her home to her apartment.

It wasn't snowing so hard as earlier, but the flakes were still swirling around in the air. We stood on the sidewalk outside her building for a few minutes while she was hunting for her key. And then right before I left her, I put my hand around the back of her neck. I didn't pull her to me but just kept my hand there. She didn't flinch, but I could feel a muscle jump in the back of her neck and her eyes had opened wide, like she knew something was coming, and that was when I knew what her eyes reminded me of. It was those dark water lagoons down in the Florida swamps, the ones they tell you to stay out of because of what might be living in them.

"Goodbye," is what I said to her. "You'll be seeing me," and I dropped my hand and turned and walked away.

All my life I never really wanted a woman unless she needed me. With Teresa I could tell pretty much as soon as I saw her face. Those dark eyes telling me a story I wasn't meant to understand. Still, it's funny when you think of it, me meeting someone like her in a bar. Especially in that bar.

The truth was, if Franco's wasn't her kind of place, it wasn't mine either. Not most of the time anyway. In my usual bar, I was a different kind of guy. Nothing special with the women and no fights either. If I stayed around the whole evening, I even got what you might call philosophical, ruminating over one thing and another. Which was the reason I mostly enjoyed my usual bar more, with a lot of guys hanging out, smoking hand-rolled cigarettes and drinking bad brandy, guys from Hungary and Greece and all those countries that got swallowed up into Yugoslavia and Czechoslovakia and later got spit out again. Those guys liked to talk theoretical. They didn't think philosophy was some bullshit for fruits and bookworms.

Or science. Or poetry either, though I never got into that. Theories of the universe and thinking about them was what I liked. I used to subscribe to a bunch of science magazines, read everything I could about astronomy and particles and antimatter and stuff like that. Dark matter and electromagnetic waves. Strong and weak forces. Unified theory. Time, how it speeded up or slowed down. And light, the way it was sometimes one thing and sometimes another. I used to talk with the bearded little gnome of a guy who owned the place. Imre was his name, or what we called him anyway. Someone told me he'd been in prison for a while in Hungary. But he wasn't Hungarian, and he didn't talk about it, either, where he was from originally or about Hungary and how he'd ended up there. He'd got out of the country in '56, that was all I knew, and he didn't ever explain about that either. But he talked a lot about other stuff. When he bought the bar, he painted the walls dark red and then he hung up a bunch of black-and-white photographs of places in Europe. Once in a while he changed one, but mostly they were the same bridges and castles and churches and sometimes a view of mountains. He used to sit up on the corner bar stool like he'd been plunked there, and whoever wanted to come around and talk, he'd talk to them, long as it was about what he thought was serious. No Quebec politics. No family garbage.

"This is not matter of interest to me," he'd say, if you tried to bring up something about an election or the government or your old lady. You'd have to picture us, him up on his stool, about as big as a grasshopper, and me four times his size and looming over him while I downed a beer or sometimes, to please him, a slivovitz or a schnapps.

He was up on his stool the time I got to explaining to him how I was a big-bang guy, big bang as opposed to a steady state theory of the universe is what I meant. It's not hard to imagine what an ordinary guy in Franco's would've thought I was talking about, but Imre knew right away what I had in mind. He didn't agree with me either, what I said about how things were changing all the time.

"Illusion," he told me shaking his head. He wasn't a conventional steady-state guy either. While he was explaining what he had in mind and how come, he made gestures with his arms like he was directing an orchestra.

"Theory depends," he said, "how far is extended. Example, what if things happen before big bang?" He went on talking about what if before all that primordial matter heated up and exploded and sent itself spraying across the universe and forming into galaxies and dark matter and so on, what if before that there was another universe from another big bang, another glob of all the matter that was, and it had exploded and gone booming out and then after so many billion years had come shrinking back into a glob, and what if before all that happened there had been another big bang and before that another big glob and so on, and what if time was so huge and long that each of these explosions, booming out and shrinking back in, was just a hiccup in what was really all just about the same universe?

"Think of waves in ocean," he said, "all time like waves travelling and changing. You watch, you watch, right? You think, change. Yes? But each time wave is made of same molecules in same place." He grinned at me then and slid off his stool and went around behind the bar. When he popped out again, he'd poured us each a shot of schnapps. "After drink, you go home," he said handing me a glass. "You go home, you think about."

He was right. I did think about what'd he'd said, and it took me a week to work it through. So you can imagine how once in a while I needed to head for a place like Franco's.

The day after I met Teresa, I went into her shop. It was a Saturday afternoon, but there weren't any customers. She was on the phone, and when she hung up and turned to look at me, her hand went to her throat. For a second I just stood there. She was wearing a long yellow skirt and over it a long black sweater, and her black hair was pulled back and tied in a curly bunch at the nape of her neck. She looked like she belonged there, like she was standing in her own garden. Plants were hanging from the ceiling and dangling over counters, and the place smelled wonderful. I thought this was where some of her smell came from. "So this is where you hang out," I said.

"This is where," she said, still not smiling but not looking so much like she thought I was there to kill her. "Do you want to buy some flowers?"

"Maybe," I said. "You want to show me what you got?" She turned full around then, very serious, and began to lead me around the shop. There were rows of green plants and flowers in vats. She named them all and told me which ones lasted and which ones had scent. You could buy the flowers one by one, pick them out of the vats. There were jars of different kinds of leaves too. And at the back of the shop there was a cold storage room with long glass doors on it where they kept the roses and some other tall, purple flowers.

"When do you get off?" I said after a few moments.

Her hand went to her throat again. "We're open till six."

"I'll wait," I said. "Take you out for dinner after you close up the place." She looked at me, sort of frowning like she was deciding what this meant, and then she nodded.

I helped her lift a few of the big pots and move some plants to different places. The rest of the time I just stood around. When customers came in, they would sometimes go back into the cold storage with her, and I would watch her bending over the vats to pick out the flowers they chose. There was condensation on the chilled glass of the doors, and I got the feeling I was looking through mist into some other time and that she was preserved in there with the flowers.

Afterwards we did go out to dinner, and it all went okay although I don't remember much of it. For the rest of winter and into spring, I went on seeing her. One thing I found out right away, though I hadn't expected it either, was that she'd been married in her teens and had two little kids. The husband was gone. He'd cleared out on her and later on she'd heard he might have been killed in some kind of accident. The kids stayed with her parents nearly all the time. Her father was mostly retired by then. His back had gone stiff, so he couldn't work in the company's truck gardens out on Laval. He couldn't walk too much either, and he hung around a lot at home watching the kids and the television and doing nothing much else.

It took me a while to convince her to go to bed with me. Longer than it usually took. I wasn't used to waiting, to tell the truth. Like I said before, I wasn't inclined to try unless I thought a woman had some kind of need for me. With some women it was easy to tell. The ones that just wanted a good time. I was a guy who looked like a man. Some of them wanted that, a big man who took up space. And for some of them, back when I was younger, it was my bikes that made the difference. I had different ones, the best being a big, 750 cc hog that I got off a guy that owed me for a couple of engine rebuilding jobs. It's a fact a big bike like that gets to a woman. Warms her up, you could say. Her thighs are already used to being wrapped around you. And she's used to hiding behind your back and breathing in your sweat and not being able to say anything in the noise and wind. But Teresa didn't much like to ride with me; the pavement flashing under her feet scared her, she said.

What got her into the sack I never did figure. It must have been a Sunday because we were both off work all that day. We'd been out shopping. She needed a frying pan, she said. Her old one was burning stuff; the bottom was warped or scraped. So we bought one, and some shelf paper, and I remember picking up a twenty-four of Molson and a drill bit for me. We headed back to my place to leave off the beer, and after that we were going to do something else, I forget what. Anyway, I remember the day was cold with not much wind. Smoke rose straight up from the chimneys. The roads were dry and chalky, the way they get when there hasn't been any snowfall for a while and what's on the ground hasn't got near to melting either. When we got back to my place, I felt ready for something. I was in my bedroom looking for a pair of shoes. I guess I even found the shoes because I remember dropping them on the floor and calling her name. She must have been out in my kitchen or living room.

"What is it, Gil? You need something?" Her face peering around the door frame looked like a kid's, all eyes and watchfulness, like she wasn't sure whether there was something she ought to know or do.

"That's about the size of it," I said. "Come in here." She walked into the room, and I took her by the shoulders and shoved her down on the bed. "It's about time for us, don't you think?" I said.

I wouldn't have jumped her or done anything more if she'd screamed or begged me not to, but she didn't do any of those things. She just looked up at me for a minute like she'd known this was coming. Then she sat up straight like a girl told to mind in school and started to unbutton her blouse. It was a long-sleeved, white one, and I can still see those thin fingers plucking the buttons out of the buttonholes, one by one, like she was playing strings on a harp. It seemed like for her, if I'd said the time had come, then it had.

But when we got to it that first time, things didn't exactly slide along easy. Even though she did anything I put her to, she acted like sex wasn't something she was used to, which didn't figure since, with an ex-husband and two kids, she wasn't in a league with the Virgin Mary.

I guess I could say I was disappointed. Although later on things went better between us. I learned what to do and when to push her around and when not to. But to tell the truth, if it hadn't got any better than that first time, I still would have been crazy about her. You can't say why about a feeling like that. Just certain things about her made my gut go hot. The way she fingered a piece of bread or a spoon or the leaf of a plant, as if she could feel what it was about, absorb it into her silence. The way she leaned against me sometimes, really leaned like she couldn't stand up on her own. The way she let me order her drinks or food, turning those eyes on me, giving me the feeling she would starve to death or die of thirst if I didn't take care of her. She had that nice voice too, sweet and a little raspy, like dry leaves rustling against each other. But she didn't talk a lot ever, and that was something else I liked about her, that she could be quiet and I could and we could still be together.

I guess you could say I needed her. Of course it looked like it was all the other way, but the fact was that in the beginning I did need her near as much as she needed me. I've always been the kind of guy who stops when someone's changing a tire. Sometimes the people'll be leery at first. Like I said, I'm big and stronger than most. But when they see I'm really going to help them, they relax and get grateful. I like that. And I like the feeling I'm taking care of them. I'm the kind of guy people talk to about stuff too, like the time they were in jail or how their ex-wife turned out queer or how someone jumped their sister in a parking lot. I hear it all. Sucked in by someone else's need, you could say. But the truth is, it takes one to know one, and like I say, I had needs myself.

I was raised in an upstairs duplex. In a bunch of them to be exact. My two older brothers ended up gone while I was real young. There was a big age difference between us, and I don't much remember them. Gary, the oldest of us, ran off when he was sixteen. My parents said he'd gone and joined the U.S. Army, and maybe he had. A year or so after that, Paul got himself killed. He lived for a while in the hospital after he pitched out of the tree, but there was something had gone wrong in his head from cracking it. I was only six, and I don't know a lot about how the thing happened. Nor any special reason he fell. The kids that were in the tree with him didn't seem to think there was any accident about it. They said he just let go and rolled off the branch, like that's what he'd decided to do. Afterwards I used to think of him in summertime, when you sometimes see a dead bird, a baby one that's speckled and scrawny and that's fallen from the nest or maybe been shoved out by the parents because it's sick or got some flaw and can't measure up.

My parents must have sold their house right after Paul died because I remember that from first grade on we never had a house again and were always moving, and the places were always the same: long, skinny hall, living room in front, then the bedrooms, theirs and mine, like it was planned so I could hear their fights and most of the time the other stuff they did too. They made a shitload of noise at whatever they did. After the bedrooms came the bathroom and at the back of the place a little scratched-up kitchen with the crummy fridge and stove my mother was guaranteed to hate. It's hard to figure why, but my folks lived in one or another duplex about exactly like that until they died. (My mother went first, and then a couple years later my father bought it too. Both of them heart attacks.) The way they lived, it was like they didn't have a real life anyway, so they didn't need a real home, but I can't say I know. Come to think of it, maybe they just plain liked renting. Anyway, they always said it was better that someone else took care of the dripping pipes and the backed-up toilets. Except for agreeing about that, my father and mother didn't get along. She had a mouth on her and little, angry blue eyes, and when those eyes started to gleam you knew you had to watch out. She liked to cut my father down, but she wanted him to pay her some mind too. It didn't take a genius to see that. Truth was he didn't pay much mind to anyone. Far as I could see, he didn't give much of a shit. But maybe there was a lot of stuff I didn't know there too. What I did know was he'd as soon hit her or me as talk to us. He broke my arm two times, which was two times more than enough, and I didn't like going to school with his bruises on me either. The teachers used to look at me funny and sometimes ask questions which I didn't answer. Around him I kept quiet mostly. It was my mother who was the screamer. She bitched at him, and when she got on his nerves he'd smack her, and then she'd throw things, and he'd smack her again.

We lived for a while west of Decarie, down near the tracks. It must have been early summer because I remember we'd finished supper, and it was bright as afternoon, and I was crazy to get outside, down to the street where the other kids hung out. In that duplex the kitchen was painted yellow, and that's where I can see her standing at the sink with her hands in the soapy water and my father sitting at the supper table smoking and writing notes in the margin of the sports page. He made bets on the races, some at Blue Bonnet's and some in places I didn't know

about. My mother was washing up, and I was drying. I'd
done the glasses and plates, the towel was already damp,
and I was waiting while she scrubbed the meatloaf pan.
Dishes were the time I always wished, since my brother
Paul was dead and my brother Gary was never coming
back, that at least I could have a sister or two. They would
be the ones, for example, doing this chore with my
mother, and I would be sitting at the table with my father
and breathing in the smoke from his cigarette, and we
would be talking about the races or even about my own
softball game that day in the park. Instead of which, he
wasn't saying a word, and my mother was the one doing
the talking, which was more or less the norm, and she was
saying how someone had rammed her leg that day in the
lineup at Steinberg's grocery store. I'd already noticed she
had a big bandage on the back of her calf and blood had
seeped through the middle of it.

"Acted like it wasn't her fault too. Cart just had a mind
of its own, I suppose. And there I am, blood running
down the back of my leg because there was some sharp
metal rod thing sticking out of her cart. The store manager got me a taxi to the General. He was sorry, he said
so about ten times, but not her, the bitch—five stitches it
took. I was lucky, the doctor said, missed that big tendon
there." All this time my father was reading and writing
stuff down and once in a while grunting as if he heard her
and knew what she was saying.

Finally I saw her turn and look at him. Her little blue
eyes got that glitter, but she went right on talking in the
same voice, and what she said was, "So I shot the elephant,
and there was this space ship with little men falling out
the windows and a giant on the ground gobbling them

up." I thought this was clever and started to laugh, and then I saw how she was looking at him, and I understood that laughing wasn't what I should be doing. He'd gone right on reading, never even lifted his head. Two red patches had popped out on her cheeks, like they always did when she was getting into a temper, and usually about now she'd start to bitch at him for not paying her any mind. But this time she didn't say anything, and that seemed worse, like we'd just skipped several stages. I watched her hand groping around in the water. A hot place began to spread in my stomach, and I got to breathing hard like I always did while I was waiting for the explosion. Now I watched her arm come out of the soapy water. A stream of drops ran off her elbow and dripped onto her apron. Drops flew from the egg beater as she whirled and let it fly. The handle caught him on the ear. He made a grunting sound, the egg beater crashed to the floor, and right at that instant, just like always, everything in front of my eyes went red.

"My leg hurts, you fucking bastard!" That was her voice. And she must have thrown something else because I could hear a smack and a clatter, and I heard his chair legs scrape the floor and after that a bang like the chair had fallen over and then thumps and her screaming, not saying words any more but just screaming. But all I could see was red everywhere, like the whole place was filled with fire, and what I felt most was a kind of relief, like when you crash into the furnace in a dream. Because even if we were all burning up, at least now she'd gone and got him to do it to her, and the explosion wasn't out there any more, hidden and waiting, like a land mine set to blow our guts out, but was already detonated here in our kitchen. Even if she ended up dead this time, which I always thought she might, at least there wasn't any more space between knowing and happening. I must have done some yelling myself because the next thing I heard was his voice right close up to me saying, "Shut the hell up," and something smashed my lip against my teeth. I don't exactly remember the pain, though I know it made tears come out of my eyes and that for a minute or two I couldn't draw breath. What I do remember is the taste of blood. And how, just after that, more pounding started, but this time it was coming from the front door where the downstairs neighbours were banging on it and shouting through the panels about how we'd have to stop the racket or else they'd call the police.

Once the neighbours had gone away again, things calmed down pretty quick. I got the tray of ice out of the fridge and started sucking on a piece of ice while my mother sat on a kitchen chair with the side of her face all red and swelling by the second. I think she made me get her some ice too because I remember emptying a tray of cubes into a dishtowel and how they kept sticking to different sections of the towel while I was trying to make a pile of them and how all the time that I was doing that my mother was sitting on the chair moaning and trying to tell me to hurry except that she couldn't make clear words. The next day she couldn't speak at all. She couldn't chew either, and she sent me over to Steinberg's to buy cans of beef and chicken broth and a box of straws.

What I don't remember is what I thought about her and him, that night or at any other time back then. Most likely, I thought nothing at all. And to tell the truth, I never did have much of an idea what made him tick. Her

I understood better because I think that in one way things might have been the same for her as they were for me. I think that even though she hated it, she wanted the shouting and the business of being face to face with him, and even being slugged by him, so that finally she could feel she had his attention. That didn't stop her from screaming bloody murder, of course, whenever he gave it to her. Everywhere we lived, the people downstairs used to complain about the noise. The time her arm got broken, they even called the police, who, after they came and trussed up her arm and told her to go to the hospital, tried to get her to press charges, which she wouldn't. For breaking bones he had a special side-hand chop. (The two times it hit me, I could feel my arm shiver and go cold, and right away I wanted to vomit.) Another time I remember her nose bled and swelled up all red and shiny like a pepper, and she had to go to the hospital then too. When he wasn't around, she used to complain about him and look for me to say how much of a shit he was to her, which of course he was. But she never made the move to leave him. She wanted to stay, I guess, and she wanted to fight with him. Maybe she even wanted to lose. Neither one of them ever talked a word about my brothers. It was like they'd never been born. The closest my father came was a couple of times when he told me getting married and having kids was his biggest mistake. He told me this like it didn't relate to me in any way, like I was just someone he knew and had got talking with. Do it like renting, was what he said to me, move on when you've had enough. I remember nodding my head when he told me that, but by that time I'd figured out whatever he said to me was probably dead wrong.

After I turned sixteen, I didn't see much of them. That was the year I got big, and the last time my old man smacked me. I'd broken some ashtray, and he bashed the side of my head when I wasn't looking. I turned around and sank my right fist into his shoulder and caught him in the cheek with my left. I would have taken him apart right then, I knew I could do it, except my mother—this was what blew me away—she came at me with a big metal spoon. I remember it dripping with whatever she'd been stirring. It was worse than him going after me. All the shit he'd given her, and she was whacking me with a stupid goddamn spoon. I grabbed it from her and threw it in the sink. He was half-sitting, half-lying on the kitchen floor, just kind of staring up at the wall and the ceiling. I think I'd knocked him silly.

"You don't fucking lay a hand on me again," I told him, and then I turned to her. "He's right about you," was what I said to her. "You're a stupid fucking cunt." Her face went kind of still. She hadn't expected that. She stood staring at me, her little blue eyes blinking like there was some fact she needed to work over. After a minute she stopped looking. She wiped her hands on her apron and took a step towards where he lay sprawled on the floor. "Did Gil hurt you much?" was what she said.

That afternoon, I packed up my stuff and got out. I figured, shit, there wasn't ever any place for me with that pair; let them kill each other. Her spoon had left a fat, purple welt on my arm, and any of the two or three times I got to feeling bad about her, I rolled up my sleeve and took a look. There was a row of bloody-looking bruises along the knuckles of my left hand too, but I didn't need any reminders to know what I thought of him. Took about three weeks for all the stuff to heal, and when it did I called them and told them I'd see them once in a while but that I wasn't coming back.

For a while I lived in a room over a greengrocer's. I was pumping gas nights. I'd told the guy at the station I was twenty. I looked it, and they didn't even suspect I was lying. I wasn't going to school much. Remembering stuff and figuring things out wasn't hard for me, but the history teacher was stupider than half the class, and I could read books on my own if I wanted. Besides, school was for kids, and I didn't feel like a kid. French I'd learned from the guys I played hockey and softball with. I took the school's business accounting course, and all the auto repair and industrial arts they had, and after another year I figured I had enough. When I got the job at the big Shell station, I found an apartment that I could move around in. But just the same, I had in mind to buy a place one day. I always wanted that. My own place where the walls and the radiators and the wires and the pipes were all mine. And I wanted a wife too. Some guys I used to talk with, they'd go on about having a million women or else some gold-plated, state-of-the-art hooker like it was their ultimate dream, but for me those women didn't smell good. I wanted a woman that was mine, one woman that needed me and wouldn't ever not need me. I wanted a woman with a dark, quiet place inside her, the kind of place I didn't have in myself. After I turned twenty or so, I was always looking, and it's a question I can't answer, how it took me until I was past thirty-five to find the woman.

I married Teresa pretty soon after I got her into bed. She was what I wanted, and I didn't see any point in dicking around. We were out walking the afternoon I got it settled with her. It was April, and the snow had shrunk back so the sidewalk was mostly dry. Just under the dead-looking trees in the parks, the snow had stayed, dirty and frozen except around its edges where it was melting into little swamps of mud and water. The side streets and lanes were a mess too, so we stuck to St. Hubert and Clark and the Main. We were passing by a bride-dress store where the front window was filled with these human-size dolls, all of them brides poking their plaster tits out of their white dresses. I could feel the sharp angle of Teresa's shoulder bone when I put my arm around her. I reached across and put my other hand on the side of her face and turned her so she could see the dresses. It was like turning one of the dolls. "You should be checking those out," I said to her. "What do you think? May or June?"

She didn't say anything for a minute, just leaned her face into my hand like she was thinking it over. Then her eyes kind of spilled towards me. It's weird to say, but I felt their darkness on my face. "You sure you really want to marry me?" she said.

"Yeah, I want to." I was looking at her face so close I could see the different browns in her irises, the black glitter of her pupils and where the lines would be coming in the hollows that ran from her nostrils to the corners of her mouth. "I'll take care of you," I said. "You know that."

She nodded, her head moving against my hand, and I knew the deal was done. I was strong and I'd stick with her. She knew that, and I think she knew she couldn't stand alone. "Tulips come in May," she said. "I like tulips."

We told her parents the next week. It was the first time I'd thought about my own parents, dead for nearly ten years by now, and I couldn't find much to think about that didn't make me feel lousy. Teresa's old man took me out and got himself shit-faced and me nearly. He kept saying things in German. He didn't have any accent speaking English, but he knew some old hill dialect from outside Vienna, which is where he was raised until he was six or so, and he kept switching into it. Half of what he said I missed, but it seemed to be confession time. Man to man, or something like that. He'd killed a man once, he said. It sounded like he'd challenged the guy and had to ante up. And he'd had himself another woman for a while, but that was a long time ago. He kept calling Teresa his princess and his little squeeze, like she'd never been married or had two kids, like she was still living with them and still a little kid herself. He cried about six different times and hugged me, whacking me on the back, hard, like really he wanted to hit me. He kept begging me to be good to his baby. By the end he damn near passed out. I had to find a taxi to get him home.

We got married at the end of the summer. Way too late for tulips, but her mother had got in the act by then. Church was out on account of Teresa being married before and the ex-husband not necessarily being dead, so we went down to City Hall on my bike, and afterwards we drove west along Sherbrooke Street to this old-fashioned mansion building that belonged to the city. Her folks had rented a room in it, and her mother and the aunts brought bowls of salads and big platters of meats and a wheel of parmigiano cheese on a stand and what her mother called a Genova cake with a ton of booze in it. With that and all the bottles of wine and beer and grappa, they had to use someone's truck to haul the stuff in. We had music too, a couple of guys walking around playing violins and sometimes singing. They sounded schmaltzy, but the music kind of wound around everything and everyone and made things feel special and once-in-a-lifetime, which of course they were. A couple of her cousins bartended, and we had ourselves a real wedding reception with her uncles and aunts and cousins and my friends, some of my old bike buddies and the ones I went fishing and rafting with, and their wives and the guy that owned her flower shop and my boss and some of the guys that worked with me. The food and drinks part was nice, and so was everybody shaking my hand and slapping my back and some of them hugging and kissing me and all of them hugging and kissing Teresa and wishing us happiness and luck. The only bad part was after an hour or so, when her dad lost it.

He'd had a snootful of grappa by then, and he came over and gave me a drunk's sly stare out the side of his eyes. "You take care of that little girl. She needs watching after, my baby squeeze. Hears music you don't hear." He kept coming back and repeating himself and giving me a big slap on the back. Once or twice I thought he was going to start blubbering.

Finally he smacked me so hard I dropped the glass I was holding. The glass smashed, and some of the women went running around to get towels, and I turned and got a hold of her dad's arm. "Now, Dad," I said, my voice real low. "Teresa's my wife now. I'll take care of her. You don't have to keep saying it." I kept hold of his arm just long enough and just tight enough, he'd figure out I had half a mind to do a lot more. I guess he knew it because after that he pretty much laid off.

Towards the end of the afternoon we all went outside and crossed over to this park that was on the other side of the parking lot. One of her uncles had brought along his camera equipment, tripod and all, and he took a bunch of shots of us standing around on the grass. At one point, while he was fiddling with some gadget on his camera, I saw my shoe was untied and bent over to fix it. I was still bent down when I heard him saying to Teresa, "Tell your husband to stand up. His shoe isn't going to show in the shot." He didn't mean anything special saying that, he was joking more or less, but up until that day I hadn't even thought the word husband. Wife yes, but not husband.

I stood up. "Yeah, okay, I'm up," I said. "Go ahead and shoot," and I heard the word again in my head. *Husband*. It gave me a feeling, I can tell you.

In the pictures, the trees are yellow and red and gold, and the grass has that trampled look. You can tell it's early fall. But I remember how it was, standing there in the park with the sun on my back, not like fall but like summer, and how after a while I was sweating in my suit and how good I felt, as though my life was warming up.

In the shots of the two of us, Teresa looks surprised, as though a wedding was the last thing she'd thought of when she woke up that morning, and I look like a guy who'd never worn a suit before, which wasn't too far wrong. Some of the pictures show her kids. The little girl, Amy, had on the fanciest blue dress you ever saw on a kid. She had a basket of flowers too, I remember, except she kept leaving it everywhere and then crying until someone found it for her. Her brother was the one who mostly went looking. His name was Phil. He must have been six that fall, and they had him wearing a bow tie and a jacket that was about three inches too short in the sleeves. In the pictures his wrists stick out of the sleeves like chicken bones. Teresa borrowed the jacket off one of her cousins, and I don't think she'd noticed it didn't fit the boy. He was a solemn kid, and polite enough, although he kept his eyes on me like he thought at any moment I might turn into some wild animal and eat them all. In one picture he's standing behind his little sister, and he has his bony, kid's hand on her shoulder, like he's her father or they're some kind of miniature bride and groom.

The kids took some getting used to, in fact. I wasn't ever too keen about having kids, and back at Franco's I hadn't counted on any kids coming with her. But now we were married I got interested in having them move in with us. Seemed like part of this big change in my life, having them to take care of. Teresa's mother made a bit of fuss, but to tell the truth, I think they were more than she could handle, and we weren't exactly far away. I'd rented a house a couple of streets over from them on Drolet. The kids moved in with us after Christmas. We picked them up one night after supper and brought them to our place. They kind of tiptoed in, the skinny, weak-shouldered boy and the little girl, both of them brown-skinned and big-eyed, her standing behind him and holding onto his pocket or the back of his sleeve whenever she could, and both of them watching Teresa and me like they weren't sure about either one of us. There wasn't much talk that night, I can tell you, not even when we showed them their rooms.

I stood in the hall and watched Teresa kind of pushing them, first towards one of the rooms and then towards the other. Both rooms smelled of paint, and they seemed extra bright and clean, as if they were full of daylight, even though it was night. "See," she kept saying. "See." She'd spent near to a month fixing them up. The boy's room she'd painted yellow and the girl's light green, and she'd bought them quilts and made bedspreads and matching curtains. Watching her do all this, I'd got the feeling she hadn't felt too much like their mother up until now and was making up something to them.

"It's nice, Momma," Phil finally said, as if he'd remembered her feelings might be hurt if he didn't say something.

Amy grabbed hold of his pocket when he said this, but I grabbed hold of her and got her hand loose and hoisted her up high. I remember she shrieked, and then she giggled and shrieked again while I carried her into her room.

The other two followed us, and when I set her on the ground, she stopped shrieking and ran around behind her brother again. "Come on, Amy," he said, turning around and taking hold of her arm. "Here's your room. Look at your room."

"Oh, here's a place I missed." That was Teresa fingering a little gap between the light-switch coverplate and the wall. "I'll just touch that up," she said. We all stared at the light switch then, and after that everything seemed more normal. We unpacked the plastic bags that held their clothes and another that held their toys and got them both into bed. I will say they seemed proud of having their own rooms. At Teresa's parents' they'd shared.

But later that night, when we went to check on them before we went to bed ourselves, Amy's bed was empty. I remember Teresa standing in the doorway and saying in this weird voice. "They've stolen her." But already I had opened his door and was looking into his room, and there they were, both asleep in his bed.

The light from the hall shone straight across their bodies. Teresa came and leaned on me, and we stood for a minute beside the bed, just staring down at the two of them. Like dogs from one litter was what I thought: the same curly black hair and long, skinny bodies—him in pajamas, her in her white nightgown—the same black eyelashes resting against their cheeks. They were lying on their sides facing one another. Her hand had reached out and got a grip on the hem of his pajama top. He had his back smack against the wall, one arm stretched out towards her, like either he was staying in touch with her the way she was staying in touch with him or else he was holding her off.

I was the one lifted her up and carried her back to her own room. She wasn't heavy, but the weight and warmth of her went right through me, the feel of her body in my arms, and I was sorry to have to set her down in her bed.

For years we went on finding them like that, asleep together in his bed, and for years I had the job of picking her up and putting her in her own bed. Her hair used to stick to her forehead in flat little curls, like someone had pasted black rings on her skin, and her face was always a little damp. While I was carrying her, she would sigh and turn her head, but she never did open her eyes. I never tried to wake her either.

The truth was Amy took to me right off; if I ever had waked her, she wouldn't have minded. She had a piping voice like one of those recorder flutes, and she used to climb in my lap and sing to me or sometimes just wriggle and fiddle with my shirt buttons or poke me in the cheeks. She was kind of a miniature Teresa to look at, small face and long legs, curly black hair, but a Teresa with the shine still on her, and I got to see what the old man had meant about Teresa being his main squeeze when she was a little kid.

I used to tickle Amy to see her squirm and giggle, her body curling and twisting like a puppy that's rolled over on its back and is getting its stomach rubbed. I liked to give her her bath too. Seeing her naked in the water gave me a feeling I never had before, and I wanted to take care of her all her life, keep everyone else in the world away from her. Phil didn't like it. He'd watch her when she was with me. I'd look around and see him standing still as a pole in the doorway. He watched her a lot. His eyes had Teresa's habit of always being on the alert for what could go wrong. And to tell the truth, I didn't much like him at first.

But after we were all living together for a while, I got to feeling sorry for him. One weekend at the end of June, he showed me his report card. I'd asked him something about school, just to pay him some mind. And right away I could see he welcomed me asking. He went off to his room and when he came back he had the report card. He was nervous to show it, I could tell from the way his eyes looked at me and then jumped sideways, and from the way he handed the report card to me, like it was too hot to hold, and then shoved his hands quick into his pockets.

The folder was small, made of blue cardboard. Second grade, terms I, II and III. His teacher was a Soeur Mathilde. I read through the subjects—*lecture, science humaine*... The kid studied in French. Maybe Teresa had told me or maybe she just assumed I'd know, but I didn't, and in fact he'd never said one word in French that I'd heard. Every mark was an A, and every comment was like he was the greatest pupil the teacher had ever seen. The boy was smart as hell.

"Not bad, Phil," I said to him and grinned to show how I meant it. "Not bad." He grinned back for a second and ducked his head again. It was only when I got to éducation physique that I read... "*manque de l'énergie et l'enthousiasme,*" which didn't surprise me. It was clear he hadn't had much practice for being a real boy. Teresa's father was too much retired for that, and Phil's father was a no-show and never coming back besides, so that was something I could do for the boy. "You know," I said to him, "we're going to toss a ball around this summer, you and me. And come fall, we're heading down to the rink." He didn't look so happy then; in fact he blinked so hard I thought he was going to cry. So I gave him a good pat on the shoulder. "You'll be okay," I said. "I'll teach you. You'll be okay."

And he was. Over the next few years I took him out and taught him to skate and stickhandle like a hockey player and to throw and field a ball, and I walloped him if

I caught him crying. After a while he learned not to bawl over stuff, and the third year he got on a good team at the rink after school, and he knew it was because of me. He stayed scared of me, but he knew I was trying to make a man out of him.

Only one place I never did trust him, and that was with Amy. There was something about the way he watched her, right from the beginning, that hand on her shoulder. He could get her to run around for him too. That was another thing that bothered me. He could get her to do any damn thing he wanted. It went on year after year, her chasing for his skates or his mitt, whatever he'd forgotten, and dancing after him like a dolly on a string. It made me crazy watching it. Philly this and Philly that. For every time she climbed into my lap, she was ten times as often running after him. Like a regular little slave.

Everything else in the house I ran like I ran the business. I'd got Teresa to quit her job soon as we were married. I think she missed it, but I didn't much like the idea of her mother and father in and out of the house looking after the kids. Besides I was the kind of man didn't want my wife working. A couple years after that, I bought the business off my boss. The loan was big, and it took most of the profits for me to keep up the payments. We didn't have a lot to live on the first few years, but it was worth it. My boss had half-retired anyway, and I was doing better at the job than he'd ever done. Turned out I was good at running things. All except for Amy. Her I couldn't say no to. Which was okay except that it made me understand how come it was that she couldn't say no to her brother, and that was an idea I didn't like.

Just once I caught Phil messing with her, and of course it made me wonder how much stuff I'd missed. The time I found them was in the summer. Once school was out, both kids used to get up crazy early and go out in the alley behind the house, where the kids in the neighbourhood all hung around. But this time he'd got her up into the attic. Maybe it was raining; I can't say I recall. Probably he got her up there with some story about reading to her. He did that a lot. She was running towards eight by then and could bloody well read a book herself if she'd a mind to.

I could see how it was, even when I was still pounding up the attic stairs. How he'd have got his hands inside her clothes and would be touching that smooth, brown skin, and how she wouldn't know what was what.

But when I got up there, I couldn't see much of anything for a moment. The attic fan wasn't working, and the whole space was so hot it nearly choked me. Then I heard their voices. The two kids had got themselves hidden behind a bunch of rubbish that belonged to the owners of the house, chair cushions that the kids must have piled up to make a wall, and a chest, and boxes, the kind of stuff that nobody wants and always gets saved anyway. I took out the boxes and cushions with one hand and him with the other. The stuff went flying in one direction, and he went skidding across the floor the opposite way, and what was left at my feet was my girl.

Cool as a little witch she was, sitting cross-legged on the floor and flashing those black, little-girl eyes up at me like I was the monster in her story book. "Daddy, you hurt Philly!" She looked over at him. "Did Daddy hurt you much, Philly?"

"You little bastard," I said to him then. "What the fuck you think you're doing with her?"

I took a step towards him and stopped because she'd grabbed hold of my leg and started screaming, "Daddy, Daddy!"

"Hey," I said to her. "Don't do that. Daddy's taking care of you."

The boy never did cry. I'll give him that. Just sat there staring up at me like a retard, with his back against one of the boxes. He put his hand to his jaw, and I could see him lick the blood off his lip. And I could tell by his eyes how he would never like me again and never trust me either. I'd lost him. That was for sure, and it made me feel bad. But messing with my little girl—he deserved what he'd got and more. There was stuff all around, those boxes and cushions, a mess of potato chips, and the kids' books he'd used to get her up there.

She didn't weigh much to lift, but she kicked her feet into me, and she twisted like an eel, and when I got a good grip on her and was carrying her away, she started screaming and beating on my shoulder with her fists. We got down the stairs like that, and I carried her right into the bathroom. "You let Phil get you dirty," I told her. "Daddy doesn't want you dirty."

I ran the water and took off her clothes, and when I'd got her into the bath, I washed her all over. That made her happy. All the while I was soaping her and touching her everywhere, she was splashing in the water and giggling like crazy. I can still hear her. "Daddy," she kept saying, "you're tickling. Daddy, stop it, Daddy, don't. Daddy, Daddy..." I can still see her too, brown and shiny as an otter. The boy had a fat lip and a bruise along the side of his jaw. When Teresa saw his face, she gave me a look, but she didn't say anything. I was the boss, she knew that, and I knew what he'd had in mind. I protected Amy. I took care of her.

I took care of Teresa too, like I told her I would. We had some good times in the first years with the kids and around the neighbourhood, and being with her in bed got to be something like I knew it would be the first time I saw her. You might even say the strangeness of her was what made it good. With an ordinary woman's flesh, all warm and heavy and full of complaint, time comes when you've had your fill. You even can't stand to touch it any more. But hers was never like that. Her body was like something conjured up out of the things she smelled of, smoke and perfume, and out of her fear and shyness and the other mysteries in her brain, out of her strangeness itself. If I couldn't keep hold of her attention, still I knew she was there, dark matter, you might say, acting on everything and everyone around it, so that I could always feel how she was there. That was the good part of it. I had her. She never said no to me in bed. Not like the other guys' old ladies with their bitching and their headaches. I heard enough about that sitting around the bars Friday nights. No, with her it was all different. Nights I came home from the garage and she wrapped her legs around me, I was in a different universe.

By then I was making good money. And I got to having myself some times with the guys I was friends with. I needed some ordinary life, and Teresa never complained when I went off with them either. She didn't take to travel herself. The one time I made her come with me to Florida, which was a place I'd been to and thought she'd like because of all the growing stuff, she was a wreck worrying for days before we left. On the plane she couldn't eat, and it was tranquilizer city while we were down there and another scene on the plane going back. I never saw anybody so scared for nothing. After that I did my travelling with the guys. There were six of us used to get a van and drive to Sept-Îles a couple of times a year and then charter a plane, fly up into Labrador with all the whisky and beer we could carry. We drank that and ate part of what we caught and then brought the rest back with us. Walleye and trout mostly. I went fishing in Florida a bunch of times too. A guy I did work for owned a discount travel agency, and he paid me in cheap Air Canada tickets. After I got into hunting, I did some climbing too, out in the Kootenays. All that she never minded, though sometimes I wondered if it was mainly she didn't notice.

Just what and when things went so far wrong with her that there was no getting them back was hard to figure. The strange got stranger, you could say. Nights I came home she would look at me for a minute, like she didn't remember me. Then her face would clear, and she'd go back to peeling or mixing something, and maybe she'd say what was for dinner. But for that first minute I used to think I had turned into another person or opened the wrong door, walked into the wrong kitchen. It happened, and then it happened more often, and one night when I was lying with her she began to cry. This was in summer, the first hot weekend in July. The house was tall and narrow, attached on both sides. You couldn't get much of a cross-breeze, and the heat rose up through the stairwell like steam from a pot, and with the windows open you could hear down in the street the drunks and the teenagers shouting and the cars revving their engines and the babble when the movie let out down the block, like the whole city was shoving its way past our house. And with all that summer noise and us sweating and the sheets twisted and pulled half off the mattress, around us the air went cold. Like an iceberg had floated up nearby and pulled the heat out of the air. Only it was her where this cold was coming from. Even though I could feel it all around me, I knew it came from inside her. Her body had gone inert lying under me, and in the light from the street, I saw the flush like a stain spreading up her throat and into her face, and I saw the shine of tears sliding from the sides of her eyes down into her black hair.

"What the hell's the matter?" I said.

Those eyes, the darkest place in the world, were looking up at me. And what she said was, "Who are you?"

I tell you it was like a bomb went off in my head. A fucking bomb. *Who are you?* Like I was some kind of stranger lying over her. I got straight up, off her and off the bed in one move, and went and got a beer from the fridge. My hands were shaking like an old man's when I opened it. *Who are you?* Like we haven't been married six years and her kids aren't sleeping down the hall. Like I don't fuck you practically every night I'm around. I even checked out my face in the mirror. But it was the same old meat-and-potatoes face, the man I always was. So what was she seeing?

I didn't ask her, not that night or any other. To tell the truth, I didn't want to know, and she didn't tell me—if she could have. I spent the rest of that night on the couch.

The next evening, when I headed home, my stomach started bunching together like someone was going to punch me in the gut. By the time I walked into the kitchen, I was ready for anything. She was standing there at the counter with a big chopping knife in her hand. I could smell the onion juice. She looked around and gave me that can-you-help-me smile of hers like there had never been any question of who I was. Her forehead was sweating and her black hair was pinned up on top of her head.

"I couldn't find the fan, Gil. You know where it is?" she said in a voice as ordinary as the kitchen. I don't remember what I answered. I think I just stared at her. She was wearing a blue shirt with short sleeves, and she held the knife by the point and the handle, the knife going chock, chock through the onion and the chopped pieces falling into a little glossy pile. Her wrists were thin as a girl's. I could have snapped them. Like one of those fancy wine-glass stems. She was thirty-two by then, and the boy nearly twelve.

It didn't happen again, her not knowing me, not for a couple of years, and I kind of forgot about it. The garage was going gangbusters. I sold a third interest to my mechanic and gave him a right to purchase on the rest, and I bought a house over behind the park, an old place that some geezer had died in. It hadn't been touched for forty years, but that meant no one had messed anything up, gutted the rooms or torn down the stuff that was nice, like the woodwork, which was yellow oak, or the plaster mouldings, and I was good at fixing things up. With the house there was more room for the kids. There was even a passable garden at the back, say fifteen feet square. It was all under snow, of course, but they told me there were some rose bushes and other stuff too.

The weekend after I closed on the deal, I took Teresa over to the place. It was mid-February with the kind of cold where the air is so still and dense you can hear the scream of the jet engines from way up high. There were ruts in the road too and about three feet of snow on the ground. We couldn't get into the house yet, but I took her around to the back. The kids stayed in the car. "It's all ours, occupancy April first," I told her. "They tell me there're rose bushes. Over there, they told me." I pointed to the mound of snow piled up against the fence. "They said the sun was good there for roses. The man was about ninety when he died."

Teresa had been looking where I pointed. She was wearing her black coat with a fur hood, and I couldn't see her face until she turned towards me. "Roses?" she said, and I saw she was smiling.

"Yeah, roses. That's what I've been telling you. They said the guy was good with them, and the snow being heavy this year is better for keeping them in good shape." Her eyes stayed on me like she wanted to be sure this was true. "Believe me," I said. "The nephew said the old guy talked and talked about them. Kept him alive, I guess. You can meet the nephew if you want."

I stopped because she was walking away from me, although walking wasn't the word. Paddling was more like it. The snow came up to her thighs, and it was like she didn't know it was there. She knelt down by the fence in all that snow, so that now it came up to her shoulders. When I got over to her and hauled her to her feet, she had snow all over her like a kid. She was crying, too, and still smiling right at the same time, and I knew it was a good thing what I'd done. I held onto her and looked around at the snow and at the back of the old house, and I was as glad as I've ever been.

Come summer we'd be well settled, and she'd have a garden. She had plants all over the place we were renting now, but this would be outdoors, and she would be digging in the earth and watching things push up green out of the mud; it would keep her connected.

Driving back to our rented place, I told her how I'd found the house through one of my customers and what I'd paid for it, how big the mortgage was and what the taxes would be. I knew she wasn't paying me any mind, I could hear her humming to herself half under her breath, but I didn't care. With the ice in the streets, the traffic was the pits, and some guy nearly side-swiped us coming across St-Joseph, and still I felt good. I didn't even get mad at the idiot.

The first summer it pretty much worked like I thought. There really were some roses. We dug them out from under piles of straw and leaves. Most of the bushes had lived through the winter. They looked like old wood to me, but she knew how to do whatever it took to clean them out and make them bloom. There were some dark red, the colour of plum jam, and others butter yellow. Come fall I helped her trim them down and cover them in piles of leaves and mud. When it got cold, I found where the house leaked heat, and I caulked a lot of joints and the gaps around the windows and shot some insulation into the space between the attic ceiling and the roof. Figured I'd start replacing the worst windows come spring. That winter I did some painting, and I stripped the stair railing down to the old yellow oak and put a new toilet and sink in the bathroom. Even on the coldest nights, when the wind rattled the loose glass in our bedroom window, I felt good. Teresa was there beside me and not acting up, and I was in my own house.

In the beginning of the spring, when we'd been in the house almost a year, I came home one night—the slush had bled into my boots while I was crossing the Esplanade, they hadn't plowed the street for a while—and I was thinking how I wanted a gin or maybe just a beer and how I needed a new pair of boots and how it wasn't that long since I'd bought the ones I was wearing. The salt and all the freezes and thaws kill the leather.

The house was quiet when I came in through the back. No TV and no voices. Just a drip from a tap that needed a new washer, and the hum of the old oil furnace. The kind of sounds you hear when the TV's just been turned off. I shouted but she didn't answer, and I went on into the kitchen.

For a moment I had the feeling that I was in the wrong place or maybe that I'd seen wrong and what I was looking at wasn't a hill of broken dishes in the middle of the floor. White dishes and green ones. All our dinner plates and cups and saucers. There were chunks of the flowered soup bowls her mother had brought us too and pieces of a yellow platter someone gave us for our wedding. Not a whole plate or bowl in the pile. The cupboard doors were hanging open, and I could see not a dish left on the shelves; it was like a hurricane had come through and sucked everything out of every cupboard and smashed it all on the floor. Except for sitting on the kitchen table, nice as you please, were these two glasses of milk and two plates of ravioli and fried zucchini. The kids' dinner. A fork was sitting in the middle of one plate and another fork was lying sideways on the table like someone had dropped it there. I yelled then. My voice sounded like a wild man's. And I ran all over the place and up and down stairs yanking open doors and yelling some more.

I found the kids in the attic behind a pile of boxes, hiding like there were burglars in the house. "Where the hell is she?" I said to them, pulling the boxes apart. I wanted to smack them both, but I felt sorry for them too.

They stared up at me with those eyes they got from her and shook their heads. They didn't know where she was. And I could see it was true, they didn't know. They said it started while they were having supper. "Momma was screaming," said Amy.

Phil looked from me to her and nodded when she spoke. "I called the garage," he told me, "but you'd already left." His voice had begun to crack, and it was hard to understand what he said. He looked worse off than she did. He was tall as I was by that time and on his way to being taller, and he weighed about half what I did. A big-eyed scarecrow was what he was. I could tell he'd been blubbering, there were big, wet smears on his face, but I didn't do anything about it. Not that time. He had something to blubber about. "She pointed at the floor," he said, "and she screamed." Amy had run out after the dish breaking started, and he'd followed her.

What was going through my mind was that Teresa was dead. I don't know why I thought that, but I did. Like she might have stuck a knife into herself. I told the kids to go down to the bathroom and wash their faces, and I went looking some more.

I found her in the broom closet off the kitchen. Her eyes were closed, and she was curled up in the middle of the mops and brooms and cleaning stuff. It was cold in there; the insulation wasn't very good at the back of the house, and she looked frozen, her bony knees pulled up to her chest and her lips blue as bruises. She was cold to the touch too, but when I lifted her hand to take her pulse, her eyes opened, and that's when I realized I'd been holding my breath since I'd opened the door to the broom closet and that I'd been sure as anything she was dead.

"Come on," I said. I could feel my heart smashing in my chest. "Come on. We got to get you out of there."

Her eyes wandered over my face and sank down shut again. While I was hauling her out of the closet, one of the mops banged down on my head, and she grabbed my arm, her eyes wide open now and staring over my shoulder and her face kind of flattened like a little kid's pressed against a pane of glass. "Is it still here?" she said. It wasn't the mop she was talking about.

"Is *what* still here? What the hell happened?" I was half-supporting her, half-carrying her, and I wasn't angry any more because it was too much for that. To tell the truth, I felt like there was some really big mistake, bigger than anything I could imagine a reason for.

She was still holding onto me with one hand, and now with the other she pointed at the hill of crockery. "It's under there. Big and wet, a thing with feet and little hands." She paused. Her eyes were still staring, and when she went on she seemed to be forcing out the words.

"I killed it," she said. "I threw and I threw. I killed it."
She nodded at me as if otherwise I wouldn't believe what
she was saying.

"Yeah," I said. "Yeah. Come on. You're cold. We'll
get some more clothes on you." I got her coat and
wrapped her in it and sat her down in the living room,
and I made her some tea, and I got myself a gin (God
knows I needed one), and I cleaned up the mess, and after
that I put her to bed. The kids came down then—I think
they'd waited until she was out of the way—and I threw
out the pasta and fixed them a frozen pizza. They had
to eat it off folded-up paper towels since we didn't have
any more plates. After that I sent them to watch the
TV. That made me feel a little more like myself, getting
them straightened away. But from that time on, to tell the
truth, things were never really straightened away, and
they weren't ever much good again either in that house.

You don't always know what's the end of something.
The doctor the next day said mostly the same things he'd
said before. A psychotic episode, as he called it, was what
she'd had. And I guess that's as good a word as any for a
hill of broken dishes and a woman huddled in a broom
closet because she thinks some slimy little monster's cruising around her kitchen. Like I said before about the
moment when everything changes, you don't know it
until a while afterwards. That little gnome guy, Imre,
would say there wasn't any change; it was just I had got
to seeing what was there all along. But that's change in a
way, and the truth is after that night I never had a real
wife. That's how I look back on it now. I took care of
her, kept her in the house except when she got so bad it

was dangerous, and she had to be put in hospital. Business was good enough I could hire someone weekdays to look after laundry and getting food in, and the kids got to be good at making supper. Rest of the time I managed.

I might as well admit that, here and there in the next couple of years, I got a little something for myself on the side. I didn't cat around on her before that, but a man has to have something. There was a woman at the place I bought my magazines and cigars; she was divorced and knew about a lot of things, and I helped her with a guy that was giving her trouble about money she owed him. And there was the wife of one of the guys I fished with. He had something else going, and his wife needed it from me, and I liked her. She had wide hips and a narrow waist and a sweet laugh. But then her husband threw her out, he wanted his piece to move in, and mine wasn't a house she could come to, so she moved across the river to Brossard, where her brother lived, and I didn't see her much after that.

Around that same period, I got back into having fights. Mostly in bars, and a couple of times in traffic, when some guy cut me off. Another time I taught a lesson to some asshole that took my space in a parking garage. I always kept one of Phil's baseball bats in the car. On my feet I wasn't as fast as I used to be, but I was still strong and I weighed more than most, and if I could land a punch or two, I was still in control. The guys I clobbered deserved it, and the fighting cleaned out my brain, left me clear to handle the things in my life.

There's just this one time I was in a bar that could have been bad. It was after a hockey game. The game had gone to overtime, and there were lots of bets going, and guys were drunk. There was some shoving. And then this one guy threw a beer in my face. I rammed my fist into his throat, and he went down like he was shot. They couldn't find a pulse, so the bartender called the cops, and while we were waiting for them to come, I pointed out a few things to my friends. Things I knew about them. Like I mentioned before, people tell me stuff. Things they wouldn't have wanted their wives or their bosses to hear about. I put it like that, how we could help each other, and when the cops came, my friends all swore it wasn't me that had hit the guy. There'd been some other guys, they said, doing most of the fighting, and they had lammed it when the guy went down for the count. After a while I got so I could see those other guys punching him and running. No one else in the bar had really seen what happened, and the cops must have figured maybe what my guys said was true or could be, because in the end they didn't charge me.

After that I sometimes got the impression maybe my friends didn't much like me any more. There was that second or two of silence when I showed up and then too much talking, but I still met them most Friday nights after I got the garage shut up. After all, they'd been loyal to me, real friends when I'd needed them, and sure enough, after a while they kind of relaxed again.

I still went to Imre's place some of the time too. He was off in the hospital a lot, something to do with his lungs. But when he was there, looking exhausted, he still sat up on his stool listening and even sometimes talking. He had books around sometimes, and he lent me one by some Czech guy. The story was about a lot of different people, but the part I remember best was when some girl knelt down on the highway because she wanted to die, and what happened was a lot of people in cars got killed swerving to avoid her. I remember telling Imre how I didn't exactly like the book but couldn't get it out of my head. He leaned back his head and laughed like he'd scored some kind of triumph. I could see the metal in his teeth. He nodded at me. "Good," he said. "You will think about. Very good."

"Maybe I'll read another one," I said then, mostly because he seemed so pleased. But this time he shook his head.

"No. For you one book good. Two you begin forget." He took a drag from his cigarette and started to cough while he was exhaling, and the guy he had tending bar had to run and get him a glass of tea.

After that he ended up back in the hospital for a spell, but the truth was, even when he was around, I didn't go to his place so often. I'd got to heading over to Franco's more and more. Everything I heard there was ordinary, and I could drink and half-listen without doing any thinking. Most of the guys I knew were married, some of them twice or even three times, and they used to lean on Franco's bar and buy drinks for each other before they headed home. Just a bunch of guys bitching, mostly about the Habs and once in a while about politics and the FLQ or even about their old ladies. Ball-breakers. Whiners. Juice dries up after you marry them. All the usual crap. And I said, "Yeah," because I didn't want to seem different, but the truth was it hadn't been like that for me. It hadn't been right, maybe, but it hadn't been like that. I laughed when the other guys laughed, but I didn't talk much on that subject, and they didn't any of them ask me stuff about Teresa. I didn't have anything to say, and they knew it.

Weekends were the worst. Friday nights, I drank shots and laughed some with the guys like I said. But when I got home, there were two days of it to come, and I didn't feel so good about things. Teresa didn't ask to be nuts, but I didn't ask for it either. Sometimes Amy was waiting for me when I came in. "Momma doesn't talk to me," she'd say. "She shut her door when I came home from school. If I bring friends, she won't talk to them."

"Yeah," I'd say while I was checking out the mail and seeing if there was anything to eat. Sometimes there was and sometimes there wasn't. Just Teresa's everlasting coffee stinking up the house. "Yeah, I know," I'd say to Amy. "She doesn't talk much to me either."

Some of those nights, I'd get myself another gin and I'd give Amy a glass with gingerale and some of the gin in it, and she'd drink it and then come and get in my lap. Just like she was still a little girl. It was nice, her doing that. Even though she was getting on for sixth grade and a long drink of water herself. She still giggled when I put my hands on her. And she didn't like it when she got into my lap and I didn't pay attention. She'd wriggle around if I got started watching the news or a game. Regular flirt, she was, and to tell the truth it might have seemed a little strange, us getting on with each other like that, but it made her feel better about her mother. I could tell that. And it made me feel better too.

By then Teresa was checked into the hospital a lot. Whenever she got bad, or sometimes when the doctors were trying a new mix of drugs and they needed to watch her, and sometimes just because she wanted to go. Sometimes I wanted her to go too.

That year Phil went away to university. He was still

kind of a weak sister, but some brain, a speed demon at math, and he got himself a special bursary from Dalhousie. The rest I paid. Studying was right for him. He wanted to be an engineer, and that was something I wouldn't have minded being myself if education had been something I'd aimed for or had a chance at. An engineer could handle anything, I figured. Not that Phil was the kind of kid who was going to get himself dirty, but computers were getting to be the biggest thing going and that was right up his alley. To tell the truth, I didn't mind the idea of having him out of the house and getting Amy more to myself either. The summer hadn't gone badly. Both kids had jobs, Amy babysitting and Phil dishing ice cream in one of those places where all they serve is sundaes and sodas, and Teresa spent all day in the garden far as I could tell. Her face and neck and forearms were brown as chocolate. But after Phil left and the weather got cold enough so the garden was put to bed, she got worse. It was like she had begun to hate herself and me too. I was thinking about this while I was driving home one night. It was the first big snow, and the driving was slow; always happens in Montreal the first storm, like everybody never heard of winter and they just learned to drive besides. I'd had some drinks, maybe a few more than usual, and there were a couple of whores on the corner before our block. One I'd seen before, and who wasn't bad to look at, was standing in the snow in her thigh boots and black tights and her fur jacket. I slowed the car, and then I thought, shit, that's dirty business; you don't know what she's got waiting for you, and besides, don't I have a wife there for me anyway? When I got home, I was still kind of hot. I was still kind of drunk too and thinking what I wanted but not thinking really, not remembering how things were.

The truth was I didn't have sex much with Teresa any more, and lately most nights I didn't sleep with her either. Sometimes she went afraid when she saw me, though not always, but the chance that she would stare at me like I was one of her monsters kept me out of the bed. It was getting creepier and creepier, being there in the house with her and not knowing what she was seeing. She'd been six weeks in the hospital this last time, and when she came home, I kind of gave her the bedroom. I don't think she noticed I wasn't coming in. There was a little room off the hall with a couch and a TV, and I slept there or sometimes in Phil's room now he was away. His was the room at the other end of the hall, and Amy had the one over the garage.

Anyway, that night I was sucking back a beer and sitting on the pull-out couch in the stupid little TV room, and what I was thinking was I wanted it anyway, even if Teresa wasn't exactly right about it. At the same time I was hunting around on the tube for something to watch, a game or a movie, and then I heard Amy coming in. Some cracked-voice teenage boy with her. I could hear them laughing, and after a while I must have stopped hearing them because I looked at my watch and thought, shit, the bastard's down there trying to poke my little girl. She wasn't little any more, of course. She was still skinny but with a pair of ripe little hooters pushing out the front of her sweatshirts, and you knew some crummy teenage kid was going to think they were sticking out there for no other reason than for him to grab on. So I thought I'd go down and be sure she was okay, say good night to my little girl that wasn't so little any more, let the creep know there was a real man in the house.

I found them in the kitchen. He was sitting at the table, a weedy specimen, sweaty around the eyes, long hair, no guts or muscle most of these kids. She was getting ice out of the fridge. She looked a little smeary around the mouth, and her hair that was like her mother's, fine and curly and a real blue-black, wasn't exactly combed, but she was dressed and he was, and I didn't say anything, just got myself a beer out of the fridge and told her good night.

I was meaning to bunk down in the TV room, but after I turned off the upstairs hall light I could see there was a strip of light along the bottom of the bedroom door, our bedroom door, mine and Teresa's, and I thought, well, why not? It's my room, isn't it? And I opened the door and walked into my own bedroom. The bed lamp was all that was on. It sent a smear of light up the wall and another onto the bed. She was lying face down, her body made a long tube under the covers, but when I closed the door, she rolled over on her side and drew up her knees.

"It's me," I said, making my voice even and quiet.

The bed shook when I sat down on it. Her body curved away from me. The move was automatic as a wave. "Well?" I said. She didn't say anything. I reached out and palmed her breast. There was a breadth of flesh there in spite of her being such a tall, thin woman, a hidden handful no one but me knew about. Her eyes closed and opened, and I could feel her skin shrinking from my hand, like I was some sort of rapist guy, like I didn't have the right. "Don't say you don't know me," I told her. "Don't fucking say it."

And she didn't, but that didn't make it nicer the way her eyes were staring at me as though I was nothing but one of her monsters and the way her body was hating my touch. "I deserve better than this," I told her. "A man deserves better in his own house. Little girl's down there in the kitchen giving some asshole kid a better time than you give me." I laughed then. "Should try my luck with her." Of course I didn't mean it. I was just trying to get her attention. And I did. She knew what I meant. I could feel it in the way she stopped breathing for a second, and I could see it in the way her eyes slid sideways, like she believed I was a guy that would do that. But the worst was a minute later when I stood up and headed for the door, and she didn't stop me.

I stood there looking down at her, and she never moved. Those eyes that I could fall into went on staring at nothing, and I understood how she had to be alone no matter what, and how anything, anything at all, was better than me pressing on her, following her into where she'd gone, into silence and the deepest part of her. I tell you it made me feel like she had locked all the doors to the house, my house, and I was outside, shut out in the street with slush in my boots and couldn't ever get back in.

In the den I kept a bottle of gin. I skipped the beer and started drinking the gin and watching some jerk movie on the tube. After a while I got out of my clothes, except for my shirt, which is how I slept mostly. A bit after that I heard footsteps on the stairs, just one set, but I knew it was the both of them climbing in sync so I wouldn't guess, and I thought, fucking wonderful. Under my own roof. A man can't get it in his own house and his little girl's giving it to some asshole teenage boy.

I waited some and had another swallow or two of the gin, and then I was out in the hall and the light was still on under Teresa's door. And, on the other side of the hall and down the two steps, there was the same strip of light. Only this was under Amy's door. I was laughing by the time I reached it. I was going to enjoy killing this punk.

Only there wasn't any punk. In the bed was just Amy in her nightgown. "Daddy?" She said it in the littlest voice. She had a magazine in her hands and under the covers her body was long and thin as her mother's, like there was hardly any difference between them any more, except that Amy looked alive. She still had that sweaty messed-up look too, and now she smiled at me. I had my hand on the doorknob, and I swear I was just going to back out of there, when she gave me that smile. It was a sneaky smile, like we both knew something we wouldn't be talking about. Then she sort of pushed down the covers and twitched the nightgown off her shoulder, like she was pretending to be in the movies or something. "Daddy," she said in this little voice and gave me that smile some more. And I thought, well, isn't this house mine? Isn't it?

You read about stuff like Amy and me, and you think, what a creep, what a bastard. Doesn't that guy know any better? But no one ever says, what about the girl? What did she do? No one asks, what did she want? I stood there looking down at her, just looking down at her. And there wasn't any question. She wanted it. But still I stood there, just stood there like a dumb ox. Get out of here, I told myself.

"Daddy," she said, "Daddy," and while she was saying that, her hand was patting the bedcovers beside her.

Of course, I knew how they got laws about stuff like that and the truth is, I'm not some pervert kind of guy either. But then she said something else. "I thought you were Philly," she said, and I thought, oh, fuck, it isn't that weedy creep that was downstairs she's giving it to. And then she was patting the bed again. "There's room, Daddy." And there was, and we needed each other, and that's the truth. I wouldn't ever have stayed if she hadn't wanted it, and that's the truth too.

After that Teresa got better for a while. You'd see her blink and try to get what I was saying to her. She tried with Amy too. But anyone could see she couldn't control what was going on inside her head. Around the middle of November I came home, and there was smoke all through the house. Amy was there hugging a pile of charred cloth to her chest and looking scared, and she told me her mother had set fire to a bunch of Amy's sweaters and skirts and had thrown them out the window while they were burning. Damn near set her own hair on fire too, from what Amy said, running around with armfuls of burning clothes like she was a crazy woman, which of course she was. I had to buy Amy a bunch of new clothes, and I had to ship Teresa off to the hospital again. The doctors said they'd try some different drugs. They did that, I guess there wasn't much choice, but when she came back, she seemed kind of inked out, like the drugs had blotted out what was her. And the truth was I didn't care so much anymore. The thing dies in you, the hope I guess I'd call it, even the wish. It dies too.

I used to visit Amy at night. Mostly she ran through her little girl, shoulder-twitch act, sort of baby-doll stuff.

And then I'd get in bed with her. One time, after I'd been with her for quite a while, she got up all of a sudden and I could hear her feet slapping along the hall towards the bathroom and then what sounded like her coughing up her supper. She didn't come back, and after a while I got up and went back to the den. That bothered me a little, but the truth was she was throwing up a lot around that time anyway, so it wasn't me that made her toss her cookies that particular night. I used to hear her after meals, especially supper, and she got even skinnier and her smile got more twisted. But we were fine together, and besides it didn't matter so much what we did or didn't do any particular time because the way things were, and even though she sometimes called me Philly by mistake, I knew she wanted me to be there doing what I wanted to be doing. I knew that, and I wanted to be there, and she knew that. Like it was the one way she could help me and I could help her fill some of the emptiness in the house, all the dark, hollow places where Teresa might have been. After Phil moved back that winter, there wasn't much chance to be alone with her, but the feeling was always there, between her and me, I mean, and it seemed like with her in the house, even if Teresa was home too, staring into the blackness inside her head and the house reeking of her everlasting coffee, and even if Phil was hanging around again and giving me killer looks like he wished he were man enough to take me on, with Amy there, with my little girl up in her room lying on her bed and waiting for the old man to come and be there with her, I wasn't a guy with nothing. I had something of what I wanted, and so did she, and that's the truth.

There isn't so much more to tell. About my theories or what changed and what didn't or how the empty places got filled. Teresa I had to put in an asylum kind of place up in Rawdon north of the river. Long-term care for the mentally afflicted, was how the doctors there put it. She was a danger to herself, they said, besides which I didn't need her killing herself or the house burned down. After she left, the dandelions grew up in the garden, higher than the roses. I didn't have the heart to weed them out, and indoors I didn't bother with much either. The whole place felt old and full of dead air.

After Phil got his engineering degree and started working at a company out on Côte-de-Lièsse near the airport, he and Amy came into the kitchen one night while I was eating my supper. A pair of cranes was what I thought then, looking up at them. They were both wearing jeans and black jerseys. "You two hungry?" I said. "There's more chili in the pot."

He shook his head. And then he said it to me, what they'd come to say. "We've found a place downtown, Dad. An apartment on Jeanne-Mance, a block above Sherbrooke. It's a sublet. The guys in it now are moving at the end of next month." He went on about the rent and the lease. While he talked, she stood a step behind him, and twice that I saw, she reached out and touched him, once laying a hand on his back above his belt and once grabbing his pocket and hanging on for a second, just the way she used to.

I'd been reading an article on plasma in a science magazine I'd got, and I'd lit some matches and watched them burn and wondered if the white centre of the flame, the part you couldn't see through, was the plasma they were talking about in the article. I lit another one now and held it up. With my other hand, I shoved the magazine aside and nodded like I was thinking over what he'd said.

They were both staring at the match, their dark eyes kind of glittery, like the flame was hypnotizing them. I blew it out and laid it on the edge of my plate with the others I'd lit, and then I looked up at them again. "Sounds like a done deal," I said. "When do you plan on moving?" I saw them both draw breath and their eyes relax and their mouths soften at the same time. It was like they'd been expecting an explosion and now none was coming.

"Besides," I added, "I'll probably be moving out of here myself one of these days. Won't need this much house with you two gone. You can probably use some of the furniture in this place."

"Sure," he said, sounding like he wasn't sure what we were talking about. "Furniture. Probably we can use some. Thanks, Dad." He shook his head and blinked.

She stepped out from behind him and smiled at me. "Thanks, Daddy."

"Don't mention it," I said, and I made like I was going back to reading my article. I was damned if I was going to let them see how hard they'd just clobbered me.

She didn't move but went on standing there and smiling, and now she was running her long-fingered hand through her hair. "I'll come and see you lots, Daddy. Philly will too."

"Sure," I said. "Sure. Any time." Fat chance he'd be coming to see me.

He hadn't moved either, and he was kind of studying me like he still had a thought I might go berserk but really wanted to trust me. "When I've saved some money, I might buy a car," he said to me after a minute. "A used one. Maybe you'd help me check it out."

"Sure," I said again. What was I going to say? I wish there'd been only her, my little girl, that came with Teresa all those years ago, and not the two of you standing there telling me what you're telling me?

The next six weeks went by kind of fast. I thought some about them and me. I'd figured that as soon as he was gone she would be too. But I didn't like them living together. And I hadn't counted on it all happening so quick either. Hearing her feet on the stairs, quick and light, and his serious tread, and then hearing nothing; it was like someone in the house had died. Of course, I could say that about Teresa getting crazier and crazier too, but the difference was that she disappeared a little at a time, so that by the time I put her up in Rawdon, she wasn't very often the Teresa I'd known, and I guess I'd got used, in a gradual way, to having no wife again.

The kids moved on a Sunday. I borrowed a truck from a friend, and a couple of Phil's friends from engineering came over. They loaded the kids' stuff in and some of the furniture from the house, and they ferried it all downtown. The whole business was over in a couple of hours. I watched the gang of them drive off, and then I went back into the house, and it was the one time I damn near cried. Later, when it got dark, I went out and got drunk at Franco's, which made me feel some better until the next day.

After that time, the silence rose up hard and dry like a wall around the house. They were gone, the both of them, and they weren't coming back. She was eighteen by then and had already tried university and quit it. She'd seen a doctor, too, about her vomiting, which must have helped because she wasn't so skinny-looking any more but just a long drink of water like her mother before her.

When they got themselves settled, which couldn't have taken too long, she found herself a job in a store where they sold tablecloths and dishes and small pieces of furniture. It was the kind of place I couldn't turn around in, but she seemed to like it. She came home to see me sometimes, and he even came along once or twice. She always called me Daddy, never Philly any more by mistake, and she smiled at me with that same funny, twisted smile of hers. But I could feel how I didn't matter to her the way I used to. Not much, anyway. Not with him in her life. Even though she'd been my little girl, I always kind of knew he was the one that counted with her. And, of course, that's the way it was for him too. Me knocking him around when he was a kid didn't ever fix that.

The surprise for me was that they didn't stay living together very long. After six months or so he moved out to the West Island. She didn't sound very happy about it when she told me, but it was closer to his work, and he had friends out that way. Those were the reasons he said. I understood then that he'd moved her out of the house not to have her with him so much as to get her away from me. He always was against me. There were women hanging around for him by that time, more than when he was in university. He'd filled out enough in his twenties so he wasn't a beanpole, and he had Teresa's eyes, and you could tell he had a brain in him. Over the next years I saw him with different girls. Amy came around with a bunch of different men too. But it never got to either one of them getting married. So I figured they might think they'd escaped me, but the truth was we couldn't any one of us escape the real thing that held us, which was Teresa, or more exactly the darkness that was at the centre of her. That was what had got hold of the three of us, and I could feel how we were in orbit, we three, just like around a black hole with its density being so great none of us would ever break free. Schizophrenia was what they said she had. They'd turned definite about that, and she had clinical depression too, and they used other words for what was inside her. But those were just words, and for me no words could say the darkness that was at the centre of her. She certainly couldn't have told it herself. And nothing any doctor ever did could cast it out either. Probably it was just as well her kids didn't have any kids themselves. What we went through, it was enough.

The year after they moved out, I sold the house for a lot more than I paid for it. I moved into an apartment on St-Viateur near where our old rental house was. Around that same time, my mechanic said he was ready to buy me out the whole way, and I told him I was ready to go. I was pushing sixty. Most of the time I had an ache like an iron claw in both my knees and the lower part of my back and sometimes down my left arm too. I figured that was from some of the falls I took climbing. And there were a couple of times, that last year at the garage, I got a stitch in my side so bad some of my guys had to help me into the chair in the office, and then I couldn't move from it for near an hour. They wanted me to see some heart doctor, but I knew I'd be right soon enough. Like people say, at my age, you wake up in the morning and nothing hurts, you know you're dead.

The next winter I bought a place down in Florida, a bungalow kind of house in one of those inland towns on the edge of the citrus country, the kind that are laid out there half asleep in the sun and still southern at heart. I fished the inland waterway and hunted with a guy that owned an airboat and belonged to a shooting club. Once in a while I went over to the coast and did a little deep-sea fishing too; a few of us, maybe three or four, would charter a boat for a day and head out the Sebastian Inlet.

These days I take it easier. I sit out here on my veranda. That's what your porch is called down here in the land of alligators. I don't ever see snow any more. That line stops somewhere north of here, even in the worst of winters. I like a gin or two long about this time of night. Eases out the pain in my arm and chest. I can see the sky going red and the sun dropping down behind the pines across the road. Big, soft, southern pines. They grow up thick along where the bayou runs, and I like to see them spreading wide against the sky.

Amy's coming down to see me in a few days. She'll take a long weekend, the way she always does, fly in through Orlando and then rent a car and mosey over here to check on the old man. She cleans the place up a bit when she comes, makes sure the woman I've got doing my laundry is doing a good job and the same with the kid who comes over and mows the lawn. After three or four days, she gets out of here again. She says she has to get back to work, which is maybe true, but I can tell she isn't easy with me, not like we used to be back when her mother was with us and we were there for each other, my little girl and me. The fact is, though, I'll be glad to see her when she comes and sorry when she leaves.

Come June when the afternoon rains hit, I'll head back north to Quebec, and like always I'll drive first thing up to Rawdon and see Teresa. She hardly looks any different each time, the same eyes and blue-black hair without any white, except at her temples where they've pulled back her hair and fastened it with some kind of plastic clips. She isn't allowed anything metal. It won't be any different being with her either. It never is. You can tell right away how there's still that dark, silent place inside her where the part of her that's real lives. She knows me too. Her eyes kind of lift to my face and follow me when I move around her room. She talks a little to me, although never about anything much, and she doesn't say my name. "Oh, hello," she'll say, very polite. "You've been away, haven't you?" And when I give her some flowers, which I always do, she buries her face in them for a few seconds and then lifts her head and says, "Thank you so much. I do love flowers." She might even smile, but the smile isn't exactly for me, and I wonder to myself sometimes, when was the last time she said my name?

The truth is I still have a feeling about her. She was my woman, the one I chose soon as I saw her that crazy winter night back at Franco's, and for all that came after, a thing like that doesn't change.

So maybe the little gnome guy in the bar all those years ago (Imre was his name; he died a long time ago, lung cancer, if I recall it right), maybe he was the ticket all along. I remember the word he used about change—illusion, he called it—and the way he waved his hands when he talked, like he was directing some orchestra. To tell the truth, how he thought, that's how I've got to thinking about things too. Just about exactly the way he said. How that big moment when you think something changes is really just the moment when you see the thing clear through for the first time. And how steady state is the bigger truth. Whether you did good stuff or bad and whether you took care of people right or not and whether you were happy or sad or even ever figured out which was which, the truth is that after enough years it all comes out more or less the same, and in the end makes up to no difference at all.

ACKNOWLEDGMENTS

The author wishes to express her gratitude to Diane Martin. She would also like to thank Gena Grove, Christina Flavell, Karen Haughian and Nancy Brown.

BIOGRAPHY

Julie Keith's fiction has been widely published in literary magazines and anthologies. Her first book, *The Jaguar Temple and Other Stories*, was nominated for the Governor General's Award for Fiction in 1995. In 2000, *The Devil Out There* was nominated for the Grand Prix du livre Montréal, and won the Hugh MacLennan Prize for Fiction. Raised near Chicago, Keith moved to Quebec in the mid-60s. She presently lives in Westmount.